"Don't ever do that again,"

she whispered. Impotent rage burned in her eyes. "Do you hear me?"

"I hear you, Marydyth, but I can't say I won't kiss you again," Flynn replied truthfully. He didn't trust her, but, damn it all to hell, he could no longer trust himself, either.

In that moment she hated herself almost as much as she hated him. She should've fought him, should've scratched his eyes out. But the kiss…

It filled her with an emotion she didn't want to feel and was hungry to feel again. She was mad and confused, and Flynn only made it worse. All of her notions about J.C. were nothing more than a foolish woman's dreams, and in the midst of all that, Flynn O'Bannion had managed to make her feel like a woman again.

"I do hate you." She spat out the only defense she had….

Dear Reader,

As the weather heats up this month, so do the passion and adventure in our romances!

Since her publishing debut in 1995, Linda Castle has gone on to write five more Harlequin Historical novels, including *Heart of the Lawman,* which is a spin-off of her very first book, *Fearless Hearts.* In this emotional Western, a woman's greatest nightmare is replaced by her greatest dream, when she is finally reunited with her daughter after being wrongfully incarcerated. And now she must face the man who put her away, Sheriff Flynn O'Bannion—not only because she's undeniably attracted to him, but also because he's her daughter's legal guardian!

Temperatures—and tempers—flare in *Plum Creek Bride* by Lynna Banning, about a German nanny whose new position leads to a marriage of convenience with a single-father physician who must grapple with a town plagued by cholera. *The Captive Bride,* a new medieval novel by Susan Spencer Paul, is the tale of a fierce knight who'll stop at nothing to reclaim his father's estate—even if it means marrying the headstrong vixen who now inhabits the keep!

Sit close to a fan while reading Ana Seymour's *Lord of Lyonsbridge,* because her sinfully handsome hero, Connor Brand, might cause a meltdown! Connor, the horse master at Lyonsbridge, teaches a spoiled Norman beauty some important lessons in compassion and love....

Whatever your tastes in reading, you'll be sure to find a romantic journey back to the past between the covers of a Harlequin Historicals® novel.

Sincerely,

Tracy Farrell
Senior Editor

Please address questions and book requests to:
Harlequin Reader Service
U.S.: 3010 Walden Ave., P.O. Box 1325, Buffalo, NY 14269
Canadian: P.O. Box 609, Fort Erie, Ont. L2A 5X3

HEART
OF THE
LAWMAN

LINDA CASTLE

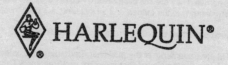

HARLEQUIN®

TORONTO • NEW YORK • LONDON
AMSTERDAM • PARIS • SYDNEY • HAMBURG
STOCKHOLM • ATHENS • TOKYO • MILAN • MADRID
PRAGUE • WARSAW • BUDAPEST • AUCKLAND

If you purchased this book without a cover you should be aware that this book is stolen property. It was reported as "unsold and destroyed" to the publisher, and neither the author nor the publisher has received any payment for this "stripped book."

ISBN 0-373-29073-X

HEART OF THE LAWMAN

Copyright © 1999 by Linda L. Crockett

All rights reserved. Except for use in any review, the reproduction or utilization of this work in whole or in part in any form by any electronic, mechanical or other means, now known or hereafter invented, including xerography, photocopying and recording, or in any information storage or retrieval system, is forbidden without the written permission of the publisher, Harlequin Enterprises Limited, 225 Duncan Mill Road, Don Mills, Ontario, Canada M3B 3K9.

All characters in this book have no existence outside the imagination of the author and have no relation whatsoever to anyone bearing the same name or names. They are not even distantly inspired by any individual known or unknown to the author, and all incidents are pure invention.

This edition published by arrangement with Harlequin Books S.A.

® and TM are trademarks of the publisher. Trademarks indicated with ® are registered in the United States Patent and Trademark Office, the Canadian Trade Marks Office and in other countries.

Visit us at www.romance.net

Printed in U.S.A.

Books by Linda Castle

Harlequin Historicals

Fearless Hearts #261
Abbie's Child #321
The Return of Chase Cordell #348
Temple's Prize #394
Territorial Bride #441
Heart of the Lawman #473

LINDA CASTLE

is the pseudonym of Linda L. Crockett. Linda is an avid reader and writer of historical romance of all types and periods. She is enchanted with the West, but is an admitted Anglophile. For a bookmark and autographed bookplate write to Linda at her address: Linda Castle/Crockett, #18 County Road 5795, Farmington, NM 87401.

This book is lovingly dedicated to my family and God, and to my legion of loyal readers. We have come full circle; we started our dance together with the O'Bannion family in *Fearless Hearts,* and we finish with the O'Bannion family in *Heart of the Lawman.* Enjoy!

Prologue

Tombstone, Arizona Territory
November 1886

"Please, please take good care of my baby." The blowing dust made Marydyth's voice crack. She stroked her daughter's downy soft hair with her fingertips, trying to memorize every detail of the baby's face. "Tuck her in at night. She likes to hear a lullaby."

"She likes lullabies sung by a Jezebel?" Victoria Hollenbeck's voice floated from under the netting of her mourning attire. Her words were harsher than the winter wind coming off the low, rugged mountains to whistle through the streets of Tombstone.

"Promise you will rock her at night." Marydyth's eyes scanned the innocent face, lingering on her upturned nose and dewy soft lips. "And—and just pick her up and hold her for no reason during the day. Will you do that, Victoria?"

Rachel's babyish cheeks were growing pink from the scuffing wind. Marydyth cursed herself for being so selfish. She had thoughtlessly begged Victoria to bring Rachel to the train depot in this weather—how she hungered for just one more minute to look at her baby. "Please help her say her prayers. Tell me that you'll help her say her prayers, Victoria."

"What kind of prayer would a gold digger like you know?" Victoria spit the words at Marydyth in a voice so bitter it singed the edges of Flynn's soul to hear it. As he watched from under the protective brim of his hat, Victoria swiveled her body, forcing her shoulder between Rachel and Marydyth's outstretched hand. The younger woman's anxious fingers reached for the child but all she grabbed was a tuft of white rabbit fur accidentally plucked from the collar of the baby's red velvet coat.

"Let me hold her. Please, Victoria. Let me feel her in my arms—one last time?" Marydyth begged.

Flynn unconsciously inhaled and looked heavenward. The scent of a storm was on the ocher coattails of clouds scudding from the hills.

"I wish there was sun," Marydyth muttered. "Her curls shine like crimson-kissed gold in the sunshine...." Marydyth's fingers managed to touch one silken curl. She leaned closer and tried to kiss the top of Rachel's head but Victoria stepped away.

Victoria was not going to give an inch—not even today, the last time Marydyth would ever see her child.

"Before you get on that train, Marydyth, there is something I want you to take with you into the walls of Yuma. Let this be your company for the rest of your life—and I pray to God it will be a long one." Victoria shuddered and took a deep breath, as if her hatred were about to consume her and render her mute. "I would've seen you hung for what you did to my boy. Hung and left for all the world to see." Her voice cracked. "But I couldn't do that to my only grandchild. I will raise Rachel to be a lady, but not for you. No. I will do it because she has Hollenbeck blood in her veins."

"I know you don't believe me, Victoria, but I loved J.C.," Marydyth whispered.

"Loved him so much you stabbed him in the heart." Victoria took another step backward.

Marydyth did not deny the deed.

Victoria trembled beneath the dark veil. "You are a murderess and a liar. Just think about this every night before you go to sleep in that place. I will do everything in my power to erase your mark upon this child. She will never know that her mother is the Black Widow."

Marydyth could not hold back the strangled sob. Rachel fastened chubby, dimpled fingers over the black lace on her grandmother's Cisele collar.

"Mama." She gurgled.

Hot, dry tears stung Marydyth's eyes, choked off the air in her lungs.

So, this is justice?

"Please, Victoria, tell her that I love her."

"I'll tell her nothing about you." Victoria's biting declaration carried on the grit blowing into Flynn's eyes. He didn't want to watch, didn't want to listen, but he had no choice.

"Marydyth, I want you to suffer as I have suffered. Your child will be alive, but to her, *you* will be dead— as dead as I can make you. Nobody in Hollenbeck Corners will ever mention your name again, I'll see to that." The black netting on her mourning hat fluttered in the wind.

Flynn felt the current of anguish, hatred and love flowing between the trio of Hollenbeck women. It was like a tainted river that threatened to overflow its banks.

It was a pitiful thing to behold, these women tearing

at each other. It was gut-wrenching and full of sorrow, and something that a man like Flynn had no belly for. His nerves felt raw. They had been that way since the trial.

He drew hard on his cigarette and wished the scene over soon.

A small crowd of people had gathered near the station. Angry murmurs and the sound of a mob made the hair on the back of his neck bristle. He crushed the stub of his cigarette into the ground with the toe of his boot.

Somebody threw a rock. It hit the side of the locomotive with a hollow ping. Flynn peeled back the edge of his coat and drew his side arm.

"Black Widow!" somebody shouted.

"Murderin' Mary, I hope you burn in hell!" yelled another bodiless voice.

"Mrs. Hollenbeck?" he said.

Both Victoria and Marydyth turned to look at him.

How the hell did I get tangled up in this mess?

It was a bitter irony that he had been drawn into this tragedy simply because he was the only lawman available to come to the Arizona Territory.

Pitiful.

The crowd sounds grew more agitated, like a swarm of riled yellow jackets. Flynn kept his gun at waist level, his finger on the trigger.

"Ma'am, we've got to go," Flynn said.

The train belched out a cloud of steam and the slithering vapor swirled around Marydyth's skirt. The relentless wind broomed along the street, driving back the crowd with stinging pelts of sand.

Flynn turtled into the warmth of his sheepskin coat. It didn't help. He hadn't been able to shake the chill that had seeped into his soul when he'd heard the verdict.

For the first time in his career justice didn't taste sweet. It tasted sour, and grew more foul each time he looked at the baby Victoria held in her arms.

It was a damn poor thing to be taking a woman to Yuma. And even worse knowing she left behind an infant.

Flynn shoved the sympathetic thoughts aside. He had no call to feel anything one way or the other about it.

He wore a badge—nothing more or less. The jury had had their say. Marydyth Hollenbeck's fate was sealed. Nothing this side of heaven could save her from the hell that waited within the prison gates of Yuma.

The train whistle blew, which sent an icy finger trailing down Flynn's spine.

"Ma'am."

Marydyth's shoulders stiffened inside the smoke-gray wool coat. Invisible fingers of wind pulled at her hat, which merely rested on her head since she wasn't allowed a hat pin.

Flynn narrowed his eyes against the sting of blowing sand and watched her turn. No bandido or high-line rider had ever managed to stare him down, but enduring the gaze of Marydyth Hollenbeck's red-rimmed blue eyes rattled him. His pulse ticked off the time as they stared across the mile-wide gulf between lawman and prisoner.

"It's time," Flynn said gruffly. "You better get on the train before this turns ugly."

She grimaced.

Flynn kept his gun pointed into the crowd and extended his hand to help her aboard, but she jerked back. The iron manacles locked around her slender wrists clanked together in a discordant peal.

"I don't need your help to get where I'm going. I

managed it all by myself this far and I'll see it through to the end,'' she said. She grabbed hold of her skirts, climbed the steps to the train and never looked back at the jeering crowd.

Chapter One

Territorial Prison, Yuma.
April 1889

Marydyth fell onto her hard cot. Exhaustion and heat sapped her strength and dragged her toward sleep.

But she never rested.

Night was the worst time in this place that men had named Hellhole. Night was when the specters of her past came to visit.

She tossed and turned on the hard mattress, willing them to stay away for just one night.

But her guilt would not abate. Andre's face floated before her. His eyes were hollow, dark sockets but his lips twisted into a hideous grin. Then Andre's face shifted and changed.

It was J.C.

Oh, J.C., I didn't do it—you know I didn't kill you. But J.C. only stared at her with dark, haunted eyes until his face transformed and became Victoria. She was laughing. Laughing.

Go away!

Did Marydyth scream aloud or was it only in her head?

Next, Andre's face returned and loomed closer, pale blue and lifeless. His eyes were empty holes.

I didn't want to kill you... I didn't want to kill anybody.

Rachel was crying. She was lost, somewhere just beyond Marydyth's reach. She turned in a circle, searching, looking for her baby.

Where is my baby? Who will love my baby?

Marydyth woke to the sounds of her own frightened screams.

Hollenbeck Corners, Arizona Territory
April 1889

"Unca Flynn!" Rachel darted down the stairs, her black leather shoes clacking out a quick tempo while she ran. She launched her body at Flynn's outstretched arms without a single doubt that he would catch her.

He spun her around and held her above the crown of his cream-colored Stetson hat.

"Whe-e-e-e!" The little girl squealed in delight.

He gave her one last turn and then brought her to his chest. She was giggling and squirming in his arms.

"How's my girl today?"

"I missed you."

"I didn't miss you at all." He pulled a face. "Not even when I went to the mercantile on the way home."

Her eyes widened. "Did you bring me somethin'?"

"Naw." He grinned. "There is nothing in my shirt pocket for you."

Rachel attacked his pocket like a hungry coon. She dug deep and came up holding the hoarhound stick.

"Shh—don't let Mrs. Young know." Rachel held one dimpled finger to her lips.

"Is it a secret?" Flynn whispered.

"Uh-huh. Mrs. Young made gingerbread men for our dessert, so you mustn't let her know." Rachel's warm breath fanned out over his face as she whispered.

"Then it will be our secret. You can count on me." He winked.

Rachel hugged him tight around the neck, and liquid warmth—love—exploded in his chest.

It had been this way for a long while now. Flynn and Rachel. *Unca* Flynn.

He deposited Rachel on her feet and she immediately wrapped her fingers around two of his. "I missed you," she said for the second time.

"I had to move the cattle, honey," Flynn explained. "It will take a few more days."

"Oh." Flynn felt as if the sunshine had been covered by a cloud when Rachel stopped smiling.

"Tell me about those gingerbread men," he said as they walked through the parlor. The tall, narrow windows were open and the evening breeze fluttered the heavy, green tasseled draperies.

It was still hot.

"I made a special one just for you, Unca Flynn. I saved it." Rachel's eyes darted toward the kitchen at the back of the house. She leaned close enough for him to feel the angel's wing of her breath along his neck. "Mrs. Young didn't like it, but I saved it anyway," Rachel whispered into his ear.

"I am mighty beholden to you for the kindness. Gingerbread is one of my particular favorites." Flynn folded himself into a chair, and Rachel scrambled into his lap. She sucked on her hoarhound when he patted her knee.

"I love you, Unca Flynn."

That hot feeling expanded in his chest again. He swallowed hard.

If anybody had told him three years ago that he would give up his badge and become nursemaid and surrogate parent to a four-year-old charmer, he probably would have locked them up for drunkenness. But sure as God made little green apples, U.S. Marshal Flynn O'Bannion was now just Unca Flynn.

"I love you too, sugar." His voice had gone husky with emotion. He cleared his throat. "I'm hungry enough to eat the south end of a northbound bear."

Rachel giggled as he hauled them both up from the chair.

"Are you done with that sweet stick yet?" he asked as she crunched the last bite.

"Now I am."

"Then let's go see what old Mrs. Young has for us tonight." He levered her up onto his shoulder and gave her a ride down the carpet-lined hall.

"Unca Flynn..."

"Yes, sugar?" he asked while he ducked the fancy chandelier. The flickering lamps made long-fingered shadows on the ornate wallpaper as he passed.

"You smell funny." Rachel wrinkled her nose when he glanced at her.

He laughed. "Yep, I guess I do. It was mighty hot out there today." Too damned hot to have to wrestle cattle all day, but there was nobody else to see they got moved to the high country for summer grass and water. When he took over caring for Rachel he had mingled his herd in with the Hollenbeck beeves. Come fall he would cut out enough for his walking-around money, and the Hollenbeck profits would go into Rachel's trust fund.

"After dinner I'll see about a bath."

"Good," Rachel agreed as Flynn reached the kitchen. He swung her down to the floor while the rowels on his spurs jingled. The smell of gingerbread and wood smoke filled his nostrils.

"Miz Young," he said to the wide back in front of the Monarch cookstove.

Mrs. Young allowed her attention to stray from the pot she was stirring for only a moment. "Evening, Mr. O'Bannion." She turned back to the bubbling pot. Her gray hair was pinned tight but one or two disobedient strands had worked free in the heat of the kitchen.

Flynn shoved his hands in his pockets. It was damned awkward but she had greeted him in exactly the same way for close to three years.

"Come lookie, Unca Flynn." Rachel pulled one hand free and yanked on his finger. He moved to the scrubbed pine table, glad for something to do until Mrs. Young was ready to leave. Rachel pointed to a blue-sprigged china plate. In the center lay a slightly gimpy, somewhat misshaped gingerbread man.

It was the prettiest thing Flynn had ever seen.

"Do you like it?" Rachel asked.

"I do, I surely do." Flynn smiled down at her expectant face. It took no effort to act as if he were pleased. He had grown a mighty soft spot for Rachel since Victoria had drawn up the papers and roped him into becoming the child's guardian.

Her voice grew serious. "It isn't very good—not like Mrs. Young's." Rachel's gaze slid to the closed pie safe with the pierced tin panels. Flynn was sure inside must lie a treasure of perfectly formed gingerbread men in precise rows upon the scrubbed wood.

Flynn's heart contracted at the searching expression in

Rachel's cornflower-blue eyes. "Dumpling, I think that is the finest gingerbread man in town—probably the whole territory."

Some of the strain left her small shoulders. "Mrs. Young said it was crooked."

Flynn's eyes slid to the housekeeper. She was in the process of folding a dish towel. When she had folded four layers she used the towel to pull a black Dutch oven out of the front of the Monarch stove. Then, as she had done every night for three years, she stripped off her apron and turned to Flynn.

"Dinner is roast beef. There is a pan of biscuits and a bowl of gravy on the warmer." She laid her apron aside and retrieved her brown bonnet from a hook by the back door. "Yesterday's loaves are in the pie safe if you take a hankering for some."

Without another word she tied the bonnet on her head and shuffled out the back door. Heavy, determined steps thudded alongside the house. The iron gate in front creaked once when it opened and once when it swung shut. They would see no more of Mrs. Young until seven o'clock in the morning.

The huge house seemed to sigh in relief.

"I'm glad she is gone," Rachel whispered.

Flynn frowned and rubbed his rough palm against Rachel's satiny cheek. "It's just the two of us again, partner."

"Uh-huh," Rachel said with another relieved sigh.

Flynn knew that Rachel was uneasy around Mrs. Young. Most of the time he was home and things were fine, but when he had business to take care of or the herd to move, then he saw Rachel become unhappy.

Maybe it was time to make a change. Mrs. Young was

old and set in her ways. Rachel had all the energy and curiosity of a normal child.

Maybe if he talked to Mrs. Young...

He wasn't sure how to ride herd over her. Still, the notion that he needed to make changes for Rachel nudged at the corners of his mind.

He yanked out a kitchen chair and helped Rachel into it. She straightened her petticoats over legs as straight and slender as a yearling filly's.

"Are you eating man-size or little girl-size tonight?" he asked as he lifted the heavy iron cover from the Dutch oven.

"Man-size," Rachel said.

He looked at her from under lifted brows. "How about we start small and work up?"

"All right, Unca Flynn."

He dished up two plates. "Did Mrs. Young snap at you again, punkin?"

"No, not 'xactly." Rachel squirmed in her chair.

"Truth?"

"No. She isn't like you, Unca Flynn," Rachel explained patiently in her young-old voice.

"I should hope not." He chuckled and tried to make light of what she had said. "I'm a tough old range bull."

"You're not old, Unca Flynn." Rachel laughed but then her expression turned serious. "You're not old like Grandma Hollenbeck."

"No, I'm not old like that, Rachel, but your grandma is very sick." Victoria probably seemed aged beyond counting to Rachel since the woman had been ravaged by her strokes.

Flynn sat down at the table. He picked up a fork and rotated it between his finger and thumb, chewing on the question that he knew had to be asked. Finally he just spit it out.

"What did Mrs. Young say to upset you today, Rachel?" He stared at his food, while he waited for her to find the words.

"I asked her why I didn't have a mama like Becky Morgan and Maizie Duncan and all the other little girls in town." Her voice was a quivering whisper as she stared down at her lap.

A hard knot took up residence in Flynn's belly. This was a day he had long dreaded.

"What did she say?"

"She said I didn't have a mama." Rachel's voice was dry and whispery. "But how come, Unca Flynn?" She looked up at him and tears swam in her blue eyes. "How come I *don't* have a mama?"

"Oh, honey, don't listen to Mrs. Young. She is a grumpy old sage hen who has forgotten how to raise a little girl." Flynn reached out and rubbed her soft cheek with his thumb. He made up his mind then and there. Mrs. Young would have to go. He would not have a woman in the house who had so little compassion.

Rachel swallowed hard and toyed with her food. Flynn tried a piece of meat but it tasted like sawdust while he chewed.

He had known this day would come—that eventually Rachel's curiosity would bring him to this point, but he was unprepared. What could he tell her?

Rachel had grown up in a town full of secrets. Victoria Hollenbeck's power and money had silenced the tongues of the residents of Hollenbeck Corners. As far as Flynn knew, Rachel had never even heard her mother's name spoken. He had said nothing because he just didn't know what to say. But as he looked at Rachel's tight little face, he knew he was going to have to find the words.

And soon.

"You do have a mama, Rachel," Flynn said softly.

Her head lifted. She stared across the blue-flowered china with a look of hope and bone-deep hunger. Her pale blue eyes burned into him.

"I do?"

"Yes, you do. You look a lot like her, in fact. She has blue eyes, just like yours."

I remember, because she turned and looked at me with those amazing eyes before she walked through the gates at Yuma.

"You—know her?" Wonder tinted every word.

"Yep, I know her."

Rachel's eyes scanned his face, as her mind gauged his words, searching for truth and meaning.

"Where is my mama, Unca Flynn?"

Straight as an Apache arrow, her question pierced his heart.

Flynn swallowed hard. Now he had opened Pandora's box and all the misery that came with his answer would come flying out.

How could he tell Rachel that her mother was in prison for killing her daddy?

Her world would shatter.

No. The world he had built around this tiny girl would shatter, if she learned what part he had played in taking her mother away.

"She had to leave when you were just a baby." The half truth rushed past his lips.

"Why?"

Something cold and mournful, like wind out of the Superstitions, swept over him. "She—she just did. There are times when adults have to do things—even if they don't want to. I—I can't really explain it all to you now. Maybe when you are a little older.''

Rachel's bottom lip trembled. She drew in a ragged breath in an effort not to cry. "Oh."

He swallowed hard. This little scrap of flesh and bone could wound him with a look. Her tears destroyed him and turned him to a babbling fool.

"She loved you, honey. That is what you need to remember and think about. Don't listen to Mrs. Young, just remember that your mama loved you."

Her face took on a sullen hurt look that cut him deep. "If she loved me she wouldn't have gone away. If she loved me she would come back," Rachel said softly.

The edges of his heart withered. "No. That isn't always true, honey. You've got to believe me when I tell you that she didn't have any choice. She had to go."

Rachel flew out of her chair and crumpled against his body like a fragile flower seeking shelter from a hard frost. He cuddled her while the sound of her sobs tore a hole right through him.

Someday he would have to explain it all to Rachel. And then he would have to live with the consequences of what it meant to have worn a badge.

A half hour later a knock at the door brought Rachel's head up. Flynn slowly rose from the chair with Rachel still cradled in his arms.

She had cried for a long time.

Her tears ate at him like acid. He was ill equipped to be a father—but he was the closest thing she had to family now.

"I wonder who would be coming to call?" He hoped he could draw her from the pain she was in.

"Don't know," she said with a hiccup.

"Well, let's me and you go find out." He gave her a kiss on the top of the head and set her on her feet. Together they crossed the carpeted parlor to the front hall.

Rachel's ragged hiccups tore at Flynn every step of the way to the door. He was too old and too much a lone wolf to be caring for her. She needed more.

She needed a mother.

When he reached the door she looked at him with such an expression of loneliness that he scooped her up in his arms again.

They looked through the frosted pane of glass and saw the glow of a lantern. Flynn opened the door and discovered Charlie Parker, Hollenbeck Corners's aging postmaster. He gripped an ancient-looking mining lantern in his deeply tanned, gnarled hand.

"Charlie?"

"Evening, Mr. O'Bannion. Sorry to bother you." Every time he spoke his Adam's apple bobbed like a cork in the water.

"No bother. Come inside, Charlie. What brings you out so late?" Flynn lowered Rachel to the floor and stepped back so Charlie could enter, but the man hung back. "Is something wrong?"

Charlie glanced down at the thick Chinese carpet beneath Flynn's feet. He dusted his boots on the backs of his pant legs before he stepped over the threshold into the big house. "Not 'xactly, Mr. O'Bannion."

The postmaster was acting so jumpy that Flynn found himself looking both ways down the steep hill toward town. J. C. Hollenbeck had built his mansion on a rocky knoll near the San Pedro River. Flynn could stand on the front porch and view most of Hollenbeck Corners below. Right now the place was pretty quiet. A horse nickered, a dog barked and a furious-sounding cat answered, and there was a faint tinkle of barroom music floating on the dry spring breeze. But there was nothing to account for Charlie's nervousness.

"Would you like some supper, Charlie?" Flynn asked as he stepped inside and closed the door behind him. "Mrs. Young left us a pot full of prime Hollenbeck beef." Charlie always looked as if he could use a hot meal and an extra night's sleep.

"No, thank you kindly. I am here on business."

Rachel looked at Charlie from her position behind Flynn's knee. He could feel her little fingers curling into the fabric of his Levi's.

"Business?" Flynn frowned and shot a glance at Rachel. "And it couldn't wait until the morning?"

Charlie's Adam's apple worked up and down a couple of times real fast. "I—I wasn't sure. Uh…a—a letter has come…." Charlie glanced toward Rachel and swallowed hard.

"A letter?" The short hairs on the back of Flynn's neck rose of their own will.

"It—it ain't 'xactly for you—" Charlie subtly nodded toward Rachel once again "—if you catch my meaning."

Flynn didn't catch Charlie's meaning, but the way he was acting the letter must have something to do with Rachel.

Marydyth.

An icy finger traced a line up Flynn's back. He was hard-pressed to keep from shivering. He looked down at Rachel, still hiding halfway behind his leg. The salty outline of dried tears was still evident on her little cheeks.

Once right after Victoria had persuaded Flynn to become Rachel's guardian he had seen a pile of letters tied with a black ribbon. They had been addressed to Rachel and sent from Yuma.

Flynn and Victoria had some strong words on the matter before she ended the discussion by tossing them into the flames of her fireplace.

"Sugar, why don't you go clean the dishes off the table? I'll finish with Charlie, then we'll wash them up and have some gingerbread and milk." Flynn gave her a wink.

"All right, Unca Flynn." Rachel unclasped her fingers from his pants and walked slowly down the long hall. She looked small and way too vulnerable as she passed beneath the crystal chandelier.

"Thanks, Mr. O'Bannion, I didn't wanna say nothin' in front of the child." He pulled an envelope from his vest pocket. His fingers worked nervously around the outside edge. He seemed undecided about whether he wanted to keep it or give it to Flynn.

"Is it a letter for Rachel?" Flynn finally asked when Charlie's fingers had trodden the same ground for the third time.

"No, not precisely." Charlie's lips parted but no sound came out. Then he took a deep breath. "It's—it's, aw hell, the letter is addressed to—to the Black Widow." The words spilled out in an awkward rush.

"I don't like that name, Charlie." Flynn took a step closer and lowered his voice. "I never did."

Charlie's eyes widened and his Adam's apple worked up and down. "It is to Mrs. Marydyth Hollenbeck," he corrected himself, and thrust the letter at Flynn. "Now who would be a-writin' to her here? I said to myself. Well, nobody who knew what happened, I answered myself. And then I says, well, I says, I better get this to Mr.

O'Bannion, right away." Charlie was staring at the paper as if he thought it might come to life.

"I figger you'd best be the one to have it—since Miz Victoria is—well, you know."

"Yes, I know." Flynn glanced at the envelope in his hand. It was dirty and ragged. There was no return address and the postmark had been blurred by dirt, greasy stains and the passage of time. It was an old envelope, and had passed through a lot of hands.

Flynn glanced back at Charlie. A hundred questions raced through his mind.

"What do you suppose you'll do with it, Mr. O'Bannion?" Charlie was still staring at the paper. "I'll tell you one thing for nothing, Mr. O'Bannion, I am mighty happy I don't have to do nothing with it. That Black Wi—I mean that Mrs. Hollenbeck, she came to no good, and everythin' that touched her was the same way."

"I'll have to give it some thought," Flynn interrupted, strangely annoyed to hear Charlie condemn Rachel's mother in her own house.

"I knew you'd know just what to do, I mean you takin' care of the little one and all. Yep, that was why I brought it to you. Well, I best be going." Charlie suddenly turned and shuffled toward the front door, as if he had used up all the words inside him and was anxious to escape.

"Thanks for coming all the way up here. I appreciate it."

"Just wanted to get it to you right off." He glanced at the envelope once again. "I figger it might be important—or it might be bad news of a kind. Bad news seemed to follow that woman."

Flynn ran his finger over the stains and dirt on the

yellowing envelope. "Charlie, I'd like for you to keep this quiet."

Charlie looked at Flynn and blinked. "Yes, sir. Whatever you say, Mr. O'Bannion, I'd be happy to oblige. It's a load off my mind just to put in your hands." Charlie ducked his head and pulled his shapeless hat back on his head. "I told myself that Miz Victoria wouldn't like me waitin', nosirree, she wouldn't like it a'tall."

"Thanks again, Charlie, and good night." Flynn closed the door behind Charlie.

He glanced down at the envelope, allowing the questions to come unhindered.

Why *would* somebody be writing to Marydyth at this address? The papers had been full of the details of her trial—the details and those names: the Black Widow and Murdering Mary.

The public had turned on Marydyth with the same vigor they had once pursued her. And the very ones that had been so happy to be guests in her home, to have attended the fancy dances and dinners, suddenly didn't know her name.

"Unca Flynn, the table is all cleared." Rachel's voice drifted down the hallway.

He shoved the letter in his pocket. He would have to deal with the letter later. Right now his main priority was caring for Rachel.

Chapter Two

As sundown came to the prison, the oppressive heat of the day vanished. Within an hour Marydyth was shivering in the cold.

She turned on her hard, rickety cot and closed her eyes. The hand she rubbed her face with was rough, callused and dry as the desert around Yuma. There had been a time when Marydyth's hands had been soft, white, *delicate,* J.C. had called them.

Marydyth smiled and thought of her husband. There had been a time when the most important question she and J.C. shared was how many beaux they would allow to call once their darling daughter began receiving. Now each night when Marydyth lay down to sleep, the first and last thought in her head was a prayer for Rachel's happiness. It was all that kept her sane.

Once more J.C.'s face came to her mind. She remembered their wedding day, all bright sun and giggling anticipation. J.C. had given her his name on that day.

"Marydyth Hollenbeck... It suits, I think," he had said. Then he had smiled, creating a dimple in his cheek. Did Rachel have a dimple? Marydyth tried to visualize

Rachel's face, how it would have changed and matured during the time she had been away.

As an infant Rachel's hair had held the promise of reddish highlights. Would it be blond or would it shine like an Arizona sunset? Would it flash with auburn fire?

A smile tugged at the corners of Marydyth's mouth. For a short march of time she was able to forget her environment. In her mind, if not her battered body, she could rise up from the depths of Yuma's hellhole and live through the hopes and dreams she cherished for Rachel.

Her little girl would be a beauty, of that Marydyth had no doubt. And she would be a lady.

Victoria would see to it.

Rachel would never have to go to bed hungry. And she would never have to worry about money.

But would she be loved?

Would Victoria be able to put aside the poison of her hatred and embrace Rachel? Or would the bitterness of J.C.'s death be a blight on Rachel's life?

The chilling question made Marydyth shiver more than the bleak cold of the Arizona desert. Would Victoria be able to love the daughter of a woman convicted of killing two husbands?

The moon rose and sent a silvery shaft of light through Rachel's frilly starched curtains. Flynn had opened the window halfway to allow a little fresh air into her room while he got her ready for bed. Now she was tucked up and listening to him with a look of pure fascination on her face.

"...and the little princess lived happily ever after." Flynn closed the slender volume and placed it on the table beside Rachel's bed. He leaned close to give her a kiss on the forehead.

"That was a nice story." She yawned and stretched, nearly giving him a shiner with her small clenched fist.

"You ought to know it by heart, as many times as you've had me read it. I think tomorrow you can read it to me."

"Unca Flynn, I can't read!" Rachel giggled and snuggled down in her feather bed.

"No? All right, then maybe I'll read it one more time—but that's all. Now it is time to say your prayers and get some shut-eye." Flynn helped Rachel out of her bed. She knelt beside it with her head bowed. Delicate pink toes peeked from under the edge of her yellow flannel gown.

"Dear Lord, bless Grandma, Unca Flynn and Carolee Martin's baby goat."

Flynn nearly guffawed, but he supposed that God was as interested in Carolee's kid as he was every other living thing.

Rachel didn't say anything else for a long time, and finally Flynn cleared his throat to hurry her along.

"And please bless my mama, and if it isn't too much trouble, Lord, please send her back home from wherever it was that she had to go. Amen." She scampered under the quilt and closed her eyes without meeting Flynn's stunned gaze.

So, Rachel had decided to enlist the help of the Almighty in getting a mother—her mother.

Flynn leaned over and tucked the covers beneath her chin. "Good night, little one."

She squeezed her eyes tight and burrowed into the softness of her eider coverlet. "Good night, Unca Flynn." She yawned again.

He picked up the lamp and walked to the doorway but something made him pause at the threshold and look at her. She was lying flat on her back with her eyes squeezed shut. The moonlight skimmed over her little turned-up nose and her square chin.

She was beginning to favor her mother.

Flynn nudged the unwanted thought aside. It would do Rachel no favor to become the beauty her mother was. In fact, he feared that the good people of Hollenbeck Corners would start treating her like a pariah if she started to remind them of Marydyth.

He shook himself and turned away from Rachel's door. It wasn't like him to be so damned maudlin. Must be old Charlie's babbling, bringing up the past.

What he needed was a stiff drink and a smoke. And now that Rachel was fed, bathed and tucked in for the night he was going to have one.

He crept down the stairs on tiptoe, taking care to keep his spurs from ringing on the treads. He went into the study—the only room in the rambling mansion that he had ever felt really comfortable in.

Flynn pulled the makings from his shirt pocket and rolled a smoke. It dangled unlit from his lips while he poured himself two fingers of good whiskey.

Old Doc Scoggins had told him that smoking shortened the life span. Course, Doc Scoggins never had a puff of tobacco in his life and he dropped dead during church services only two months back. But Flynn had not wanted to take any chances—for Rachel's sake. He had stopped smoking—at least he had stopped lighting them—but he hadn't stopped rolling them.

Every night as he went through the ritual he told himself it was foolish to cling to his tobacco habit like a sugar-tit, but he got a certain amount of stubborn comfort from rolling a smoke, even if he never lit up.

He laid the unlit cigarette in the ashtray and took a drink. The first sip blazed a hot trail down his gullet and sent a flash of hot lethargy to his limbs. There had been some days in the past two and a half years when he had wondered how women managed to raise a houseful of children without getting roaring drunk once a week.

The thought had finally come to him that men and women were different in more ways than the obvious one—otherwise they would be a pack of falling-down drunks. Motherhood was damned hard work.

He collapsed into the big easy chair by the fireplace, cursing the leather for creaking like a riled cat under his weight. He held his breath and cocked his head, listening.

When the house remained silent, he let out a relieved breath. The noise had not woken Rachel. Perhaps tonight she would sleep.

He took another drink and drew the envelope from his pocket. The paper was of good quality—or had been when it was new. The fancy watermark was still visible beneath the stains.

Flynn stared at the travel-stained paper until a strange feeling crept over him. He felt as if he was violating Marydyth Hollenbeck in some way. Once he even glanced behind him, unable to shake the feeling that he was being watched.

With a snort, he tucked the letter back in his pocket.

What am I going to do with it?

The sensible thing would be to just throw it away.

No, I am not like Victoria Hollenbeck. But there had been times when he wondered if that were true. Maybe he was as cold and cruel as Victoria.

Flynn took another drink and mentally argued with

himself about the letter. What if it was important? Charlie had been worried enough to come out in the night to bring it....

No, he wouldn't open the damned letter.

He finally decided to take it to Moses Pritikin, Victoria's attorney. He could make the decision about whether to open it or to send it on to Marydyth at the Territorial Prison.

Flynn took another drink. Outside, the familiar scratch and whisper of the wind pushing a tumbleweed across the front porch caught his attention. He allowed himself to relax—as much as he ever relaxed in this house.

Since he had gotten tangled up with the Hollenbeck family there hadn't been one truly worry-free moment that he could remember. By day he worried if he was doing a proper job managing little Rachel's estate. And by night...well, at night the demons that most lawmen lived with came to haunt him.

"Only Rachel makes it all worthwhile," he muttered. Rachel's welfare was the tie that bound him tightly to the life he now led.

Rachel's terrified scream jarred Flynn awake. The empty glass shattered on the hearthstones as he jerked to his feet. He bounded toward the stairs. He took them two at a time, his spurs clanging with each impact all the way to Rachel's room.

The moon had moved on but her frantic thrashing and whimpers guided him through the dark to her bedside.

"I'm here, honey, I'm here." He untangled the sheets from her little body. He kept up a steady stream of chin-wagging, not even sure what he was saying, but saying it in a voice intended to soothe and calm.

"Mama!" Rachel whimpered and fought him while he pushed sweat-soaked strands of hair from her brow.

"It's all right, honey," he said, while he wished his hands weren't so big, clumsy and rough—while he wished that he knew more about raising a little girl.

Damn it all to hell—she needs a woman's touch.

"Mama! Mama!" Rachel screamed, as if she had read what was etched into Flynn's heart.

He pulled her close to his chest, knowing that she was still locked in that dark place where she went every night.

"Where are you, Mama?" Her voice had the tone of a lost soul. It bit right into Flynn's heart.

"It's all right, sugar. Uncle Flynn is with you…shh."

So tonight her nightmares were of Marydyth.

Two nights ago she had dreamed she was lost in a great black hole and Flynn could not find her. The nightmares were never exactly the same, except that Rachel was alone and needed somebody to help her.

He kissed her forehead and started to rock her back and forth, humming some tune that had lain in wait since his own childhood.

Too damned long ago to know how to do this.

"I can't find my mama…. Mama…" Her voice trailed off. Within a moment she dragged in a sobbing, ragged breath, and then she finally became still. Her breath came deep and slow as she fell into the blessed peace of slumber. The only sound was the creak of wood and bed ropes as Flynn rocked her.

Morning dawned gray and thready. The clouds overhead were salmon on top and a dirty tarnished silver beneath, streaked as if a child had dipped her fingers in paint and dragged them across the eastern horizon, thought Flynn.

There was no wind yet, but Flynn knew the respite was only temporary. Yep, it was going to come a blow by noon.

He tugged the brim of his Stetson hat down tighter on his head, as if he felt the wind pulling at it already. Jack snorted and broke wind and the chin on the curb rattled as he shook his head. Flynn swung into the saddle and gathered the reins, wanting to get the last of the herd moved today.

"I know, you'd rather stay in the stall and eat cracked corn. You're getting downright lazy since we retired," Flynn told his mount. They had been together so many years that conversation seemed natural, maybe even required. Jack had been his partner on many manhunts and had shared a cold camp with him beyond counting. The big horse flicked his ears back and forth as if he were listening to Flynn.

Flynn pointed Jack southeast and kicked him into a ground-eating lope. When they reached the rest of the herd, Jack worked hard, as if he sensed Flynn's need to get done early. The first-year heifers were separated and put in an upper pasture, but Flynn took the breeding cows and the one-eyed bull to a nice meadow that lay in the squat hills just past Brunckow's cabin.

There were no windows left now and a part of the roof had blown off during the last dust devil, but the cabin and meadow provided a good place to water Jack and take a rest. The cabin had been standing since 1858 when Frederick Brunckow had come looking for riches. What he got was his body tossed down his own mine shaft by a band of renegade Mexicans. It was ironic that Ed Schieffelin had discovered a rich vein of silver only seven miles away in 1870. Poor old Brunckow.

When Flynn had still been riding for the law he had

come to the cabin more than a dozen times looking for outlaws. The raw pockmarked adobe walls helped give it the name that the *Epitaph* newspaper had perpetuated— the bloodiest cabin in Arizona Territory.

Flynn stepped off and let the horse wander around the perimeter of the old building, nibbling grass as he went. He shaded his eyes from the sun, and leaned against the side of the cabin while Jack had a good rest. His eyes roamed the countryside, picking out a jackrabbit and a covey of quail as he rested.

It struck him that he was only a few miles from the Lavender Lady Mine. Since he was so near he decided to go check on it. A lot of men had remained out of work since the big strike that closed the Lady.

And brought him here.

Flynn's mouth twitched at one corner. If it hadn't been for the mining strike he wouldn't have been in Hollenbeck Corners.

And he wouldn't have had to be Marydyth Hollenbeck's escort.

All these years it had stuck in his craw. He had never had to take a woman to prison before. And now he was taking care of that woman's daughter.

It was a hell of a thing.

Flynn leaned away from the side of the cabin and gathered Jack's reins. He had enough daylight left to make it to the mine and still be back home before Rachel needed to go to bed.

Flynn saw the yawning black hole of the shaft from a long way off. There was something about a mine that made his flesh crawl. He supposed he was a bit of a coward when it came to working underground.

"Easy, boy." Flynn steadied Jack and peered into the

rocky outcrop that ringed the Lady. The horse was acting spooky and he couldn't shake the feeling that he was being watched.

A few years ago he would have bolted into the rocks and got prepared to fend off Apaches, but since Geronimo was gone that was no longer a worry.

Still, he couldn't quite shake off the notion that eyes were trained on his spine.

Flynn rode Jack close and did a quick once-over on the mine. It appeared to be in fairly good shape—from the outside. He gnawed on the inside of his mouth while he thought. If the Lady could be reopened it would surely help Hollenbeck Corners.

"Well, that's another thing I can speak to old Moze about." Flynn spoke and Jack worked his ears back and forth in response. That was the only kind of conversation they ever had: Flynn talked and Jack listened.

Flynn heard the distinct sound of a twig snapping. He swiveled in his saddle and drew his Colt at the same time. Nothing but lonesome prairie and cactus met his eye. He sat for a moment while his pulse ticked off the time. Then when he heard and saw nothing, he kicked Jack up and headed back to Hollenbeck Corners.

But he kept his gun drawn.

That evening went much like the one before it. Mrs. Young left after saying her usual dozen words, Flynn and Rachel spent a quiet evening and then she went to bed. At one o'clock in the morning she woke up crying for her mama. By three o'clock in the morning Flynn had decided that he would go see Moses as soon as Mrs. Young showed up at seven.

Flynn was riding down the hill when he came upon Clark's Dairy wagon.

"Morning, Flynn."

"Morning, Amos."

"Did you hear the news?" Amos asked with a happy grin.

"Can't say as I have." Flynn rested his wrist on the saddle horn while Jack took a disagreeable nip at Amos's old bay wagon horse.

"My cousin in Tombstone was getting ready to start delivering milk yesterday when his wagon fell through the street," Amos said with a chuckle.

"I'm sorry to hear that." Flynn tried not to laugh along with Amos.

"No, don't be. My cousin was still on his own land—when they got the wagon out they found a vein of silver. He's gonna be a rich man." Amos chuckled again.

Now Flynn laughed. "I guess I better start taking care where I walk, eh?"

He had heard tales that there was a honeycomb of tunnels beneath Tombstone and Hollenbeck Corners.

"Yeah, I'm hoping I'll have the same kind of luck." Amos Clark smiled and touched his finger to his white cap. Then he clicked his tongue and the bay started off at his plodding gait toward the mansion.

Flynn laughed one more time before he urged Jack on down the slope. Hollenbeck Corners was becoming civilized. It seemed like only yesterday that Geronimo was raiding; now they had door-to-door milk delivery and two daily newspapers and a fire pumper—but no sheriff. The mayor and citizens had decided that John Slaughter, marshal of Cochise county, was near enough. And besides, J.C. was the only man who had ever been murdered, and everybody knew who was guilty even before the trial.

Or so they said. Flynn had never been that sure. All

through the proceedings and even after he had taken Marydyth to Yuma, something had nagged at him.

Times were changing in the territory. Every day it seemed that things became more modern and the world to the east had more of an effect. With news arriving on a regular basis, people in the territory were becoming more political and talk in the saloons was often about what was going on in Washington.

Flynn guided Jack down the main street and stopped at a tall, narrow building with an impressive wooden false front. Sunlight rippled across the fancy gilt lettering in the picture window of the law office. Moses was mighty proud of that window. He had paid a pretty penny to have it shipped by rail from back east and installed by a glazier from Tucson.

Flynn dismounted and loosely wrapped the reins around the hitching post. "Don't go hightailing it back to the barn on me, or I'll take Harold Benson up on his offer. And you'd make a piss-poor livery horse." He softened the threat with an affectionate pat.

He stepped up to the boardwalk and made his way to Moze's office. He heard the sound of two men's voices from the inner office as soon as he opened the outer door and walked inside.

Flynn didn't want to be listening to the conversation so he busied himself pouring a cup of coffee from the gray graniteware pot on the potbellied stove in the corner of the room. His back was to Pritikin's private office, but the men's voices suddenly grew too loud to ignore.

"I'm tellin' you, Ted, I have no authority in this matter. You'll have to deal directly with Flynn O'Bannion."

Flynn turned. Now it wasn't somebody else's business, it was his. He took a step toward the partly open door. Through the crack Flynn could see Moses behind the desk; on the other side, all he could see was the toe of a boot with a fancy double-eagle design.

"Who needs to deal with me?" Flynn drawled as he entered the doorway.

Moses Pritikin's head swung around. The lawyer's sharp eyes were as clear and quick as a red-tailed hawk's, set in a face tanned and cured by a half century of Arizona wind and sun. His hair, white as cow's milk, was a shock against his swarthy, angular face.

"Speaking of the devil... Come in, Flynn, come in." Moze's overlarge hands always seemed to stick too far out of his shirtsleeves, and today was no exception as he gestured.

Flynn crossed the threshold and finally got a look at the man inside those double-eagle boots. Ted Kelts, J.C.'s former partner, was sitting in the red leather chair opposite Pritikin's desk.

"Ted here is interested in buying the Lavender Lady Mine," Moses said.

Pritikin's office was on the skinny side of small from the get-go, and the massive desk he had squeezed into it left scant room for more than one client at a time. Flynn sidled into the room as best as he could and found a place against the wall.

"The Lavender Lady?" Flynn asked after he took a sip of the too-strong, bitter coffee.

Ted Kelts nodded. "I've been thinking it would be good to open the mine. A lot of men in town are out of work. Prices on copper are a bit better now." Ted Kelts grimaced. "I'd kind of like to see what the old girl has left hiding under her skirts."

"Funny you should ask about the Lady, Kelts. I was just out there yesterday looking it over," Flynn said.

"You don't say. How'd it look?"

Flynn shrugged. "I'm no miner. I don't like being underground."

"Well, I am a miner. Sell her to me," Ted said with a smile.

Flynn studied his face for a long time. "I don't think so."

Ted's dark eyes flashed in anger. "But why not?"

"I'm thinking of reopening it myself." Flynn studied his face. "And Victoria really wanted me to keep all the Hollenbeck holdings in one piece."

Ted nodded. "Yes, I understand, Mr. O'Bannion, but J.C. had decided to sell to me—before he was murdered by that woman. By all rights I should own the Lavender Lady." Kelts fingered the gold chain on his watch fob. "Moses tells me that you have complete control now."

Flynn pushed the Stetson hat back on his head with his index finger. The last thing he wanted to do was get into a chaffer with Ted Kelts over some hole in the ground.

"Victoria put me in charge of all the Hollenbeck family holdings," Flynn said, but there was no pleasure in his admission.

Kelts smiled and leaned toward him. "Let's discuss terms, O'Bannion. How much do you want for the Lavender Lady?" His navy brocade vest puckered at his middle, but Ted tugged the cloth down tight until it was smooth and wrinkle free. He was a tall, rangy man, strong as a bull, with hard muscles that had been honed by swinging an eighteen-pound sledge for years before he hit his first strike. "I'm sure Victoria intended to take care of this oversight before she had her last stroke. It would be a matter of you signing the papers, O'Bannion, righting a wrong, you might say."

Flynn's gaze followed the sharp crease along the fancy

pin-striped trousers to the handmade Justin boot propped up on the knee of his opposite leg. If price was the issue, Ted Kelts could afford whatever was asked.

His eyes slid up to meet Ted's gaze. "'Tain't for sale."

Kelts stiffened. "What do you mean it ain't for sale? Everything and everybody has a price. Just name yours."

Flynn narrowed his eyes. "Sorry, the Lavender Lady ain't for sale." The more he talked to Ted Kelts, the less he liked him. "Not today or any day."

Ted uncrossed his legs and sat up straight. "You're a cattle man, O'Bannion. I know you're running your own head along with Hollenbeck stock. Why would you want a broken-down mine to worry over? It's probably worthless anyway, but I'd be a whole lot more able to get it open again than you would."

"Maybe, maybe not," Flynn said.

"Then...why won't you sell?" Ted looked perplexed.

"I'm riding for the Hollenbeck brand now. Victoria made it plain she wants Rachel to have all the Hollenbeck property—just as it is. And just for future reference, I haven't got a price."

Kelts snapped his head around and looked at Moses. "Is this legal?"

"Legal as Victoria's money and my skill could make it." No small amount of pride sparkled in the dusky depths of Moze's eyes and he was working hard not to grin. "I'd like to see somebody find a loophole in one of my documents. Damned near ironclad.... Write them so nobody can break them," he added under his breath.

Ted sat motionless as a tombstone. His eyes narrowed for half a second, then he stood and tugged his vest down. "Well, I guess that's my answer—for today, O'Bannion. But I'm a man who usually gets what he goes after, so I'm sure we'll be talking again."

Flynn leaned away from the wall and nodded. "About anything you want, Kelts, but when it comes to the Lavender Lady, the answer will still be no. That is my last word on the subject."

"I didn't get where I am by giving in easily." Ted extended his hand to Flynn. "No hard feelings?"

"I wouldn't fault a businessman for doing what comes natural to him."

"Glad to hear it." Ted pulled his watch chain and drew a fancy pocket piece from his vest. "I'll take my leave now." Ted nodded at Moses and Flynn. "Thanks for the coffee, Moze."

"Don't mention it. By the way, Ted, I heard you was headed back east?"

Kelts frowned and slipped the watch back where it came from. "News does travel fast in Hollenbeck Corners. Yes, I have some business in Washington."

"Taking up politics, are you?" Moses smiled like a fox.

"The thought has crossed my mind." Ted smiled and turned to Flynn. "Think about what I said, O'Bannion."

When Ted closed the outside door, Flynn eased himself down into the solitary leather chair.

"More coffee?" Moses offered.

"Naw." Flynn shook his head. "This stuff would rust a horseshoe, Moze."

Moses blinked and stared at his own cup. "Really?"

Flynn shook his head and set down his cup. With Kelts gone, his thoughts settled firmly on the letter in his pocket.

"Whiskey, then?" Moses offered as he opened his desk drawer and brought out a brand-new bottle of Cutter and Miller.

"A little early for that, wouldn't you say?" Flynn frowned at the attorney.

"You tell me? You look like a dog chewing on a tough piece of hide." Moses leaned back and laced his fingers behind the shock of unruly white hair. "Maybe you need a woman. Beatrice has a new girl over at the sportin' house. Name is Annabelle—ain't that a hoot—such a fancy name for a whore? Has hair the color of molten copper."

Flynn's frowned deepened. "I didn't come here to get directions to the cathouse, Moze."

"And here I was thinking that maybe you had lost your way. I happen to know you haven't visited Beatrice and her girls for two years," Moses went on, ignoring Flynn's glower. "It ain't healthy, Flynn. A man can get all backed up...ruin your digestion—shorten your life. It's a medical fact. Dr. Goodfellow over in Tombstone told me so."

"I don't need a woman," Flynn repeated with a flinty voice.

"I haven't seen a look so mournful since the last lynchin' bee over in Millville. If it isn't a woman you need, then what has put that hangdog look on your face? Trouble with your cattle? Little Rachel?"

"No trouble with Rachel or the cattle."

"Why don't you get rid of those critters? They're more trouble than they're worth."

"Easy for you to say. That's what I do for a living now, Moze. A grown man has to have a livelihood."

The lawyer snorted. "You don't need the money." Moze's hand fell to the desktop and he shook his head in amazement. "Guardianship of Rachel pays you a nice annuity—I write out the bank draft, remember?"

Flynn shifted in the chair and scowled at Moses but he didn't say anything.

"You haven't touched it, have you?" His brows rose until they nearly touched his hairline, and his eyes widened. "It's all just sitting there in the bank, isn't it?"

Flynn shook his head. "I didn't come here to talk about that damned money. I didn't want it in the first place."

"You are a strange duck, Flynn O'Bannion." Moses shook his head in disbelief.

"Look, it's bad enough to be living in the Hollenbeck house like it was my own...." Flynn's voice trailed off. It was hard to put into words the way he felt about caring for Rachel, but he sure as hell wasn't going to take money for it.

Moses laughed and rocked back in his chair, then laced his hands behind his head again. "You are a dying breed. All right, if that isn't what's stuck in your craw, then tell me what is."

Flynn drew the envelope from his shirt pocket and held it out.

"What's this?" Moses unclasped his fingers and leaned forward across the mammoth desk.

"Look at the address." Flynn shoved the paper closer.

Moses took the letter. His eyes flitted across the tattered envelope. When he glanced back up at Flynn he was frowning; all traces of humor were gone. "Why haven't you opened it?"

Because I felt like I was violating Marydyth Hollenbeck's privacy just looking it. Because I have never been able to forget the hatred in her blue eyes or how she held her head high when she walked through the gates of Yuma.

"You're the Hollenbeck attorney," Flynn answered

with a careless shrug of his shoulders. "I brought it to you."

"Victoria Hollenbeck's attorney—not Marydyth's." Moses handed the envelope back to Flynn. "This is your domain. You better open it."

Flynn drew back his hand as if the letter were afire. "It's probably...personal."

"Maybe, but it looks like it has taken the long way round coming here—how personal could it be when the sender didn't even know the Black Widow had been sent to prison?"

A muscle in the side of Flynn's jaw began to work. He hated the name the townspeople had pinned on Marydyth. For Rachel's sake.

"It doesn't seem right."

"Fine, I'll do it." Moses snatched up the envelope and ripped open one end. A page fluttered to the top of the desk. He carefully unfolded the brittle paper. It was a heavy cream-colored stationery. He held it up to the light. Flynn could see the distinctive watermark of a clipper ship. Then Moses squinted his eyes, ducked his chin and started to read.

A hard knot formed in Flynn's gizzard. He didn't feel right about any of this.

"Well, now this is a fine kettle of fish," Moses said as he let the paper slip from his hand.

"You look like somebody died."

Moses never spoke, he just slid the single page across the desk. "Read it for yourself."

Flynn picked up the letter, his eyes darting quickly over the large handwriting. He looked up from the page and swallowed hard.

"What are *you* going to do?" Moses asked.

"So it's all up to me, huh?" Flynn stood up. He would

have liked to pace, but the cramped office wouldn't allow it. "What would you do if you had to deal with it?"

Moses grimaced and read the letter again. "Claims complete responsibility for the murder in Louisiana." He mused aloud as if he had not even heard Flynn's question. "Could it be possible?"

"If it is, then Marydyth Hollenbeck..." He couldn't finish his sentence.

Moze swallowed hard. "Now, let's not be too hasty. At the worst it may mean that she didn't kill her first husband, Andre. This second part could be a confession of guilt, I suppose, if you are inclined to interpret it that way."

"And it could just as easily not be. Is that what you're saying?" Flynn searched the attorney's face with narrowed eyes.

Moses sighed and placed the letter in the middle of his desk. "Any way you look at it, it's a judgment call, Flynn. The decision and the responsibility are all yours, I'm happy to say." The words fell harder than the judge's gavel had on that fateful day. "Victoria made it real clear—any and all decisions regarding Rachel and the Hollenbecks are yours alone."

Flynn picked up the letter and stared at it. "Did you notice the signature?"

"Yes, I did. I have to admit it shocks me. I thought Murdering Mary was all alone in the world. If she had an uncle, then why didn't she tell anybody?"

Flynn glanced up. "Kind of sticks in your craw, don't it?"

"I don't want to even entertain the notion that we might've separated Rachel from her mother and sent an innocent woman to prison," Moses replied. "In fact I don't like to think about that a'tall."

Chapter Three

Flynn gave Jack his head as they rode out of town. The bay enjoyed the run and Flynn was glad to let him pick his own trail so he could wrestle with the problem of the damned letter.

If he decided to interpret the letter as a full confession for both murders, Andre Levesque's and J. C. Hollenbeck's, then Rachel could have her mother back.

The memory of the child's latest nightmare brought a shiver coursing through him.

And if it isn't a confession? the voice of the cynical retired U.S. marshal prodded. Years of training, years of single-minded devotion to the law, made it difficult for Flynn to forget that big *if*.

The letter was vague on J.C.'s murder. That was God's honest truth. But it was blunt and to the point about the first one—about Andre, Marydyth's first husband.

But if Marydyth were innocent of killing Andre Levesque and she had an uncle, then why didn't she defend herself at the trial?

Flynn shook his head, realizing finally what it was that had bothered him about that damned trial.

Day after day Marydyth had sat there in silence. She

had grown more pale and drawn as the damning evidence was revealed, and not once had she raised a finger or uttered a single word to defend herself.

She had stood there dry-eyed and silent while the town judged her guilty.

Why?

That question hammered at Flynn's brain. It was a question he had no answer for.

He rode for hours, and with every mile the letter nagged at him. It would be so easy. If Flynn chose to read between the lines, he could give Rachel what she needed most in the world.

If he chose to.

Was it possible that he *wanted* to see Rachel reunited with Marydyth so badly that he could, or would, turn a blind eye to the weakness in the wording of that letter?

"Hell no, I wouldn't," he declared with hearty conviction. "And I'd have harsh words with any man who thought otherwise." The sound of his raspy voice started Jack's ears working back and forth again. "If I believed Marydyth killed J.C., I'd let her rot in Yuma and damn her to perdition without a second thought," he assured himself and his horse.

But do you really believe that? the stubborn voice asked. *Or are you like Moze?—afraid that you escorted an innocent woman to prison and mighty unwilling to face that possibility? Even if it means leaving her there?*

Later that afternoon, Flynn had made a big loop around Hollenbeck Corners and ridden through Sheepshead. He had checked on the herd and felt satisfied that the grass would hold through the summer. While he rode, he had argued with himself over and over, and still he had not made a decision about the letter.

He pulled his Stetson hat from his head and used his bandanna to wipe the moisture off the inside of the sweatband. A white ring of crystallized salt had stained outward onto the brim.

If he believed the letter was genuine, then he was beholden to see the territorial judge about Marydyth's sentence. But he hadn't quite come to that decision—just yet.

The sun was a red-gold disk when Flynn unsaddled Jack and rubbed him down. The expansive adobe stable behind the Hollenbeck house was cool and dim. It was big enough to hold four horses and two buggies but Jack lived all alone inside. The smell of hay, dust and cracked corn surrounded them.

It was a comforting odor, a familiar one that had drawn him to this spot many times since he came to live in Hollenbeck Corners. Flynn rolled himself a smoke and let it dangle unlit from his mouth.

Flynn brushed the horse and ran an empty gunnysack over him to give him a shine. He tossed down his unlit cigarette, picked up each of Jack's hooves, one by one, and carefully cleaned them, taking particular care with each frog.

An hour had passed while he kept his hands busy, and still he had not come to a decision. Flynn walked toward the mansion, still lost in thought. He was near one of the tall colonnades at the back of the house when the smell of smoke reached his nostrils.

He turned his head and lifted his nose like a feral animal. He inhaled deeply, narrowing his eyes and allowing the scent to guide him to the source. The smoke was coming from the direction of the stable.

Flynn ran to the well and grabbed up a bucket of water. It sloshed over his Levi's as he ran. When he threw open the double doors a column of smoke roiled out. One bucket doused the smoldering manure and straw, but as the smoke wafted around his head a tendril of suspicion wove around his mind.

It was damned hard to start a fire with a cold cigarette. Flynn made sure the blaze was well and truly out before he went to the house. A nagging sense of unease was his constant companion. He hadn't started that fire, so who had? The stable was behind the house, a damned long way from any road or alley. If someone had been smoking around there, then they were hiding.

As soon as Flynn opened the door a streak of calico ruffles and bouncing russet curls flew at him.

"Unca Flynn!" Rachel squealed. She hugged his knees so tight he thought they both might go end over teakettle into the hallway.

"Whoa, little lady." He untangled her arms and lifted her up. Her cheeks dimpled when he tickled her.

It never ceased to amaze him that in the light of day she had no memory of her nightmares. As long as she was awake she was a happy, laughing child.

"What's goin' on, dumplin'?" he asked as he walked the same path he took every day, through the foyer, up the hall, across the parlor and finally through the kitchen door.

Mrs. Young was already tying on her bonnet. "Evening, Mr. O'Bannion."

"Evening, ma'am." He shifted Rachel's weight to his bony hip, tickling her as he did so.

She giggled shrilly.

"Chicken and dumplings on the stove, cobbler on the warmer. See you tomorrow at seven."

"Thank you, Mrs. Young," he said to the flash of

white petticoat that showed beneath the Scotch tweed muslin of her skirt before the door slammed with a rattle.

Flynn had been so busy chewing on the problem of the letter that he had plumb forgotten about looking for another housekeeper. He had to find somebody who would be better with Rachel. At least now that the cattle were moved he would be home with Rachel more during the day. Until roundup in the fall he would have time aplenty to spend with her.

"I been waiting for you," said the golden sprite clinging to his neck. Excitement telegraphed through her body and up his arm. She gnawed at her bottom lip, as if she were about to explode. "I've been waiting a long, long time." She sighed as if to emphasize the extreme hardship it had been.

"What's got you hopping like a Mexican jumping bean?" He left the kitchen and went into the study. He folded his body into a big padded chair.

Rachel scrambled up and positioned herself squarely in his lap. She stared him in the eye and then she leaned close as if she was about to tell him a secret. "Mrs. Young wouldn't help me get into the attic today."

He felt his eyebrows rising.

Then cool smooth palms clamped on either side of his beard-stubbled jaws. "She said I had to wait for you...so I waited."

Flynn felt the strain of the day winnow from his bones as he stared into cornflower-blue eyes. "What in tarnation do you want to go into the attic for?"

"'Cause I need baby clothes." She patted him with those tiny hands that felt softer than goose down. Then she impulsively kissed his cheek and giggled. "You are an old silly, Unca Flynn."

He laughed with her. "Yes, I guess I am, sugar." Rachel was like a ray of sunshine all bottled up in a Mason jar. "'Cause I can't figger out why on earth you need baby clothes. You've been out of nappies for a long while now." He chuckled at the expression that flitted across her face, a combination of horror and embarrassment, as he teased her.

"I am a big girl now—they aren't for me. Mary Wilson's mama had another baby girl. Mrs. Young said my baby clothes are in the attic." She turned serious. "Could we take the baby some?"

Flynn didn't know whether to laugh or moan. There were so many things that he didn't know about little girls. Was this the kind of thing he could look forward to, crawling around in the attic for baby clothes to give away?

"Please, Unca Flynn."

"All right, punkin. As soon as we're through with supper we'll go into the attic and find you some baby clothes."

"I knew you'd say yes." She grinned triumphantly. "I *told* Mrs. Young you would say yes."

"You just wrap me around that little finger of yours, don't you?" He rose from the chair with her in his arms. Rachel clung to his arm as he swung her around and perched her up high on his shoulders. He gripped her ankles above the high buttons on her black leather shoes. The rough skin in his palm snagged against her white silk stockings and the lace on her pantaloons.

"Hurry, Unca Flynn, hurry. Let's eat fast so we can go to the attic."

He added a little speed and a lot of bounce to his walk. "I'll hurry but you may be sorry you asked when we run—" he ducked low to miss the threshold of the study "—into a big—" he dipped again to miss the chandelier in the hall "—fat, hairy spider!" He flipped her off his shoulder and tickled her ribs when they reached the kitchen.

Rachel's screams of glee echoed through the house. His laughter mingled with the savory odor of chicken and dumplings, and for a while Flynn was able to forget about the damned letter.

When the dinner was eaten, the dishes washed, wiped and put away, Flynn and Rachel lit a lantern and went in search of the attic. He had never been in that part of the Hollenbeck house—the closed off wing where Marydyth and J.C.'s bedroom had been—and it took a few minutes to locate the right set of stairs that led to the attic.

Flynn held the lantern high and swept his hand across the gauzy veil of cobwebs when he opened the last door.

A hundred feminine articles met his gaze in the flicker of the lamp. Frilly doilies were piled on top of an armless rocker, the kind that women favored. Three dome-topped trunks were shoved in one dark corner.

By the time Victoria had had her stroke and wrangled Flynn into becoming Rachel's guardian, Mrs. Young or some other hireling had packed away every trace of Marydyth that had ever existed. The day he had walked into the house it had been clean and completely devoid of anything personal. Over the years he'd had regular tintypes of Rachel taken to put on the piano and the mantel.

So far Rachel had not asked him too many questions, but her nightmares told him that she was asking questions in her mind. She had a natural curiosity about her folks, and the day was coming when somebody was going to have to give her some answers.

Flynn had a flash of memory of his own childhood.

He remembered sitting on Sky's lap and listening to the story of her life over and over. Victoria's hatred and bitterness toward Marydyth had left a great big hole in Rachel's life. And no matter how hard he tried, Flynn hadn't been able to fill it.

While he was preoccupied with his own thoughts, he stumbled over a big hatbox and staggered against a chest. The pain in his shin snapped him back to the present. A table with a cracked marble top provided him with a convenient place to set the lantern so he could rub his barked shinbone.

"Unca Flynn, can I come in?" Rachel's voice sounded hollow as it echoed off the discarded furniture and trunks.

"You can come in, honey, but you be real careful." He scanned the area with narrowed eyes. The cool, dry attic would be a favored nesting site for spiders...black widows.

Black Widow.

The name brought a bitter taste to his mouth. He froze for a moment, knowing that the letter in his pocket could remove that brand from Rachel's mother. If only he could put aside his doubts.

"Looky, Unca Flynn!" Rachel's excited voice brought him spinning around on his boot heel. She was stroking the hair mane of a carved wooden pony. The horse was white with black spots painted on its hindquarters.

Flynn took a step toward her but his boot caught on a red fringed shawl that was draped over something. The more he tried to free himself the more the shawl tangled around his foot. Rachel watched him wide-eyed while he did a dance with the thing hanging from his spur. But suddenly her frozen expression halted him in his tracks.

"What is it, honey? Are you bit?" He knelt down and

gathered her to his arms. Her face had gone pale as chalk. She was quiet as death. "Tell me, does it hurt, Rachel?"

She shook her head in denial. "No." Her eyes were wide and unblinking.

Fear of a kind Flynn had never imagined squeezed around his heart. "Rachel? What is it? Talk to me, honey." His chest contracted while he searched her hands and arms. He could find no marks, but if Rachel was quiet, something had to be wrong. "Rachel, answer me. What is the matter?"

She lifted her tiny hand and pointed. He swiveled around to see what she was staring at. It was a portrait. The flickering lantern light caused the azure-blue eyes to look as if they were alive. A cascade of flaxen curls tumbled over one shoulder and down out of sight at the bottom of the painting. Artfully painted stones glowed at the delicate ears and encircled the slender column of throat.

Smoky topaz and diamond earbobs with a necklace to match.

In a voice colder than the grave, Victoria had read the inventory of missing jewelry at the trial. Marydyth had sat silent, never denying her guilt, never defending herself. But now Flynn had the nagging question at the back of his mind. The letter that was signed "Uncle Blaine" mentioned that jewelry, even went so far as to talk about J.C. giving it to him as some sort of payoff.

But why wouldn't Marydyth have mentioned that? Even when Flynn brought in the old Wanted posters and they spoke of a man she had been seen traveling with, she never said a word about having an uncle.

Why wouldn't she have fought for her innocence?

"Who is that lady?" Rachel whispered.

Flynn jerked himself away from the memory of the trial. He searched his mind and heart. If he told Rachel she was staring at a likeness of her mother it would open a floodgate of questions, questions he didn't want to have to answer. It would be even worse than the other night.

If you don't tell her it will be the same as lying, his prickly conscience accused. *You'll be no better than Victoria.*

Flynn tightened his jaw against the thought. He grasped Rachel's pointy little chin and tipped her face up. Trust glowed in eyes the exact shade of the ones that silently watched him from the painting.

Flynn O'Bannion had the power to give Rachel a piece of her past. But his mouth grew thick when he thought about what he was about to do.

He could change her life. But was it fair to tell her the portrait was of her mother and then turn around and leave it and all of Rachel's questions like discarded furniture in the attic? If he told her about the painting, then wouldn't he have to tell her more?

Could he ignore the letter in his pocket and leave Marydyth behind those thick walls of Yuma when Rachel needed her so much?

The confession wasn't so vague; in fact, now that he thought about it, it was plain as day. Marydyth had an uncle named Blaine, and he had her missing jewelry. He killed her first husband and then had come to Hollenbeck Corners and killed again. It was not so hard to follow.

It might've happened that way. I can believe it happened that way for Rachel.

"That's a painting of Marydyth Hollenbeck, sweetheart. That is your mother."

Night sounds filled the Spartan cell. Marydyth had been unable to sleep even though her body cried out for rest. She had been plagued by thoughts of Rachel—plagued and comforted.

She turned over on the cot and put her face toward the wall. If she tried real hard and concentrated with all her might, she could almost feel the texture of Rachel's satiny skin beneath her fingers. She did it now, ignored all that surrounded her and thought only of Rachel. Her sweet blue eyes, her soft downy cheeks, the way a little dimple appeared when she giggled.

Suddenly rough hands jerked Marydyth around, and she raised her hands to protect herself. As she struggled, the moonlight coming through, she felt the edge of a blade.

The complicated machinery started to turn right after Flynn met with the territorial governor. He had moved as quickly as he could, but he had been careful to make sure that nobody knew what he was doing.

He didn't want to see the Hollenbeck name dragged through the newspapers again. And he intended to talk to Marydyth first.

Prison changed people and he wanted to make sure that the woman coming out of Yuma had the same kind of affection for Rachel as the one that went in.

Marydyth was innocent, the indicting voice of his conscience kept reminding him.

He shook his head, not allowing himself to dwell on that too long. Flynn could not change the past, but he was doing everything he could to change the future—Rachel's future.

Protecting Rachel was his only thought. She deserved to meet her mother under the best of circumstances. He made arrangements for Rachel to stay with Victoria, under the care of her nurse and housekeeper, so he could ride to Tombstone to meet Marydyth to make certain the woman would be good for Rachel. He wanted to have a talk with her first, to prepare her for the changes that had taken place while she was gone and the way things would have to be for the future.

It wasn't a chore he was looking forward to.

Marydyth dragged her hand across her forehead to wipe away some of the sweat. Her dry throat begged for water, but it was hours until the guard would ring the watering bell. Until then she was expected to toil in the inferno of the prison laundry silently.

Or else suffer the consequences.

A strand of her short, jaggedly cut hair fell into her eyes. She impatiently nudged at it with the back of her wrist, breaking her rhythm on the washboard for only a second. When she thought of the horror of her hair being sliced away by that wicked blade, a hot burning pain constricted her throat.

She had thought she was going to die that night.

Had been sure that her throat would be the next target of the blade. But the poor demented woman who attacked her had only wanted the blond curls. After she had them in her trembling hands she had shrunk against the adobe wall, cackling and mumbling incoherently. Marydyth had felt nothing but pity for her when the guards came to drag her away.

Marydyth shoved away the soft thoughts and rubbed the cloth hard against the cake of strong lye soap, then she dipped it and repeated the process. Steam rose from the water. Her flesh burned as she washed the garment.

She had no more pity for the woman—or for herself. It was not something she could afford to have in here.

Pain was not a sensation she responded to any longer

either. Her fingers bled in spots while she rubbed the fabric along the perforated ridges of the scrub board, then rinsed it in the scalding water. Doing the prison laundry was considered a privilege by the committees and people who came to visit the facility, but in truth it was like toiling in the humid bowels of hell.

Marydyth's stomach growled. She wondered what time it was. In the dim confines of adobe walls five and half feet thick there was no way of knowing. Being inside Yuma was like being entombed alive. She felt as if she had been swallowed by the earth. There was no light, no air.

And no way out—ever.

She bit her lip. Only by concentrating on the repetitious task in front of her was she able to slow the pace of her pounding heart. A drop of sweat dripped from the end of her nose. She watched it fall on the stone floor beside her foot, wetting the dust for a moment before it dried away.

Today the heat was searing but tonight when the sun went down the prison would turn freezing cold. She would shiver in her bunk with the thin blanket pulled up to her chin and she would dream.

Her life had settled into a routine of suffering. The only thing that kept her from taking her own life to end the torment of this place was the memory of her beautiful child.

Rachel.

She whispered the name aloud, surprising herself with the sound of her own voice. A smile tugged at her dry lips causing them to crack and sting.

She didn't care. Thinking of Rachel was like having enough to eat and drink. It was like being clean, and not lying awake in terrorized exhaustion, waiting for a dirty guard to come or another prisoner to hack off her hair.

Rachel was the only bright spot in Marydyth's existence.

She clung to the hope that God might take pity upon her and let her see Rachel again someday.

Hadn't she paid enough for her crime? Wasn't the time she had missed with Rachel enough to pay for what she had done?

Marydyth finished scrubbing Superintendent Behan's shirt and folded it end over end, twisting the material until a steady stream of water gushed out. When it was wrung as dry as she could get it, she tossed it into another tub of clear water to rinse. Over and over she repeated the task—scrubbing, wringing, rinsing.

She had not had a change of clean clothes in so long she could not count, but Superintendent Behan wore a clean shirt every day, just like Superintendent Gates before him and Superintendent Ingalls before that. She had counted the march of days and months through three different superintendents.

How many more she would see come and go before she died within these earthen walls?

Memories of her life in Hollenbeck Corners rose unbidden to her mind. Images of her fine clothes and the house J.C. had built for her flashed through her consciousness. She had been rich, and, if not liked by the townspeople, she had at least been respected for the position her husband held. But that was long ago, before Flynn O'Bannion had found the Wanted posters. Before the terrible thing she had done came back to haunt her, before God found a way to punish her for her sins.

Marydyth shook herself and focused on the washing, forcing her emotions to the edges of her mind. When she was sure the blaze of rage was subdued, she allowed herself to think again.

It was odd. When she came to Yuma she was a bundle of emotions. Then she slowly changed. First her compassion had died, followed by her ability to feel pain. The only defense against the crushing brutality inside these walls had been to stop caring, stop feeling. Marydyth had been thankful when she stopped experiencing those emotions, it made each day more bearable. She had allowed herself to retain only two emotions in this place; her love for Rachel and her hatred of Marshal Flynn O'Bannion. Two emotions, as different as hot from cold or ice from fire, but both had kept her sane.

And both were of equal measure and intensity. She hated Flynn with the same passion that she loved Rachel.

Marydyth was bent over the washtub when the short hair at the back of her neck prickled.

She stiffened, suddenly alert and aware. Living in this pesthole had required her to develop senses and hone instincts she had never known she possessed. Even when she had been on the run after Blaine had forced her to marry Andre, she had not felt as *hunted* as she did within these walls.

She gripped the sides of the washboard, ready to use it as a cudgel to defend herself. She partially turned, keeping the tub of hot water at her back for protection.

Marydyth met the fetid breath and unwashed stench of one of the prison guards. "Superintendent wants to see you in his office."

The information refused to register in Marydyth's brain. "See me? Why?"

"If I knew, I sure as hell wouldn't be tellin'. Come on." She received a bruising prod from the thick oak stick the guard carried.

"Move out," he barked.

Marydyth released her grip on the edge of the wash-board. She wiped her hands on the front of her dress. Putting one foot in front of the other she blocked out the pain in her side as she made her way through the darkness of the thick adobe passages.

Flynn rose from the wing-back chair in the lobby and sauntered to the front window of the Russ House. It afforded him an unobstructed view of the main street of Tombstone. Nellie Cashman and Mrs. Cunningham had done a fine job of making their hotel a success. The flooding of the mines in '86 had dealt a hard blow to Tombstone, but as Flynn stared out the window he saw the town bustling with the usual assortment of bad men and businessmen. The place was fighting its way back with a mighty roar.

Idly he wondered if reopening the Lavender Lady would restore some of Hollenbeck Corners' former glory. The idea rattled at the back of his brain as he scanned the street.

A painted cat entered one of the saloons across the street with a provocative flash of her turkey-red petticoats. A rowdy cowboy answered her invite, yelling hearty whoops into the dry air as he dismounted his horse on the run and nudged the swinging doors aside.

Flynn found himself smiling at the randy hombre. It seemed a lifetime since he had followed a woman like a buck in full rut. And longer than that since he had whooped in anticipation of bedding a whore. Since Rachel had come into his life he had been too busy to indulge in those pleasures.

His gaze fell upon a woman with a sedate blue bonnet walking from the direction of Schafer and Lord's Mercantile. A gentle breeze made the feather on her hat sway back and forth.

He never did find a housekeeper to replace sour Mrs. Young, and it was just one more thing he had to deal with. He dragged off his Stetson hat and raked his fingers through his hair while he was chewing on the notion.

A whistle blew. His worry about Mrs. Young drifted away on the fading sound. The train from Yuma had arrived.

Marydyth Hollenbeck looked up and tried to stop the pounding of her heart. She was nearly home.

Home.

The word practically took wing and flew!

She gripped the seat in front of her with her work-worn knuckles and waited until everyone else had gotten off the car. Then she rose, trying not to tremble, and headed for the door.

People stared at her and pointed, whispering about how she looked, but she didn't care. They could not see beneath the jagged hair or the shabby dress the superintendent had given her before they let her out. They could not see her heart leaping with joy, or the tears of happiness threatening to pour forth. They did not know that the pitiful, threadbare creature who walked among them had a daughter named Rachel.

Marydyth inhaled air, fresh, free air, and nearly pitied the people beside her because they were not even aware there was a difference. How could they know the simple joy she felt by being able to walk where she chose?

Her feet were light as her heart as she made her way through the streets. The instructions had been simple. She was to use the money provided to buy a ticket to Tombstone. There, somebody would meet her and take her to Hollenbeck Corners.

Home.

A hundred plans flew through her head when she thought about it. She was so happy. She wanted to break into a run, to hurry to the hotel to get on her way to Hollenbeck Corners.

Who would meet her? Victoria? Moses Pritikin? But really she didn't care who. All she could think of was collecting Rachel. Then they could begin their lives anew. They would pack only a few things, and then leave all the bad memories behind. She would get them on the train and they would just go.

Maybe Denver—or perhaps San Francisco. J.C.'s fortune would certainly buy a simple house in a respectable neighborhood. She could see that Rachel had a good education. Piano and dancing lessons—a proper finishing school.

Maybe she should learn a language. French?

France would be nice. Paris. There was nothing to stop her now—no bars, no ghosts. Marydyth was free. God had seen fit to show her mercy. She was going to be the very best mother any child ever had. There was only the two of them, but it was enough.

Dear God, it was enough to be a family.

She mumbled a prayer of thanks that the Lord had forgiven her for her sins as she put her feet on the boardwalk and hurried down the street toward the hotel.

Flynn chewed the inside of his jaw and searched every face that went by the hotel. He had made sure Marydyth had been told nothing, given no particulars about her release.

There were things he wanted to say himself. There

were things that she would have to know before she saw Rachel.

Flynn was staring unfocused at the sunbaked caliche street when Ted Kelts stepped into his line of vision. The dapper businessman was the last person Flynn expected to see in Tombstone, but then the memory of Moses and Ted mentioning Ted's trip to Washington flitted through Flynn's mind. He started to step outside and speak to him but a clutch of people gathered on the boardwalk outside the window blocking his way. Kelts nearly collided with a thin woman who seemed to be in a big hurry. She crossed the street and opened the door to the hotel, then stepped inside the lobby. The threadbare dress was of poor quality and hung on her thin shoulders. She looked around at the lobby and turned.

He felt as if he had been kicked in the ribs by an Army mule. For the first time in memory, his knees went weak as water. He reached out for the back of a nearby green velvet chair for support.

The gold hair framing her face was jaggedly cut and no longer than his fingers, hanging limp and stringy. Her indigo-blue eyes were haunted, yet they glittered in a way that was chilling. Her skin was gaunt and pale from lack of sun.

"Mrs. Hollenbeck?" Flynn took a step forward. "Marydyth?" he asked in a softer voice.

She rocked back on her heels at the sound of her name. The last trace of color in her face drained away. Those indigo eyes hardened until they resembled shards of Bisbee turquoise.

"You." She hoped the one word held all the contempt she could manage. Time seemed to stop while she stared at him. He looked at her, unblinking. Marydyth studied the lean weather-beaten jaw as it jerked spasmodically.

His eyes were as cold as ice-slicked sandstone and they bored into her. For the first time today she was ashamed of her plain prison-issue dress. For the first time today she felt a pang of dread.

Flynn tried to school his features, tried to hide his shock at the change in her. His stomach was knotted up, and it was hard to draw enough air into his lungs.

Dear God, what have they done to you? he thought, but all he said was "Ma'am."

She moved suddenly, digging frantically into the pocket of the drab gray dress. She jerked out a folded paper and brandished it at him like a weapon. "I am free—my sentence was commuted by the governor. Go find somebody else to consign to hell, you bastard." She continued to hold the paper up, as if it were a shield against hurt and harm.

Flynn flinched at the word "bastard," and felt his pity turn to a hot flash of anger. He would have killed any man for saying that.

"Did you hear me?" she said. "I am free."

"I heard," he grated out. But when he didn't reach to take the paper that she waved in front of her, she shoved it back into her pocket. Her hand hovered near as if she were fearful he—or someone—might take the precious document away from her. "I am not a wanted criminal anymore. You can get on your horse and—" her voice cracked "—just leave me in peace."

"I came here to meet you, Marydyth, to take you back to Hollenbeck Corners."

Her eyes narrowed. "I'd rather walk."

She took three steps and closed the distance between them. She slapped him hard across the face. The blow echoed like the crack of doom.

He grabbed her wrist and held it with enough pressure

to still her. "Are you sure you want to do this?" he asked in a voice that was barely a whisper. "Here? Now? With everybody watching?"

Her eyes darted around the room.

A young man in a pin-striped suit, who had been carrying baggage through the lobby, stopped in his tracks and stared openmouthed. An elderly couple descending the stairs turned and hurried back up, whispering words of disgust and dismay.

She thought of Rachel, and a strangled sob escaped her lips. Marydyth had no reputation left...but her daughter—her sweet innocent daughter would have to live with the sting of rumor. Marydyth drew herself up and tried to find some dignity and pride within the hatred and anger she felt.

Flynn kept hold of her hand, noticing how raw and red it was. Her knuckles were barked and there was not an extra bit of flesh anywhere on her. She glared up at him through a blur of tears, and he felt the venom of her loathing.

"I hate you," she whispered as if she had heard his thoughts and needed to make herself clearer. "I hate you more than anybody on God's earth."

A muscle in his lean jaw twitched.

"Do you hear me? I hate you for what you did to me." Her voice was raspy and harsh. "You, the noble Marshal O'Bannion, had to find those Wanted posters, had to bring them to the court and let everyone know..." Her voice broke and she started to tremble.

He turned so quickly she had no time to do anything but let him pull her along. His boots dug into the carpet, and he dragged her toward the stairs while he maintained the viselike grip on her wrist. "Come on."

"I'm not going anywhere with you."

"Yes...you are." His husky whisper was like iron striking against stone. "We are going upstairs."

Upstairs.

"I would rather die," Marydyth said as she struggled against him.

"Don't be a fool, Marydyth," he said tunelessly.

It was useless. She was no match for his superior strength. He dragged her up the stairs as if she weighed no more than eiderdown. Desperation folded over her as she searched the faces of the people in the lobby.

She knew it would do no good to scream for help.

Nobody in the town would lift a finger to help her, especially not when they found out that she had come from Yuma. And the way she looked, compared to the austere respectability of Flynn's appearance, also worked against her. She was nothing more than an ex-convict fresh from Yuma. It showed in her face and in her clothing. The residents of Tombstone were accustomed to seeing those convicts when they came out of the territorial prison. Once again, public opinion was condemning her.

The feeling that choked and strangled her during her nightmares engulfed her. She tried to remember to breathe, to slow down the frantic pounding of her heart.

She had lived through hell for three years—she could stand whatever degrading thing Flynn O'Bannion had in mind.

He forced her down the hallway to the last door and dug into his Levi's pocket for a key.

He twirled her through the door. The momentum sent her backward across the made-up bed. "I hate you," she repeated.

"So you've said." His voice was as dry and hard as the walls of Yuma.

Panic threatened to undo her when he turned the key and locked the door.

"Open that door this instant." She sat up and faced him down. "You bastard."

Barely contained fury glowed in his brown eyes. "I wouldn't make a habit of calling me that if I were you." His voice was steady and low, belying the turbulent expression in his eyes.

"Just get it over with," she said. "Take what you want and get out."

Flynn took off his hat and tossed it hard upon the bureau. "Son of a..." He turned and glared at her. "Is that what you think? That I brought you up here to...*rape* you?"

Her chin came up a notch. Defiance glowed in her eyes. "What other possible reason?"

"Son of a bitch," he muttered.

"Well, if you are not going to rape me, then let me out of here. I want to get Rachel and put as much distance as I can between me and this damned territory."

His eyes widened. He raked a long-fingered hand through his hair and muttered another epithet. "We need to talk."

"There is nothing we need to talk about, Marshal. Everything you needed to say was said in the courtroom."

The reminder of the trial sent a strange jab of guilt through him. "My name is Flynn, and I'm not a marshal anymore so I suggest you stop calling me that."

"If you are not the law, then you have no right to keep me here. Open the damned door. I am a free woman."

"I know." He took two long steps toward the bed. "Damn it all, Marydyth, I know about your release—I arranged it."

Icy hands squeezed her chest. "I don't believe you."

"Suit yourself."

With a vicious oath he turned and grabbed the straight-backed chair with one hand and spun it around backward. Then he hooked one leg over and straddled the seat, staring hard at her while he did it.

Her rapid intake of breath sent chills skittering over his arms. He didn't want to fight with her. Flynn dragged in a deep breath and started again.

"The governor commuted your sentence. But that isn't why I am here." He had intended to tell her all the details of the letter and explain how everything had come about, but the look in her eyes changed his mind.

"I came here because of Rachel," he said bluntly.

She drew herself up and stood stiff as a poker. "Rachel?" She twisted her fingers together in a way that made his insides cringe. "Is—is she all right? Noth—nothing has happened to her?"

Hellfire and damnation. Flynn saw her expression go from angry wildcat to helpless kitten in the blink of an eye.

"Please, tell me. Where is she?" She swayed unsteadily on her feet as if her strength were ebbing away.

"At Victoria's house."

She reeled back as if she had been slapped. Hurt etched itself into her thin face. She sagged onto the bed, clinging to the foot rail. "Of course, she is with her grandmother. I haven't forgotten…how could I forget?" A bitter, nearly hysterical laugh escaped her lips. "After all, Rachel is a Hollenbeck, as Victoria pointed out before I—went—away."

"She is with Victoria for the day only, Marydyth. She lives at home." Flynn didn't know why he bothered to explain. Maybe it was the lonely, haunted look in her face.

"Home?" Marydyth looked up. She appeared to be bewildered, as if the word were foreign. "Rachel lives in her own home? My old home—the house J.C. built for me?"

Flynn swallowed hard. Now was the moment, the right time to put all his cards on the table.

"Yes. She lives with me. I am her legal guardian." He took no pleasure in the words or the horror that flitted through Marydyth's eyes.

Chapter Four

Marydyth recoiled as if she had been slapped. Her bottom lip began to quiver. He had known she would react badly, especially after the way she went to pieces in the lobby, but this—this silent collapse of all her hopes—well, it nearly unmanned him.

"Oh, you are a cruel bastard to tell me such a lie," she hissed while she advanced on him.

He sat in the chair, watching her glare down at him. *I wish she would hit me again.* He could deal with her rage, but the forlorn look in her eyes clawed at his soul. He maintained his position, backward in the chair, staring up at her until she stopped right in front of him.

"Haven't you caused me enough pain?" she whispered. "Won't you be happy until I am completely broken?"

"None of this was my doing, Marydyth."

She shuddered as if someone had tromped across her grave. "Why?" she asked in a small, tight voice.

"Victoria is not in good health. Rachel has been in my care for some time now."

"Victoria Hollenbeck *gave* my child to you?" Her

blue eyes widened in disbelief. "Just how long have you had Rachel?"

"Almost since you went to Yuma," he said quietly.

"She gave my child away?" Disbelief rang in her voice.

"Good Lord, Marydyth, she didn't *give* her to me. You make Rachel sound like a stray kitten." He snorted in frustration. "The child needed me."

She reached out and grasped the back section of the chair that was between his hands. Her knuckles turned white with the effort she was exerting to control herself. "Rachel needed me."

He could not deny that. She had needed her mother then, but the fact was, she needed her more right now.

Marydyth leaned close and glared down on him. "Hating you kept me alive in Yuma. I was certain I could never hate you more than I did when you took me from Rachel—but I was wrong." She lifted her brows and her face became a mask of deceptive calm. "I have never hated you as much as I do this moment."

"Unfortunately, that doesn't change a thing." He dragged his palm down his face. "We are stuck with each other."

She blinked rapidly and backed up two steps. "What do you mean we are stuck with each other?" A chill of fear was snaking its way up her spine.

Flynn closed his eyes for a moment, then he shoved himself up from the chair he had been straddling. "This is not going the way I figured. You look all done in, Marydyth."

"Tell me what you meant," she insisted.

He stared down at her. "I am Rachel's guardian."

The unsteadiness of a moment ago was gone as she tilted her chin upward to meet his gaze. "You said that."

"I'm not sure you understand. The guardianship is legal and permanent."

She released the chair back and strode to the door. "Give me the key to this door. I want to get to Hollenbeck Corners and see Victoria. I want those documents changed immediately."

Flynn shook his head from side to side. "It isn't going to be that easy."

Her eyes narrowed down to slits of blue flame. "What do you mean, it won't be easy? I am her mother, for God's sake." She squared her shoulders.

"You make it hard for a body to go easy on you, don't you, Marydyth? You've got to keep poking and prodding until you have the whole damned story out right now, don't you?" Flynn shoved the chair aside and advanced on her as if she were prey and he a hungry wolf. "All right, damn it, you'll have it all. I didn't want to tell you this way, but you are determined so here it is. Victoria had you declared an improper parent. Because of how you lived—what had gone on in your past—and because you never offered a word in your own defense at the trial. It's done and it's legal. You can't ever get Rachel's guardianship back."

"But...but my sentence...the pardon... "

"Didn't have a damned thing to do with Rachel or those guardianship papers. Victoria had Moze Pritikin do them—he made sure they were binding. The charges—loss of guardianship was because of the riverboats, the gambling...the things that happened before you married J.C."

And because I murdered Andre, an accusing voice in her head screamed. *God is making you pay for killing Andre.*

Her throat worked for a full minute while she tried to

swallow. She thought that the whole nightmare was over, that she had paid enough, but now she saw that she was wrong. Not only was she still paying for what she had done, her daughter was going to suffer for it as well.

A strangled sob escaped her lips. Flynn could see unshed tears in her eyes. Finally she locked her trembling hands together and clenched her fingers so tight her knuckles whitened.

"But why...*you?*" She said the word as if it left a bad taste in her mouth.

"I've asked myself that same question more than once." Flynn raked his fingers through his hair. "God knows it was the last thing I wanted."

"What?" Flynn O'Bannion was caring for a child he didn't even want? Her heart rebelled at the thought.

"A few people came knocking on Victoria's door, volunteering to take Rachel in, but most folks were interested in the Hollenbeck money and not Rachel. I was getting ready to leave town, only stopped by to pay my respects because of Victoria's health, but while I was there I played with the baby. Before I knew what had happened Victoria had sent for Moses to draw up the papers and I was roped in and hog-tied."

"You could've said no," Marydyth said bitterly.

"Yep, I could have." Flynn speared her with a withering look.

"Why didn't you?" She was vibrating with pent-up rage.

"And where would that have left Rachel? Would you rather see her with a pack of money-hungry vultures?"

She could not answer. One part of her wanted to scream that anybody would be better than him, but another part of her knew that was not true.

Flynn O'Bannion was as rigid as iron—unable to stray

from his notion of the truth. But the one black sin that Marydyth could not lay at his feet was greed.

Two hot tears spilled over her lids and ran down her cheeks. She hated herself for letting him see her weep.

"Can I—" She shuddered visibly. "Will you at least let me see her?" It cost her dearly to ask that question, but Rachel was worth the humiliation.

Flynn stared at her in silence while the muscle in his jaw worked rapidly. Marydyth thought he was a low-down son of a bitch. He tightened his jaw, unable to trust what wanted to come out of his mouth.

Her eyes narrowed when he didn't answer. "I will see her whether you allow it or not."

Flynn stalked toward her. "What kind of man do you think I am?" He whirled away from her, cursing under his breath. "Do you think I would hurt Rachel by keeping you from her? Damn it all to hell." He jerked the bandanna from his neck. "Well, I am not that kind of man, Marydyth. You've turned hard and bitter."

"Prison makes people hard." She flinched and jerked back when he tried to wipe away her tears. "Losing my child has made me bitter."

Flynn could only stand there and stare at her with the bright red bandanna dangling from his fingers. She made him mad enough to spit, with her accusing eyes and sharp tongue. But she was also cutting him to the bone with her words. He had never met a woman who could rouse so many conflicting emotions. He cleared his throat and tried to get his own temper under control. Neither would benefit by their tearing into the other.

"Marydyth, I brought some of your old clothes. Let's try this again, after you've changed and dressed. We can get something to eat and talk."

"I'd rather go hungry." She practically spit the words in his face.

"Suit yourself." He turned away, then turned back. Each time she opened her mouth another insult, sharp as an Apache war lance, flew in his direction. He had never thought of Marydyth Hollenbeck as strong or hard but the woman before him now had ample portions of both qualities. "Go hungry if you wish, but I intend to have the biggest steak in Tombstone. If you change your mind, I'll be in the hotel dining room."

"I won't."

He stared at her with his fingers on the key. "After a decent meal we might both be in a better frame of mind to discuss Rachel."

Marydyth raised her chin and glared up at him. "You really are a prizewinning bastard, Flynn O'Bannion."

Ten minutes later Marydyth was still staring at the door that Flynn had slammed behind his back. The room seemed to reverberate with the sound of it, or perhaps it was her own thudding heartbeat she heard echoing in her ears.

She thought back to the morning, when she had believed that freedom was hers. Now her dreams of taking Rachel away were nothing but a cold pile of ashes.

Marydyth shook herself, trying to get rid of the chill that had entered her blood. She had to do something. She could not just give in—she had suffered too much to let Flynn O'Bannion win now.

He is hard and he is dangerous. Don't rile him or he might not let you see Rachel.

"He'll have to kill me to keep me from her," she whispered. But her words were full of false bravado; inside she was quaking with fear. He had all the cards on his side of the table. She was a convict and he was the law.

How could Victoria have chosen him? A mean-spirited marshal to raise a sweet baby girl?

She knew Victoria despised her, but could her hatred run so deep that she had wanted to see Rachel suffer?

Part of Marydyth acknowledged that her hatred of Flynn O'Bannion was somewhat misplaced. After all, it had been a jury that found her guilty.

But it had been Flynn O'Bannion who recognized her likeness on the Wanted posters. It had been Flynn O'Bannion who had put her past together and uncovered it for all the world to see. It had been Flynn who found out the truth about Andre.

He had uncovered a crime that she could not deny. She *had* killed Andre, and it haunted her day and night. But when Flynn O'Bannion told the jury, her fate had been sealed. She knew she deserved to be punished for what she had done. In a way she had been relieved to finally have it all out. She had thought when the world learned of what she had done and she went to prison, that she would at last be free of the nightmares and the guilt.

She had been wrong.

Every night she had relived her crime. Each time her head touched the pillow she saw herself hitting Andre with the lamp and saw herself running from the riverboat. The entire time she had been in Yuma not a single night had gone by when she had not dreamed of Uncle Blaine coming to tell her that he had found Andre dead and she should run for her life.

And now Flynn O'Bannion had the one good thing in her life.

She wrung her hands together and let her thoughts fly

in all directions. She fought to control herself before she succumbed to hysterics.

She was tired—worn ragged. That much of what Flynn said was true. And she was weak as a kitten from hunger.

But the thought of trying to eat at the same table with him made her stomach revolt. How could Victoria have done this terrible thing?

The sound of footsteps preceded a knock at the door. Marydyth clenched her fists. It was probably that bastard O'Bannion, returning to plunge the knife a little deeper into her broken heart.

"Damn you to hell!" She flung the door open and found a boy of about thirteen standing there, balancing two steaming buckets of water at the ends of his gangly arms. His eyes widened and two bright spots of color rose on each cheek.

"Ma'am? I—I brought hot water. Orders from Mr. O'Bannion, ma'am."

She blinked at him a couple of times, trying to digest what he was saying.

"For washin', ma'am." He averted his gaze, never looked at her again as he shuffled past and put the buckets near the washstand.

He was gone with the door shut firmly behind him before Marydyth recovered enough to speak.

"Thank you," she whispered to the empty room. It had been so long since anyone had done anything nice for her. To find that Flynn O'Bannion—the bastard—had sent up hot water made her want to weep. Instead she laughed, loud hysterical peals of laughter that echoed off the wall. It was all too much. She couldn't take it all in. Her nerves all raw and exposed, the simple act of having somebody give her hot water was more than she could take.

* * *

The rose-scented soap and clean hot water was like heaven. Marydyth washed her whole body, then did it again just to savor the feel of being clean—and truly alone.

She soaped her hair and rinsed it three times, not satisfied that the taint of Yuma was gone until her hair squeaked when she pulled along the wet strands. Finally, as she fluffed the short irregular tresses with a fresh towel, she drew up her courage and approached the looking glass.

Marydyth gulped audibly. Seeing her reflection for the first time since she had left for Yuma was a staggering moment.

Her eyes were still blue, her hair still golden, but there the resemblance to the woman she had been before ended.

With trembling fingers, she touched the dark smudges beneath her eyes. They no longer winked with laughter and happiness. Now they were deep-set, hollow and haunted. Her fingertips slid over cheekbones that were too sharp and lips that had long ago lost their dewy softness.

J.C. told me I was more beautiful than the Arizona sunrise... I doubt he'd think so now. She smiled ruefully. She stared into her own eyes for half a minute.

Yuma had not been kind to her.

What would Rachel think? Did she even remember her? Could she recall the mornings that Marydyth bathed her and cuddled her? Or had Victoria made good her threat and removed every trace of Marydyth from Rachel's life? These were questions that burned at her, but she could only get the answers by facing Flynn O'Bannion.

Marydyth turned away from the mirror and picked up the valise Flynn had brought. She tossed it on the bed and opened it, pushing aside the knowledge that he had handpicked each item. She could do this—she would deal with Lucifer himself to see Rachel again.

One by one she took out the carefully folded items. Her fingers lingered on the primrose India silk and a flash of memory entered her mind. J.C. had picked the fabric and the pattern when they were in San Francisco. Touching the intricate ruching on the full sleeves brought back more bittersweet memories of how gay her life had been. She shoved them and the pain they brought to the back of her mind, refusing to think about the past.

With grim determination she laid out her wardrobe. When it was all spread upon the coverlet she did a quick, critical inventory.

The corset had yellowed a bit and the dress was probably woefully out of fashion, but everything was fresh and clean. To her surprise there was one silk chemise, a single pair of silk stockings and a clean bandanna folded carefully around two plain horn hair combs that were new. At the very bottom of the case was her green serge traveling suit with the matching bolero jacket trimmed in black velvet piping. Flynn had even had the presence of mind to put in a pair of black shoes.

The thought of his having access to her intimate articles made her flesh crawl. But what choice did she have?

Three years of her life were gone, and all she had to show for it was a threadbare dress and tortured nightmares to keep her company at night.

A poor wage for so much misery.

Flynn sat in the lobby alternating between red-hot anger and chilling guilt. He crushed the unlit cigarette into a shapeless mass and rose to his feet. He had tossed back three fingers of whiskey in an attempt to take the edge off his anger.

It hadn't worked.

He was headed toward the bar for another try when his gaze marched up the staircase for the fiftieth time in as many minutes.

"She won't come," he muttered. "She hates me too much to come."

Marydyth had made it damned plain. She would rather go hungry than sit at the same table with him. She would rather do without than be in his debt.

He shivered involuntarily, and a strange feeling gnawed at his gut. He knew where her anger came from—where it had always come from—but that didn't make it any easier to stomach. His mind drifted back over the years, allowing himself to remember the series of events that had brought him to this hotel lobby.

Geronimo and the continuing Apache problem had meant the Cochise County marshal was called away. Flynn had been sent to Hollenbeck Corners to help quell the violence of the miners' strike. That was when he renewed his old friendship with J. C. Hollenbeck and was introduced to Marydyth. From the start there had been sparks between the two of them. She had been openly hostile, and avoided Flynn whenever possible. His lawman instincts had prickled from the first. She acted like somebody trying to hide her past. Then, when J.C. had been murdered, Flynn gave in to his instinct and started digging into the mystery that surrounded Marydyth.

The Wanted posters from Louisiana had turned up within a week. Then came telegrams from other lawmen who had come close to catching her and the man she had been seen traveling with.

If only I had recognized her sooner, the haunting voice of his conscience said, but he shook the thought away.

She never made any effort to defend herself, and it wouldn't have mattered if her past had shown up sooner or later. That was what nagged at him now since he had read Blaine's confession. Had she kept her silence and gone to Yuma to protect her mysterious uncle Blaine? If so, it was a damned misguided thing to do.

If she was innocent then she should have proclaimed it loud and long.

If she was innocent.

He shook his head. That kind of thought was best left alone. She had to be innocent. She had been pardoned—she was going back to Hollenbeck Corners.

Because Rachel needs a mother.

Flynn looked at the big round-faced clock on the wall. Almost two hours had passed by since he slammed out of Marydyth's room. People were coming and going through the lobby and most of them were heading for the dining room.

He took a deep breath and practically tasted the tang of sourdough bread and sizzling meat at the back of his tongue. His stomach growled.

She wasn't coming.

He should just accept it and go get a steak. It wasn't going to work out and he had been ten times the fool to ever think that it would.

Let it go.

He took a step toward the dining room but an image of Rachel's sweet face popped into his head.

He knew he would have to try again with Marydyth—for Rachel. Flynn simply couldn't go back to Hollenbeck Corners without settling things for Rachel.

A prickly sort of peace settled over him. As much as

it surprised him, he decided that he would apologize first—even though she should be the one to say she was sorry for calling him a bastard. Then he would find a way to talk some sense into her.

Flynn picked up his Stetson hat from the marble-topped side table and started toward the stairs. He had taken one step when Marydyth appeared on the stairs.

She was wearing the clothes he had selected. The dress did not cling to her body as he remembered it doing in the past, but there were still curves beneath the soft material that shimmered like an August sunset when she moved.

No doubt about it, she was still a looker. Even Yuma hadn't changed that.

Her hair was pulled up on either side in the combs he had bought at the mercantile. The way the short curls tumbled together hid the uneven strands and did not look so unconventional.

She met his gaze and their eyes locked for two heartbeats. He could read the hatred even at this distance.

But it didn't matter. He was Rachel's guardian, and she was Rachel's mother. That bond was stronger than their enmity.

He could and would deal with Satan himself, if it would make Rachel happy.

Chapter Five

Marydyth stood on the stairs overlooking the lobby and tried to keep her knees from shaking.

Dear God, this is so hard.

All her dreams of returning to a real life, of walking into a hotel lobby and ordering a meal like any other ordinary person were evaporating like dew on a hot day.

People were turning to stare at her. A few had even openly pointed and made comments behind their hands. They knew her, remembered the horrible stories in the *Chronicle* and the *Epitaph*. She was a fool to hope they would have forgotten. She was big news—"the Black Widow"—"Murdering Mary"—the woman who had put two husbands in the ground for money.

Her trial had been the biggest news in the territory. Only Geronimo's subsequent surrender had garnered more room in the local papers. Women who commit murder are almost as interesting as Apaches, and Marydyth had been the newspapermen's dream come true. Not only was she younger than J.C., she had a *past*.

Nobody ever stopped to consider that she might have been innocent of J.C.'s killing, or that long ago she had done terrible things in Louisiana because she had had no choice.

She had been convicted because of where she was born and the way she looked. She had been convicted even before Flynn O'Bannion brought in the Wanted posters.

The awful monikers had followed her all the way to Yuma and back again.

It didn't seem fair.

Dear God, make my feet move. Please don't let me stand here, frozen, while they cut me to little pieces with their whispers and their stares.

Bitterness rose in the back of her throat. She could not let Flynn defeat her because she was too weak to challenge him. If she did not force herself to make a stand, then she would never see Rachel.

Her feet began to move of their own accord. Not because she was no longer terrified—she was—but because she could not lose her daughter twice in a lifetime. And particularly not to the likes of Flynn O'Bannion.

Flynn looked at Marydyth over the glass of Jose Cuervo. He rarely drank tequila, but tonight he indulged himself in a shot. Maybe it was the constant buzz of whispered voices behind his back or maybe it was the contempt that shone in Marydyth's eyes. Whatever the reason, he knocked back another shot of liquid fire, closing his eyes against the burn as it slid down his gullet.

When he opened his eyes he noticed an unshaved youth smiling at Marydyth as he walked by the dining table. She shyly smiled back. A new rush of indignant whispers swept across the dining room.

"I suppose I should get used to this," she said softly as she ducked her head and took another bite of steak.

He had flatly refused to discuss Rachel until after they

had eaten. He wasn't sure why he did it, but damn it all, she was thin as a rail and he couldn't think of any other way to persuade her to eat.

Flynn narrowed his eyes and studied her. On the outside she was cool beauty but the quiver in her voice showed him just how much she was bothered by the gossip. "It won't be so bad in Hollenbeck," he heard himself say.

She looked up. "And what makes you think I am staying in Hollenbeck?"

"Where else would you go?" He met her chilly gaze.

"Anywhere. There is a whole big world out there. J.C. left us well-fixed, and..." Her voice trailed off.

The candle in the middle of the linen-swathed table guttered for a moment. He wondered if the cold he felt sweeping across the table was real or imagined. Didn't she know the terms of J.C.'s will?

"Now I am curious, Marydyth." Flynn fixed his eyes on her face. "What exactly did you think was going to happen when you got out of Yuma?"

She smiled sadly. "I had planned on getting my daughter and my money and putting this place far behind me."

She didn't know. She had no idea that J.C. had left every cent in trust to Rachel, and that Flynn controlled the money too.

He shook his head and poured another jigger of tequila. He had been hungry as a bear but his appetite had left him. He shoved the plate away and stared hard across the table.

Marydyth must have felt his eyes upon her because her head slowly came up, and she met his gaze.

"I think we better talk about Rachel now," he said softly.

Marydyth swallowed hard.

Flynn pulled a tobacco pouch from his pocket and rolled a cigarette. Telling her was harder than he had imagined, and he damned well wasn't going to mention the money. She had had enough for one day.

He never looked up as he rolled the smoke. "I'll bet you have things you would like to know about her." He pulled the yellow pouch string taut and slipped it back into his shirt pocket.

"Yes, of course." Marydyth tried to latch onto a single question about Rachel, but her mind was swarming with things she wished she knew.

How did she look?

Did she remember her? Were her teeth straight? A hundred things a mother should know popped into her head.

"Is—is she happy?" she finally stammered.

Flynn's head came up but there was a hesitation in him that made Marydyth's pulse pound.

"Most of the time, I believe she is happy."

A relieved tiny smile tugged at the corners of her lips. She leaned forward a bit in the chair; excitement made her tremble. "What did she want for her last birthday?"

"A pink dress with two ruffled petticoats," Flynn answered without a pause. "It was the talk of the town for a while, me taking Rachel in to Sarah Ferguson's for fittings."

For a moment Marydyth wondered why Victoria didn't do that for her only grandchild, but then she realized that if her grandmother cared so little for Rachel that she would *give* her to O'Bannion, then she would not be inclined to take her to the dressmaker.

A bitter taste filled her mouth. She had worried over what Victoria thought about her during the first years of her marriage to J.C. What had it gotten her? The old woman hated her and had taken that resentment out on Rachel.

Maternal protectiveness flared inside Marydyth. She had to know her daughter, had to be there for her—even if it meant knuckling under to Flynn. "I—I want to be a part of her life," Marydyth blurted out. She searched his face, hoping against hope that he might have a particle of decency in his black heart. "If you will let me."

Flynn's brows pinched together. "Why do you think I came to Tombstone, Marydyth?"

"I...I don't know." She was wary of him.

"Rachel needs a woman's influence in her life. She needs a mother."

"Rachel needs *her* mother," Marydyth corrected.

Flynn stared at the remains of his dinner, fighting for control. "All right, Rachel needs her mother. She needs you."

"Are you sure? You're going to let me have her, let me take her away from Hollenbeck."

Flynn's head snapped up. He glared across the table. "I don't think you understand my meaning, Marydyth."

"What? But I thought..."

"Rachel does need you but she is not *going* anywhere."

"But you said she lived with you..."

"And that is the way things will remain." His words fell like an anvil.

Marydyth gripped her hands together at the edge of the table. "Oh, you are a vile, low-down—"

"Stop." He cut her off in midinsult. "I don't think you want to do this right here. But if you don't care about your own reputation, Marydyth, then think of Rachel," Flynn warned. "She has to grow up in this territory. She has had enough of a burden from the past. Let's not make her future another millstone around her little neck.''

Marydyth clamped her lips shut but her eyes darted from table to table around the dining room. More than one pair of eyes were trained on her and Flynn.

He held himself rigid but his voice was low and controlled. ''You are welcome to pick up the pieces of your life, to get to know Rachel again.''

''That will be no hardship,'' she whispered stiffly.

''You may not think so when I tell you what my terms are.''

''I'm listening.''

He nodded. ''You are welcome to live in Hollenbeck House with Rachel, but I am part of the package.''

She inhaled and drew back. Her eyes widened and she looked at him as if he were something that had just crawled from under a slimy stone. ''Do you mean you want me to be your *whore?*''

Flynn's gaze never wavered. The corners of his mouth lifted in a wry grin. ''Lady, I have stepped over better prospects when I was out looking.''

She drew back as if he had hit her.

He kept right on talking. ''If a willing woman was what I was after I am sure I could find one with a lot sweeter tongue and nicer disposition than you, so don't flatter yourself.'' Flynn's mouth twisted.

''Damn you.''

He crushed the cold cigarette and leaned near the middle of the table. ''You can move into Hollenbeck House and be Rachel's mother in every sense of the word. I will have no contact with you above the normal comings and goings of the household, but know this: I am now and always will be her legal guardian.''

Her bottom lip began to quiver and her eyes filled with
a wash of tears.

"Make no mistake about this, Marydyth. *I* don't really
care one way or the other what you do. But it could mean
something to Rachel and the way she grows up." He sat
back in his chair and released a rush of breath. "The
decision is yours. If you want to live in Hollenbeck
House, the door is open."

Her eyes narrowed down to slits of blue fire and she
blinked rapidly to keep the tears from spilling over her
cheeks.

Flynn shoved back his chair and rose. He leaned over
the table and kept his voice low so nobody else would
hear.

"You sleep on it. If you decide you can live with those
conditions and abide by *my* rules, then meet me tomorrow
morning. The stage for Hollenbeck Corners leaves at six
sharp, and I'll be on it."

Cold. Merciless, blinding cold.

The thin blanket was not enough, never enough to keep
out the bone-chilling cold.

Marydyth shivered, trying to keep her teeth from chattering.

Then she heard the sound of footsteps echoing through
the thick dark corridors of Yuma—only it wasn't Yuma.
She whimpered as her surroundings shifted and changed.
Now she was in the corridor of the paddleboat going
toward her cabin. The boat was churning its way down
the big wide river. The footsteps were getting louder,
stronger...*closer.*

*He was coming. Andre was coming to her. It was her
wedding night.*

Measured, heavy treads drew nearer...a flicker of lantern light flashed along the thick, adobe wall—no, it was not an adobe wall, it was wallpapered and wainscoted. A man's shadow played and danced in the light. There was the sound of waves lapping against the side of the riverboat.

It was Andre. He opened the door and staggered inside. Drunk...big...threatening. What was happening? Didn't he understand that she was young and inexperienced? Oh, why was he hurting her so?

The pain. She was so frightened of the pain that she grabbed a lamp and brought it down hard.

She woke before the scream had quite bubbled up from the back of her throat. Her hair was slick and matted to her head with sweat. She twisted her fists in the sheet, afraid she would fly apart if she didn't have something to anchor her.

Marydyth gulped in deep breaths and tried to orient herself. She felt as if she'd dragged herself from a great pit when she sat up and looked around at the pale shapes of her room.

The sound of laughter and piano music drifted through the open window. She was not in Yuma. She was in Tombstone. Andre was long dead.

And Rachel needed her.

Marydyth collapsed back into the pillows with relief. She closed her eyes and counted to twenty, hoping her pulse would slow down.

She was not in danger—not tonight.

Never again, she screamed inside her head.

Relief and latent terror mingled in her chest, made her weak and queasy. She had hoped once she was free from Yuma the nightmare would stop. But it had come tonight. The first night of her freedom and she had been visited by her demons.

Her hands were shaking like leaves in a strong wind when she tossed back the sheet and rose naked from the bed. Flynn had packed a nightrail, but she didn't wish to sleep in a garment *he* had chosen. She measured each tottering step until she reached the washstand. More water ended up on her feet and her thighs than in the bowl, but she ignored it and splashed the tepid liquid on her face and over her hair and let it run down her breasts.

Marydyth moved cautiously toward the window, standing a little to the side so as to not be seen. She drew back the lacy curtain and sighed when the cool desert breeze washed over her.

It was the first night breeze she had felt in three years.

Tears sprang to her eyes when she glanced up and saw the moon hanging low in the western sky.

The moon.

And it made her cry with joy just to be able to see it.

"Damn you, Flynn O'Bannion." She cursed into the night air. There was no question what her decision would be, there was no *decision* to make.

Rachel was her child and she would walk through fire for her. And that arrogant bastard knew it. He knew she would agree to his terms because she had no choice, but the thought of living in the same house with a man she loathed beyond reason left her shaken.

How could she do it?

How could she not?

Marydyth stepped away from the window and started to dress. There was not a chance in the world that she would sleep any more tonight. She might as well pack and prepare herself to get on that stage.

The only hope she had, the one that kept her from screaming aloud in frustration, was the hope that once she talked to Victoria she might convince her to change the guardianship.

There was always a chance, and it was that slim hope that made her calmly shake out her clothing and prepare to face the day.

Flynn leaned against the rough wood wall of the depot with one boot heel hitched up.

All night long he had lain awake and stared at the ceiling, trying to decide if he wanted Marydyth Hollenbeck to show up or not. She had been as cantankerous as a grizzly, and the prospect of having her in the same house filled him with dread.

But what about Rachel?

That was the nut and kernel of his problem. Rachel was hungry for a woman's affection.

Her mother's affection. Marydyth's strident voice intruded upon his thoughts like a rock hitting an empty bucket.

Hell, it didn't matter what he thought about Marydyth. If she'd tough it out and live in Hollenbeck House with him and Rachel, then he could damn well do the same.

"Damn her, she had better show up," he swore under his breath. If she didn't show up he'd go and drag her down here. She had no right to turn her back on Rachel because she didn't want to deal with him.

What kind of a mother is she? the angry voice in his head asked. He shoved himself away from the side of the building and started to pace. With each metallic ching of his spurs he glared down the dusk-shrouded street.

Rachel had done without so much—too much. It would make him the happiest man in the Arizona Territory if he could introduce Rachel to her mother and see her little face light up with happiness.

He pulled his timepiece from the small pocket in his Levi's and peered at it.

If she isn't out here in two minutes, I am going to that hotel and bodily drag her back to Hollenbeck Corners.

He shoved the watch back in his pocket and looked up. Light footfalls drew his gaze. Her golden hair was pulled back from her face and caught with the combs. She looked pale and lost beneath that crown of yellow curls. When she reached him she stopped and tilted her chin upward defiantly.

"I am willing to abide by your terms, Mr. O'Bannion—just see that you stick to them yourself."

"I always keep my word. *Always.*" There was a threat in that soft-spoken voice. "You would do well to remember that fact."

The stage appeared from out of nowhere. The horses were snorting and pawing the ground, stirring up so much dust that Marydyth could taste it on the back of her tongue.

Her stomach suddenly twisted. Just a few more hours and she would see her baby again.

"Let me have that." Flynn lifted the carpetbag from her hand. She blinked and tried to rein in her thoughts. There was such a storm of emotion going on inside her she was afraid to speak, afraid to move for fear it would all come pouring out. Marydyth closed her hands into fists, fighting to control herself.

When Flynn touched her elbow she jumped, then felt her face flame bright red. She wished she would quit reacting to him, but it wasn't easy. She was so aware of his presence—and it was more than just his tall, lanky body and intimidating size. Each time he fastened that cold, agate gaze on her face she felt herself cringe. It was maddening that he had that effect on her. She knew what it was, of course; it was still her guilt over what she had done all those years ago.

But she had paid her dues and done her hard time in Yuma. The slate was clean now—the governor had evidently thought so too, because she was free. Yet as she looked at Flynn's face when he helped her inside, she realized that she had not forgiven herself for what she had done and Flynn affected her because his eyes reflected her own guilt.

He closed the door and stood there with his wide fingers curled over the edge of the stage door.

"Aren't you getting in?" she heard herself ask. It had taken twenty minutes of argument with herself before she'd been sure that she could bear to sit with him for the length of the journey.

"We'll be seeing more'n enough of each other very soon," he said with a narrowing of his eyes. "I'll ride up top with the driver."

She caught herself before she expelled a sigh of relief. His hard straight mouth curled up on one side but he never quite smiled.

"I thought that would make you happy," he said with a snort, and then he was gone.

Marydyth collapsed back against the squabs. Living with him in the same house was going to be like having a jailer again.

She pressed her palms into her lap and tried to calm herself. An excitement such as she had never known threatened to squeeze the life out of her. She closed her eyes and tried to count to twenty, but it was useless. She didn't want to miss out on seeing anything. The only other passenger—thankfully—was a taciturn old man who squinted at her once, then pulled his hat low over his eyes and fell asleep. She was left alone, not required

to make conversation or withstand the scrutiny of somebody who recognized her.

She sat back in the seat and stared out the window,
watching as the familiar and yet somehow forgotten landscape of the Arizona desert rolled by.

The day-long ride in the stagecoach passed pleasantly
enough for Marydyth. At sundown they pulled into Hollenbeck Corners. Again she was relieved to find the depot
almost deserted. The people that were there had business
of their own and never even blinked an eye at her.

She stood nervously looking around the town, trying
to reconcile memory with reality while Flynn retrieved
her carpetbag and got a buggy.

"I thought I would take the luggage to the house."
Flynn's voice jarred her. She turned with a start to see
him sitting in a buggy. He studied her from under the
concealing shadow of his pale-colored Stetson hat.

"Of course," she said. He started to get down and help
her into the seat but she scrambled up, not wishing to
give him any excuse to touch her. He must have realized
her motive because he stood with one boot on the ground
and one in the buggy and watched her with an amused
grin tickling his lips.

"If you don't want to do this, Marydyth, all you have
to do is say so. I'd be happy to get you a room at the
hotel."

"Not on your life," she grumbled, and pulled her skirt
in so it would not snag on the buggy wheel.

"Suit yourself." He flicked the reins, and she lurched
backward and bumped her head on the bar around the
seat. It had been so long since she rode in a buggy it all
felt strange and awkward. The horse seemed to be going
incredibly fast and Flynn seemed to be taking corners

with reckless abandon, but she clung to the seat and bit her tongue, determined not to say anything to him.

Marydyth tightly gripped the side of the buggy seat. She wanted to look at every inch of Hollenbeck Corners, but she didn't want Flynn to see her excitement, so she sat there, still as a statue while her eyes roamed over the town.

It was bigger. A new dressmaker had opened near the Grand Hotel. And a butcher shop was on the corner near Mullin's Hardware. There was a new livery and several saloons, one named the Flying Nymph. But overall the town had a shop-worn appearance. None of the buildings was wearing fresh paint and it all looked a little sad and run-down. Bigger, but not brighter. Flynn clicked his tongue and urged more speed from the horse.

Was he anxious to get home or was he simply trying to frighten her? She opened her mouth to ask the brute that very question, but then the house J.C. had built for her came into view. It loomed up on the hill, as if by magic, and she was stunned to speechlessness.

Her throat tightened so much she thought she might gag. Marydyth had a terrifying moment when she actually thought she could not live with so much happiness.

But while her eyes were taking in every inch of the house, she managed to compose herself at least a little.

It was just as she remembered. The ground floor was solid and square, built of adobe, with only a narrow porch and balcony above to soften the line. But the top...that was where J.C. had allowed Marydyth's imagination to run free.

He had denied her nothing when it came to the house. No request was too outlandish, he had said. Her misty eyes followed the line of the steep pitched roof upward to the point where it was trimmed with fanciful woodwork and a turret room like the one that sat atop the Tombstone Courthouse.

Marydyth's eyes filled with hot tears. The tall windows winked at her like long, half-open eyes. J.C. had paid extra to have the window glass shipped in and a hand pump put in the kitchen along with the most modern cookstove he could find. *All for her—because he had loved her.*

It was a great house—a house built to last.

Her home.

J.C. had understood her need from the first. He had seemed to instinctively understand her craving for a home that was solid and lasting. She had yearned for a place to put down roots so she could finally take root herself. Marydyth had grown up like a stunted vine, unable to grow and mature because she had no roots to grip the soil and keep her anchored.

J.C. had done his best to remedy that lack.

Flynn felt her stiffen beside him. He slanted a look at her from under the brim of his hat. The expression on her face was made from equal parts of happiness and pain. A ragged, halting breath escaped her lips, and she shuddered. He felt as if he were intruding on private thoughts just sitting beside her.

"Do you want to get down?" Flynn asked in a voice so rough and dry it would have taken the paint off wood.

"Is—is Rachel here?" Marydyth asked while her heart thudded painfully against her ribs.

"No."

"Then I don't want to stay. I want to see Rachel as soon as possible." She never looked at Flynn, just kept her eyes on her house. Knowing that it was here, that it had weathered and survived as she had, gave her a renewed sense of strength.

She had to remain strong for herself and for her child. Besides, after she spoke to Victoria she was certain that Flynn O'Bannion would be packing his bags and leaving Hollenbeck Corners forever. For even a woman as cold as Victoria would yield now that Marydyth had been vindicated and freed. After all, Marydyth had given Victoria a granddaughter...J.C.'s daughter.

Chapter Six

"After I take these bags inside we can go pick Rachel up at Victoria's." Flynn never looked at her when he spoke.

Marydyth wrung her gloveless hands together and forced herself to look at Flynn. His face was wreathed in shadow and it made him look even harder. "Maybe you should take the time to pack all your things." Marydyth found the courage to smile at him. "Because I am certain once I speak to Victoria she will see reason and change the guardianship papers."

Flynn tilted his head and stared at her in silence. She wished she could read his thoughts, but his impassive face betrayed nothing.

"I'll only be a minute," he said as he took his bag and hers and marched up the steps to the front door. Marydyth thought he opened it with the ease of someone who felt at home—something she was going to change.

That thought sent an arrow of anger flashing through Marydyth. Then to her surprise he turned and speared her with a penetrating gaze before he stepped inside.

"I hate you," she mumbled under her breath. "I really hate you, Flynn O'Bannion."

* * *

All the way to Victoria's house on the other side of Hollenbeck Corners Flynn carried on a running argument with himself. One part of him wanted to stop the buggy and take Marydyth by the shoulders and tell her some hard truths. The other part of him didn't want to be the bearer of bad news again. She really believed Victoria would welcome her home. It was foolish, he knew, but he wanted to avoid seeing that pained look in Marydyth's blue eyes for a while. Something about the way she bit her bottom lip and held her body straight as a post made him feel worse than when she cussed him and called him a bastard.

But there was a part of him that knew he should tell her about Victoria's strokes. And that Victoria had no knowledge of what was in the letter that persuaded the judge to free Marydyth. He and Marydyth were bound together now and nothing was going to change that.

If only she didn't believe there was some easy way out. Then at least she wouldn't feel it so hard when she saw for herself the way things were and would remain.

No, even if he told her right now, she probably wouldn't believe him. She didn't trust him, and that wariness made it necessary for her to see with her own eyes. No matter what he said she would think it a lie.

The prospect didn't make him happy.

And what would she do when she realized that their situation was permanent? Would she stay or would her hatred of him drive her away from Hollenbeck Corners and Rachel?

A million questions ran through his head. He couldn't find a good answer to even one of them. This was turning out to be much more complicated than he had imagined. He vowed he'd see it through—for Rachel—so he set his jaw and concentrated on guiding the horse down the nearly deserted streets.

Marydyth's stomach dropped to her feet when Flynn drove through the big arched gate and up the long, winding drive toward Victoria's house. Every turn of the buggy wheels made her heart ache with sorrow and impotent rage.

Three years of her life had been wasted.

No matter. The past was past. She intended to collect her daughter and try to reason with Victoria. And if that didn't work she would fight them both in court. She would petition the territorial governor if need be, do whatever was necessary to reclaim her child and her shattered life.

A horse nickered, and Flynn saw that Moses Pritikin's buggy was outside Victoria's house. His presence might make things a little easier.

"You'll find Victoria somewhat changed," Flynn heard himself say.

"I doubt anything less than Armageddon would change my mother-in-law," Marydyth replied. The memory of Victoria's words on the day she was sent to Yuma had burned deep scars in her soul.

"Maybe on the inside," Flynn muttered. There was no point in trying to soften the shock. Marydyth was hellbent to do all this her way.

Flynn tightened his jaw. He jumped down and wrapped the lines around the hand brake. He was headed to the other side but Marydyth didn't wait for him. She hit the ground hard and he heard a little whimper of pain.

"Are you all right?" he asked with a frown. Why did she have to be so damned hard? Why couldn't she give just a little?

"I am fine." Her words were full of ice.

Marydyth drew herself up but she still felt small in the dusky shadows in front of Victoria's house. She had a feeling of foreboding.

How would she face Victoria if she couldn't even look at her house?

Marydyth forced herself to look it over. It was after all nothing more than brick and wood, a shelter from the elements. It was not a living thing. Yet as she stared at the house a hundred memories came flooding back. She remembered the day J.C. had brought her home, and Victoria's tight-lipped disapproval of such a young wife. The house held all those memories, and so for Marydyth it was almost a living thing—almost another enemy that she had to face.

She inhaled a deep breath and tasted the desert on her tongue. It was time. She had waited for this moment for three long years.

Marydyth walked up the dozen wide sandstone steps toward the front door, with Flynn following close behind her. Victoria Hollenbeck's house was one of the first true mansions built in the Territory, paid for by one of the richest copper strikes Arizona miners had ever seen. The Hollenbeck mines were still producing, making a tidy profit, Marydyth supposed, although she did wonder why the town seemed so shabby and run-down if that was the case.

"Have you changed your mind about coming inside?" Flynn's brusque question jarred her back to the present. Marydyth looked up the steps to see that he had walked past her and was standing by the front door.

"No. I haven't changed my mind." She gathered her skirts in her hand and hurried up beside him.

He put his work-hardened knuckles to the door and knocked. It opened almost immediately. A tall woman with a quick smile and winking blue eyes opened the door.

"Mr. Flynn, how nice it is to see you. Little Rachel is in the kitchen with Gertie—I think they are making pudding. The madam likes pudding, you know."

"Yes, I know," Flynn answered as he took one step inside the house. "How is she today?"

"Same as usual. Nothing much changes around here, but I tell you it has been a pure pleasure having Miss Rachel. You are doing a fine job of bringing up that child, Mr. Flynn."

Flynn's eyes flicked to Marydyth's. They locked gazes for a moment, and she could feel the hot current flowing between them. Did he know how much she hated him? Could he feel the contempt?

"If you'll come right in here."

Flynn followed the woman but Marydyth was rooted to the spot she was standing on. She looked down at the threshold of the house she was certain she'd never see again when she left for Yuma.

"Are you coming?" Flynn turned and asked, but before Marydyth could answer a bundle of energy, wearing a gingham dress, came flying through the long hallway.

Rachel.

Her heart constricted painfully and a hot lump lodged itself in her chest. She couldn't breathe—couldn't think. This was more joy than she could stand. Marydyth tried to swallow and couldn't. She tried to move and couldn't. She thought she'd die of happiness. The child had blue-green eyes and a riot of coppery ringlets.

Then, Rachel flung herself into Flynn's waiting arms.

Marydyth died a little inside to see such trust and devotion shining in her daughter's face, and all of it directed toward Flynn.

"Unca Flynn—you're back."

Uncle Flynn?

Her baby—her little girl—called him *uncle?*

"I missed you but I had a good time with Grandma and Gertie."

"Is that a fact?" Flynn asked. He slid a quick look at Marydyth and saw that she had gone pale as chalk. Was she about to turn tail and run. Was that fear he saw in her eyes?

"Uh-huh, we cooked and I got to play with the barn cat's new kittens."

"Sounds like you had a gay old time." He set her on her feet and stood up. His eyes fixed on Marydyth's face. "Darling, I brought somebody back from Tombstone with me." Flynn's eyes seemed to be burning with an unspoken question.

Marydyth had the most overwhelming desire to turn and run through the open door. She couldn't do this. Now that she saw how beautiful Rachel was and how much she had grown up—and how attached she was to Flynn...her courage deserted her. She felt cheap and old and incapable of meeting her child.

"Rachel, honey, this is your mama." Flynn's voice sluiced over Marydyth like ice water.

Rachel turned and her curious eyes bored into Marydyth like hot branding irons. Marydyth had been certain that she long ago stopped feeling such things as regret or shame, but as her child scanned her face she felt a thousand new degrees of those torments.

"You're my mama?" Rachel whispered in awe.

The woman who had answered the door made a little O with her mouth. Then she fumbled with her apron and bustled away.

Marydyth looked from Flynn to Rachel and back

again. She swallowed hard and found her voice. "Yes,
Rachel, I am your mother."

"You don't look 'xactly like your picture." Rachel's
words held no recrimination; it was just a simple statement of fact.

Marydyth glanced up at Flynn, silently begging him to
help her.

"Rachel and I found your portrait in the attic recently.
We rehung it over the mantel," he explained. "And Rachel is real proud to have it there," he added with a smile
tilting his lips.

"Oh." Marydyth wanted to crush her daughter to her
breast, wanted to smell her hair, to touch her skin, to feel
her in her arms, but she forced herself to stand there by
the open door.

"Have you come home now?" Rachel asked softly.

Marydyth nearly sobbed aloud. She drew in a ragged
breath and twisted her fingers together. "Yes, darling. I
have come home." She glanced at Flynn to see if he
would dispute her words, but to her surprise he gave her
a little smile of reassurance.

Rachel turned to Flynn and jerked on his Levi's-clad
leg several times. He frowned and bent down so she
could lean close to his ear.

"I'm not sure this is my mama, Unca Flynn," Rachel
whispered in his ear.

Flynn glanced at Marydyth and she thought something
like pity might have clouded his brown eyes. "'Course
she is, honey."

"But she looks...different."

Marydyth took a halting step forward and allowed the
door to close behind her. "I picked your name, Rachel.
Did you know that?" Her fingers ached to touch the copper curls, to caress the velvet-soft cheek, but she would

not do it until Rachel showed her that she was ready for such contact.

"Do you remember when I was born?" Rachel asked with a hint of suspicion in her voice.

"Uh-huh." Marydyth swallowed the thickness in her throat. "I remember the day very well."

"If you are my mama, then how old am I?" Rachel's chin came up and the glint of challenge twinkled in her eyes.

"Rachel, honey, that is not polite…" Flynn said as he eased himself up from Rachel's level.

"Three years, seven months and eight days, Rachel Irene Hollenbeck," Marydyth said with a little catch in her throat.

Those words rolled over Flynn and he felt as though he had been hit between the eyes. His insides clenched and knotted in knowing that Marydyth had counted the days of her child's life—counted them and missed them.

He looked from mother to daughter. All of a sudden he longed to be somewhere else—anywhere else. He couldn't deal with this kind of naked emotion. He was an ex-marshal, for God's sake. He didn't know what to do or what to say to these two Hollenbeck females.

Damn it all.

Flynn bent down on one knee and drew Rachel close. "Honey, have I ever lied to you?"

"No, Unca Flynn." Rachel's curls swayed as she shook her head.

"And I'm not lying now. This is your mother—she's come a long way to see you and I think you should be more respectful."

"It's all right. I don't…I don't want to force her." Marydyth nearly choked on the words but she managed a weak smile. She bent down until she was able to look at Rachel eye to eye. "For now, could we just be friends, Rachel?"

Rachel glanced at Flynn for confirmation—or was it permission?

"Rachel, your mama asked you a question." Flynn's voice was lovingly stern.

"Yes, ma'am. I'd like to be your friend." Rachel kept hold of Flynn's hand but she extended the other to Marydyth.

She was very polite—and very distant. Marydyth knew she had a deep gap to cross to reach her daughter's heart.

"Fine, Rachel. We'll start out by just being friends, but I want you to know that I love you very much." Marydyth blinked rapidly. This was no time for tears. "I want you to know that."

Rachel tilted her head and studied Marydyth as if she were sizing her up. Then she smiled a little but she never relinquished her hold on Flynn's wide, work-worn hand.

"Yes, ma'am," Rachel said.

Marydyth inhaled deeply and stood up. What had she expected? Rachel had been so little when she left. She had no memory of her, and undoubtedly Victoria had made sure that nobody filled in the gaps. She blamed Victoria and Flynn for the pain she was feeling.

Flynn wanted a smoke—and a drink. He couldn't quite ignore the misery he saw in Marydyth's eyes before she so carefully hid it, and he couldn't banish the image of her quiet dignity when Rachel had rejected her.

He could see she was hungry for Rachel, but to give her credit, she was holding herself in check. He felt as though he should do something, some magical thing that would bond mother and daughter, but he couldn't think of what it might be. Mercifully Moses Pritikin came clomping out of the front parlor and saved him.

"I thought I heard voices." Moses looked from Flynn to Rachel to Marydyth. "Uh—I didn't mean to interrupt."

Marydyth faced Moses with the same icy dignity that she used in dealing with Flynn. "Mr. Pritikin."

"Miz Hollenbeck. You are looking well."

Marydyth's brows shot upward. Flynn watched Moze's neck redden. The stain rose all the way to his silver hair. He had seen the attorney stare down hardened criminals in the courtroom, but today he blinked and looked away when Marydyth Hollenbeck met his eyes. He experienced a certain twisted satisfaction to know he was not the only man who was a coward around womenfolk.

Moses coughed. "Uh, well, anyway—welcome back to Hollenbeck Corners."

The tension in the air grew thick enough to cut. Flynn could feel the worry telegraphing its way from Rachel's hand to his.

"I'd like to see Victoria now," Marydyth said without ceremony. "We have a lot to talk over." She looked longingly at her daughter. "A lot."

Moses glanced at Flynn, who shook his head from side to side.

"I—that is—" Moses started. "Victoria is…"

"Don't bother to make excuses for her. It is time we two had a reckoning." Marydyth stood away from Rachel, allowing her hand to linger lovingly on the child's head. "Is she in the front parlor?"

"Uh, yes," Moses said.

"Good, I'll just announce myself if you don't mind." Her skirts swished as she turned on her heel and marched through the grained oak double pocket doors before either man could react.

"I guess that is that," Moses said softly.

"It was bound to happen. Maybe it's best if she gets it over with quickly," Flynn replied.

Marydyth entered the front parlor and found herself engulfed by darkness. One solitary lamp burned by the front window that overlooked the street.

Had Victoria been sitting here watching Marydyth in the buggy? She drew herself up and lifted her chin. It would not do to meet Victoria with any timidity, not if she expected to change the situation with Rachel.

The soles of Marydyth's shoes clicked on the bare floor and then were muffled by the thick hooked wool carpet. Victoria had always liked the comfort of carpet beneath her feet, Marydyth recalled. She approached the single high-backed chair that was facing the windows. Even though Victoria had not yet shown herself, Marydyth knew she was in the room. She could practically feel Victoria's disapproving presence all around her. It took all the love she had for her child to pluck up her courage and step around to face the chair.

This was the moment Marydyth had waited for. Now she could face Victoria, her most ardent accuser, as a free woman.

"Victoria?" She peered at the motionless form. "I know you can hear me."

Victoria never moved. Her hands were folded in her lap, her lacy dress arranged in a graceful bell around her ankles.

"You'll have to face me sometime. It might as well be now." Marydyth paused for a moment.

"I am a free woman, Victoria. What have you got to say about that?" Marydyth challenged.

But as she studied the frail woman before her the knowledge slowly began to dawn that Victoria was unable to say anything. Marydyth frowned and allowed her eyes to see what her heart could not accept.

Victoria was indeed changed, just as Flynn had said. Her right hand was twisted at an odd angle in her lap, and it appeared to be as lifeless as the muscles in the right side of her face. Only her eyes remained bright and alert, and those eyes burned with loathing.

Marydyth stood there staring at Victoria while bits and pieces of Flynn's conversations came floating back to her.

When Victoria had her first stroke...

She was searching for the woman who had always been her nemesis, her enemy and her rival for J.C.'s affection, but all she found was the shell of a woman, alone and miserable, locked inside her own kind of prison.

"Victoria?" Marydyth whispered, but she found herself kneeling beside the chair. Tentatively, as if she were reaching out to a wild animal that might bite her, she touched Victoria's arm. The skin was as dry and thin as the last leaf of autumn.

"Oh my God, Victoria, I didn't know."

A flicker of something clouded the old woman's eyes, and she blinked at Marydyth.

Marydyth tried to swallow the painful catch in her throat but the events of the day were becoming too much. Like a heavy burden they crushed her down and threatened to suffocate her. "You can communicate by blinking?"

One long blink was her answer.

"How...how long have you been like this?"

Three rapid blinks of the eyes.

"Three years? Almost three years?"

A single blink that was held for half a second longer than the others.

So Victoria, the tough old matron who had wielded power and dictated the pace of life in Hollenbeck Corners, was alert and alive within a body that would no longer do her bidding.

Marydyth felt a wave of pity and compassion. She fought it, and told herself that she shouldn't care, that Victoria Hollenbeck did not deserve her sympathy.

But she did feel it.

A glimmer of understanding about Rachel, and Flynn's total guardianship of her, crept into Marydyth's mind. Victoria must have known, or at least feared, that she would end this way, and her last unselfish act was to make sure that Rachel was cared for.

"I am free, Victoria."

Two blinks. Marydyth realized Victoria was unwilling to believe the truth before her.

"Yes, I am. The governor has commuted my sentence. Did you know?"

Two blinks and a hate-filled glare, the final proof that two blinks meant no.

"You didn't know, did you?" Marydyth grabbed a straight-backed chair that was near and pulled it close. She sat down beside Victoria and picked up the old woman's blue-veined hand.

"I thought of you often—thought of you and J.C.," Marydyth said softly.

Three blinks.

Marydyth felt her lips twisting in a wry smile. "I didn't defend myself at the trial because I felt so much guilt over the things that I had done. But that is all over now, Victoria. I have paid a heavy price. I have a second chance at life and I want to raise my daughter."

Two blinks.

"I deserve a second chance, Victoria."

Two blinks.

"Everyone deserves to be forgiven," Marydyth whispered.

Two blinks.

Marydyth inhaled deeply, then let out the air in a great rush. All the bad feelings she had carried for Victoria left with that sigh.

"I hated you, Victoria. For what you and Flynn O'Bannion did to me, I loathed you…but now it doesn't seem so important." Marydyth looked at the thickly veined hand lying lifeless in Victoria's lap. The huge topaz and diamond rings seemed to hold the frail digits as iron shackles had once bound Marydyth. "I forgive you, Victoria, and I pray to God that someday you will forgive me."

Marydyth closed her eyes and didn't watch Victoria's eyes while she bent over and deposited a gentle kiss to the old woman's forehead. She rose from the chair and carefully put Victoria's hand back where it was.

She was ready to go, to leave this unhappy house and all the hatred she had harbored. "You were wrong, Victoria, about a lot of things, especially about me."

Outside the double doors Flynn was pacing. Moses and the nurse had taken Rachel to the kitchen for cookies and lemonade as soon as Marydyth had gone inside the parlor. Now Flynn's curiosity was eating him alive.

What was she doing in there?

He kept looking at the doors and telling himself that it was none of his business.

But it might affect Rachel.

He walked quiet as an Apache to the doors. Marydyth had slid them almost together but there was a crack about half an inch wide. Flynn squinted his eyes and looked into the darkness, but he couldn't see anything. He could, however, hear Marydyth's voice clearly.

"So," Marydyth said, "I wanted you to know, Victoria. I did what I had to do—as God is my witness, I had no choice. I took his life but I wouldn't call what I did murder—not now."

An icy finger traced a line up Flynn's spine.

I did what I had to do.... I took his life.

He stepped back from the crack in the door wishing he had not heard what she had just said. But deep inside, the kernel of suspicion had taken root and was already beginning to grow. Marydyth had just confessed.

Chapter Seven

Marydyth rocked Rachel to sleep after bathing her and reading her a story, but she was still unwilling to leave her child for even a moment. The wonder of being with her, of actually *being* a mother again, was too new—too fresh.

The memory she had carried with her through the hard times at Yuma had been of a round-faced baby. The little girl in the pretty bed with the ruffled canopy was not a baby anymore.

She felt a painful tug on her heart when she thought of how many birthday celebrations she had missed. All the days of teaching Rachel, all the moments of marveling as she changed from an infant to a toddler and the little girl she was now.

She had missed so much. But she was here now and Rachel was sleeping soundly as she watched. Marydyth focused on that positive thought as she forced herself to rise.

Seeing Victoria had put things into perspective for her. Now she realized with painful clarity that she could remain bitter and vengeful about what had happened, turning herself into a withered old woman—as Victoria had done—or she could move on, build a life and future for herself and Rachel.

Marydyth had spent enough time locked inside Yuma; she vowed she was not going to carry that place locked inside herself. She was not going to be a victim anymore.

Rachel was here and that was all that mattered—that and starting the process to revoke Flynn O'Bannion's guardianship.

Making sure not to wake the child, she allowed herself one last loving touch. Then she turned toward the door. She needed to rest so she would be ready for all the wonderful things she had planned to do with Rachel tomorrow.

With the lamp in hand, Marydyth backed out of the bedroom. Shadows capered on the ornate rose wallpaper as she climbed the stairs to the west wing of the house. There was a sort of sleepy quiet to the house, as if it had not been disturbed for a long while. She knew in some deep, inner place that she was treading on stairs that had gone unused since her departure.

She didn't like being so far from Rachel, but she could not disrupt her life by changing her bedroom immediately. Things were delicate enough. Each time she touched Rachel, there was a momentary wariness that clawed at Marydyth's insides. Several times Rachel had asked Flynn—*Unca Flynn*—if it was all right for Marydyth to do things for her. As much as Marydyth hated to admit it, he had been wonderful. His manner with Rachel was easy and matter-of-fact. He didn't make a fuss, didn't dwell on the unease, he simply nodded or smiled at Rachel in that crooked, boyish way. His manner encouraged Rachel to allow Marydyth to do for her.

She owed him a debt of thanks, as much as it rankled her to admit it. Not only had he taken fine care of Rachel—that was evident—but he was doing what he could to help her adjust to a mother she could not remember. It was a lot to be thankful for, Marydyth acknowledged as she turned the last corner toward her room.

She pushed open her door and it was as if the old house sighed. There was a quiet about it, but it was a different kind of quiet than the oppressive, fearful silence she had known in Yuma.

When Marydyth entered her bedroom suite she felt a thickness in her throat. It was foolish, but she trailed her fingers over the draperies, the dark wood of the poster bed, along the brocade comforter to the fringe on the bellpull—just to assure herself that she was really home.

Home.

Her room looked just as it had when she saw it last. She wondered how that could be.

Marydyth sat down in the small, armless chair by the window and looked outside. The town below was different in some small way she could not place immediately. Then it struck her that it was well lit. Gaslights flickered at regular intervals. Hollenbeck Corners was a pretty town. J.C. had been so proud of it when he brought her here.

Memories of her former life nudged at the corners of her mind. And now that Rachel was tucked in bed Marydyth was alone for the first time and able to look at her memories, to examine them in a way she had not done in three years. There was no unwanted, untrusted cell mate in the room. And the lock on the door was to keep people out—not in.

She shivered in relief. For the first time Marydyth had the freedom and the privacy to grieve for her husband and all that she had lost. Here in her own home, with pieces of furniture that she had handpicked surrounding her, questions nipped at the corners of her mind. So many questions without answers.

Like her release, for instance. How had that all come about? She had been so giddy and gripped by the fear it was all a pipedream that, up until this moment, she hadn't allowed herself to question how it had happened.

But now she wondered.

Did the governor hear of her plight and review the case? Had Victoria somehow been instrumental in obtaining mercy? As the image of Victoria's hate-filled eyes remained in her mind, she doubted it. Perhaps somebody had found Blaine and the stolen jewelry, but Marydyth doubted that since she had kept his name out of it.

Only now, after three years in Yuma, had she realized her foolishness. But at the time, she had hoped—prayed—her silence would prevent Andre's death from coming up. Then, it had been too late to matter. Nobody believed her—"The Black Widow." She didn't even have her wedding rings. All the wonderful presents that J.C. had given her, things she had wanted to pass on to Rachel, were gone—all gone. She glanced at her work-worn hands. The thought of her jewelry made the thickness in her throat reappear.

Marydyth sighed and forced herself to relax. That was part of the past. And she could either mourn for something that could not be changed or let it go. She had her daughter and her life. And a million questions.

And there was one person who had all the answers.

"Flynn," she said harshly. She'd sooner walk over hot coals than ask him.

No. Marydyth decided she would not ask him anything. She would just wait and maybe the pieces of the puzzle would fall into place on their own. Deep-down inside, she didn't trust him.

Marydyth opened the clothespress and found a gown, looking and smelling as if it had been freshly laundered. She took off the dress that Flynn had selected and slipped the white cotton over her head. It felt good to be in her own clothes, and in a garment of her own choosing after so long.

She sat down at her dressing table and looked at herself. Time and events had taken their toll upon her, but tonight there was a light in her eyes that had not been present in Tombstone. She knew what it was, of course, it was hope. For the first time since J.C.'s murder Marydyth had hope that she and Rachel would be all right.

Flynn stared into the cold hearth over his unlit cigarette and sipped at some Mellwood whiskey. When Marydyth insisted on reading to Rachel and tucking her in, he had found himself prowling through the library looking for something—anything—to take his mind off it.

It was the last thing he wanted to admit, but it had stung to be replaced in Rachel's nighttime ritual. It was foolish. Damned foolish, he admitted, but knowing that didn't make it any easier for him. And the awful truth was, he didn't one hundred percent trust Marydyth Hollenbeck.

And you feel guilty about it.

Guilty and responsible. He simply couldn't shake the memory of what he had overheard her say to Victoria.

"Damn it all to hell." He took a long drink of the whiskey, hoping it would burn away his concerns as it went down.

"That's the wage for a man who listens behind doors," he accused himself aloud, but it was more than that. It all came back to the letter, which, as Moses had said, could be interpreted many ways. Flynn realized now that he had chosen to interpret it in a way that would give Rachel her mother back.

But was that the right thing? Had he put a cold-blooded murderer back in this house?

He flopped down in the big chair and put the whiskey on the side table. Using his own leg as a bootjack, he eased off one boot and then the other. Flynn wiggled his toes inside his socks and crossed his feet at the ankles. Then he stared, unfocused, at the cold hearth.

After an hour of considering every possibility and looking at his problem from every possible angle he had come to a decision.

There was only one thing he could do. He was going to have to watch Marydyth Hollenbeck like a hawk. There were things about her that he couldn't let himself trust. There were too many unanswered questions, but most of all, it was the sound of her voice speaking to Victoria that would not allow him to do anything else. It gave him an uneasy feeling—sneaking around watching—but he couldn't find any way out of it.

Marydyth Hollenbeck couldn't be trusted.

Before the thought even settled in his brain, Rachel's bloodcurdling scream had him on his feet and running for the stairs. His heart was pounding like a locomotive while images of Marydyth pummeled his brain.

Was she capable of hurting her own child?

Marydyth had not been able to sleep, and she found herself walking toward Rachel's room without even realizing that she was doing so. She was right outside her door when the scream made her blood congeal in her veins.

She had heard screams like that many times in Yuma.

It was the sound of hopelessness. It was the sound a soul makes when it is lost and has no hope of being found.

Marydyth wrenched open the door and flew inside. Her only thought was of helping Rachel.

The thin, bluish shaft of moonlight added an eeriness to the room. Marydyth went to the bed and found Rachel wound up in the sheet, covered with a sheen of sweat, thrashing in torment. Marydyth knew what it felt like to be trapped in the hellish reality of a dream.

She picked Rachel up, sheet and all. The child swung her arms wildly, desperately trying to escape some nameless horror. Her elbows and tiny fists connected with Marydyth's neck and face more than once.

"Shh.... Darling, I am here now. Mama is here," Marydyth whispered.

"Mama!" Rachel shrieked.

Flynn rounded the corner and stepped into the doorway but froze on the spot.

What in the hell are you doing to her, Marydyth?

The question, however, did not reach his tongue, because as he watched he saw not a murderess but a mother's tender hand stroking Rachel's forehead.

And then something else happened.

A twining sort of awareness crept from his socked feet to a spot below his navel. He swallowed hard.

The air between him and Marydyth became electrified as his eyes adjusted to the light and he made out more details. She was wearing a gown, and the moonlight shimmered on her uneven curls and down her slender back. He wanted to turn and leave but he was rooted to the spot.

He could sense her—smell her. It was a sweet, feminine odor, a mingling of hard-milled soap, fresh scrubbed cotton and *her*.

The blood in his veins became thick and heavy. He put one palm flat against the fancy printed wallpaper and closed his eyes tight.

It didn't help.

With his eyes closed he imagined her body and how it would look if he pulled that gown over her head.

"Mama is here, Rachel. I love you and I will keep you safe. Now sleep, my darling—I will never leave you again."

A rustling sound brought his eyes open with a snap. Flynn stepped back into the deep shadows of the hallway. He didn't want her to see him.

A great struggle began to war inside him. He didn't want to believe what had just happened to him, but it was useless to deny it.

He wanted her. And it disgusted him to want a woman who, by her own admission, had taken a life.

At seven o'clock when Mrs. Young showed up, Flynn was on his second cup of strong, bitter coffee. He had spent a restless night, weighing what he had seen against what he had heard.

He was not in a good mood.

"Mornin', Mrs. Young," he said without looking up from his cup. He wrapped his fingers around the cup and held it in both hands.

"Maybe it is and maybe it's not."

He turned to see her clamp her palms against her wide hips. She stood there glaring at him with her bonnet still on her head.

"Is something wrong, Mrs. Young?"

"Yes, there most certainly is something wrong. Mr. O'Bannion, I've had no complaint with you and your ways these past years. You've been a proper influence on that *child*.''

Flynn felt his jaw tighten. He squeezed the tin cup harder between his hands.

''Lord knows, with the tainted blood flowing in her veins she needs a proper upbringing.'' Mrs. Young waggled her head and compressed her lips into a thin line.

''Just what are you trying to say?'' Flynn asked.

''I am a respectable woman.''

''I've never had any doubt of that,'' Flynn said stiffly to his cup.

''Then you'll understand that I cannot abide staying in this house a minute longer.''

''What?'' His head came up and he frowned at the housekeeper. ''What is that?''

''And I can tell you this, Mr. O'Bannion, there is not a decent woman in Hollenbeck Corners who will, no matter how much money that uppity Moze Pritikin promises to pay. No one will spend a minute in this house with the Black Widow.''

So, Mrs. Young had talked to Moze before Flynn. It did not really surprise him; the old attorney knew the pulse and rhythm of everything that happened in Hollenbeck Corners.

''Sorry you feel that way, ma'am,'' Flynn said with absolutely no sincerity.

''Maybe Miss Uppity-high-and-mighty will do her own cooking. 'Course if'n I was you I'd think twice about eating anything she cooked. Probably be laced with poison.''

''She was never accused of poisoning anyone,'' Flynn said dryly.

''That don't mean she mightn't try it. That is Murderin' Mary in there, or have you forgotten there was a dead husband before poor J.C.? God rest his soul, he should'a had more sense than to go chasing after a woman half his age." She wagged her head back and forth while she kept her arms akimbo.

"There was not that many years' difference between them." Anger flashed in Flynn.

"Well, I just wanted you to know from me, so there'd be no misunderstanding. And don't try and offer me more money to stay, 'cause I won't."

"I wouldn't think of offering you more money to stay." Flynn shoved his chair back with his knees and stood up. He glared down at her.

She shivered under his chilling gaze. "Good. 'Cause more money wouldn't make a bit of difference—not one bit."

"Believe me, Mrs. Young, after hearing your thoughts on the matter, I wouldn't consider having you stay a minute longer in this den of Satan."

She blinked twice and took a tottering step backward. Her mouth worked as if she were trying to formulate something to say. "I'll be off," she managed to croak.

Flynn slammed the door behind her—hard. "Goodbye, you haughty hypocritical old bitch...."

A sound made him whirl around. He found two pairs of blue eyes watching him. For an instant Flynn could only stand there and blink. It was more than just being caught cursing that froze him to the spot.

It was *her*.

The Arizona sunshine blazing through the tall kitchen windows bathed her in an almost heavenly glow. She was wearing a butter-colored silk morning wrapper that skimmed over her slight figure and caused his mouth to go dry as dust.

"Rachel, honey, would you check and see if the newspaper has been delivered yet?" Marydyth asked.

"Sure." Rachel bounced from the room, oblivious to anything that was going on around her.

Flynn marveled that Rachel was so innocent that she could not feel the white-hot current flowing between him and Marydyth. "How much did she hear?"

"Only the goodbye," she said with a lift of one brow.

"How much did you hear?" He focused on her face, studying it, trying to read her thoughts.

"All of it."

"I'm sorry." He was shocked to realize that he meant it.

She managed a crooked smile with one side of her mouth but she gave a little snort. "Don't be. I've heard worse." Marydyth walked into the kitchen. The yellow silk wrapper fluttered around her ankles like butterfly wings when she moved. It whispered a little sound that raised the flesh on Flynn's arm.

He drew a breath through his tightly clenched teeth and fancied that he could taste her on his tongue—a combination of sweet and hot spices.

She got a cup from the cupboard and poured herself some coffee while he tried to pull his gaze from her slender form.

"Mmm...this is good." She turned her eyes on him again and he felt color rise in his throat.

"Mr. O'Bannion, if you are able to find a replacement for Mrs. Young, and I assume what she said about my cooking would make you wish to, I want it made clear that whoever is hired will be working for me."

"What?" There was a buzzing in his ears. He blinked and focused on her face, hoping it would be less distracting.

She frowned at him.

"I don't want anyone in this house to have divided loyalties. I heard Mrs. Young mention that Victoria was paying her, or at least Moses Pritikin has been. I want no more of that. Whoever is hired will be on my payroll."

"Your payroll?" Flynn repeated dumbly. He blinked and tried to dispel the image of her delicate ankles.

She looked at him as if he were simple in the mind. "Today I intend to go to the bank and get my affairs in order." She drew herself up straight. "I need to find out what shape my finances are in and exactly what my situation is."

"Your finances?" Flynn could only repeat what she was saying.

"Yes, I'll tell you straight out, I intend to see Moses Pritikin and hire him to revoke your guardianship of Rachel."

Her words settled on him like a cold blanket, driving the crazy, lust-filled thoughts from his head.

He swallowed hard and his brain slowly processed all that she had said.

She doesn't know about the terms of J.C.'s will.

He stood there staring at her. She had survived Yuma, but what would it do to her when she found out the truth about J.C.'s will—the fact that *she* didn't have a penny to her name?

"I need to go out for a while—"

"That's fine." She cut him off before he could finish his thought. "Rachel and I will do very well without you."

There were at least a dozen things that he wanted to

say to her, but he knew he'd live to regret every damned one of them so he just clamped his jaw tight and left the house.

An hour later Flynn was sitting across the desk from Moses Pritikin. "You must've left in a god-awful hurry, Flynn."

"Why do you say that?" Flynn was still thinking of the strange sensations he had experienced that morning.

"'Cause I've never seen you out without your hat. Hell, you look practically naked."

Flynn felt his face color as that truth set in. He had been so rattled by Marydyth and his stunning awareness of her that he had not even realized he didn't have his Stetson.

"I want to talk to you about Marydyth," he blurted out.

"Is she giving you trouble already?" Moses leaned across the desk, all business written in the craggy lines of his weathered face.

"No, it's not like that." Flynn fidgeted beneath Moze's steely gaze.

"Then what's the trouble?"

"Hell, Moze, she intends to hire you to try and fire me."

A burst of laughter erupted from Moses. "Fire you?" His thick white brows shot nearly to his equally white hairline. "Does she really think that she can?"

"Yep." Flynn slouched in the chair, suddenly angry at himself and Moses. "I can't blame her. I'd do the same thing in her position."

"Except she doesn't have a pot to make water in or a window to throw—"

"That's where you're wrong, Moze." Flynn avoided Moze's gaze.

"What do you mean? I executed J.C.'s will—she had nothing. And since her jewelry never turned up she doesn't even have that to fall back on."

"She does—now," Flynn said dryly.

"She—? No. Tell me that you didn't do what I think you did." Moses leaned back, his face a mask of incredulous wonder.

"I transferred forty-five thousand dollars into an account at the bank—in her name alone—no strings attached."

Moses narrowed his eyes. He leaned back in his chair and laced his fingers together. "Where did you get forty-five thousand dollars on short notice?"

Flynn flicked a brown agate glance his way.

"I'll be damned." Moses exclaimed. "You put all the money from the annuity in an account for her." It was a statement of fact, not a question. "Why, for Christ's sake?"

"I dunno." Flynn squirmed in the chair. "It seemed like the right thing to do."

"J.C. evidently didn't think so," Moses pointed out.

"Perhaps J.C. didn't know her as well as he thought," Flynn heard himself snap sharply. "His will should have stated that Marydyth would inherit—not Rachel's 'guardian.'"

Moses drew back, his eyes narrowed while he studied Flynn's face. "I hope you know what you are doing."

"I never wanted that money. Marydyth is entitled to it." Flynn shifted in his seat. "But that isn't what I came here to tell you."

"Well—surprise me!" Moses shook his head from side to side, obviously in total disbelief.

"Marydyth wants to try and have the guardianship revoked."

"She doesn't have a snowball's chance in hell. Those papers are unbreakable, Flynn." Moze's eyes narrowed down to slits. "I made sure of it, myself."

"She is still going to hire you."

"Can't be done. I am Victoria's attorney."

Flynn sat in the chair and stared at the pressed tin ceiling overhead. He could just imagine what Marydyth would think if Moze told her that. She would believe that it was all a plot to prevent her from trying to revoke the papers.

"Is there anybody else?" Flynn heard himself asking. It was crazy. Hell, he wasn't even sure he trusted her.

"What do you mean?"

"I mean that I want you to recommend somebody anyway. How about Foster in Tombstone?"

"Have you gone loco since I saw you last? You want me to recommend somebody to *help* her?"

"Yes—no—hell I don't know what I want." Flynn stood up and stared at Moses.

"You and I are the only ones who know exactly what was in that letter, Flynn."

"I know."

"Are you so convinced of her total innocence that you are comfortable doing this?"

"That's just it, Moze. I'm not convinced of her innocence at all."

Chapter Eight

It was late afternoon when Flynn finally returned to Hollenbeck House. The minute he opened the front door he was met by Rachel's smiling face. He scooped her up and inhaled the fragrance of lilac toilet water.

"Mmm...you smell good." He made an exaggerated game of sniffing her neck and the tender flesh behind her ear.

"Mama put some stuff on me." Rachel's smile slipped and she frowned at him. "Do you like it?"

"Very much." Flynn kissed her soft cheek and inhaled deeply again. He laughed when she shivered.

"Then it's all right? You don't care if Mama combs my hair and puts water on me?"

Flynn looked into Rachel's innocent pale eyes. It tore at him to know how very much she wanted to care for her mother, but how her little heart was guarding itself, trying to spare itself pain and hurt. He didn't fully trust Marydyth, but something inside him wished that Rachel could.

"Punkin, it suits me just fine when she does nice things for you," he finally said.

"I'm glad, 'cause I liked it. Now carry me into the parlor and see Mama's company, Unca Flynn."

"Company?" Flynn asked as he shifted Rachel up to his shoulders for her piggyback ride.

"Uh-huh. He wanted me to call him Unca too, but I said no."

"Uncle?" The signature at the bottom of the letter flashed through his mind. Had Marydyth's mysterious uncle Blaine showed up? A flash of anger surged through Flynn. Could the bastard really be so bold as to enter this house after letting Marydyth take the blame for Andre's murder?

Flynn strode into the formal parlor, ready to physically eject the man. But he stopped in his tracks when he saw Ted Kelts sitting across from Marydyth, sipping what appeared to be a cup of tea.

"O'Bannion." Kelts stood up and set his cup on the marble-topped table. "Nice to see you again."

"Kelts?" Flynn glanced at Marydyth. She looked like a different woman than the one that had sent his mind spinning this morning. Now she was dressed in a demure mauve-colored day dress. The smudges beneath her eyes were almost gone, and she had smeared a little rouge on her cheeks. Her golden curls were gathered and caught by the two combs he had purchased at the mercantile.

Flynn shook himself. What the hell was he doing, worrying about what she was wearing—whether or not she was looking rested?

"Ted stopped by to say hello and to welcome me back." Marydyth smiled warmly at Kelts, then she turned to stare coldly at Flynn. "I am sure he will be the only one in Hollenbeck to make such a gesture."

"Nonsense, Marydyth." Ted reached across the wool rug separating them and patted her hand. "Give people a chance. They'll come round," he assured her in a voice that Flynn thought was a mite too syrupy.

"I doubt it, but I thank you for trying to make me feel better, Ted. You were always a good friend to both J.C. and me." Marydyth's gaze slid across Flynn. Then she turned her attention upward to Rachel, still perched on Flynn's shoulders. There was an easy bond between them. Seeing the way Rachel clung to Flynn, the way she trusted him, she felt a hot stab of jealousy.

"Marydyth, I need to go, but I want you to think over my offer," Ted Kelts said.

"What offer is that?" Flynn asked bluntly. He wasn't too damned happy to hear Ted Kelts wanted Rachel to call him Uncle—especially since Kelts had never so much as asked about Rachel all the time Marydyth was gone. His concern now seemed hollow and false.

"Ted has made an offer to buy some of the Hollenbeck mining property," Marydyth said.

"What's propty, Unca Flynn?" Rachel asked from her perch on his shoulders.

"It's land and copper mines—like the Lavender Lady," Flynn said coldly as he turned to stare at Ted Kelts.

Ted only shrugged and smiled, making no attempt to act as if he were sorry to be caught. "I told you I was accustomed to getting what I want, O'Bannion. Now that Marydyth is home I'll be able to deal with her, and I don't think I'll be getting the same answer now."

"We can talk about it later, Ted, after I give the matter some thought." Marydyth stood and brushed the wrinkles from the front of her tiered skirt. "Let me walk you to the door."

Flynn turned and watched Ted and Marydyth disappear into the hall. He wondered how in the hell he was going to tell her that J.C. had ensured she could never sell or manage any Hollenbeck interests? He had made sure that Marydyth would never have a say in how the business was run. He had thought his young wife beautiful and incapable of understanding finance. Now the die was cast; Marydyth could never manage Hollenbeck Holdings as long as Rachel or Flynn were alive.

Marydyth came back into the room and was relieved to see that Rachel had scampered off somewhere.

She advanced on Flynn and did not stop until she was practically touching his boots. "Just who in the hell do you think you are?" she demanded.

His eyes narrowed. His already stone-hard jaw clamped tighter, giving his rugged face a stony look. "What do you mean?"

"Victoria appointed you Rachel's guardian, but you are nothing more than hired help, Mr. O'Bannion. I think you may have forgotten that."

His cold, agate eyes narrowed and a muscle in his jaw twitched.

She waited for him to answer—to defend himself, but he just glared at her. "Well? What have you got to say?" Marydyth sounded braver than she felt with those unsympathetic eyes fixed on her face.

"I don't."

"What?" She blinked back her surprise and found herself backing up a step.

"I don't have anything to say, Marydyth. If you want answers you'll have to go see Moze Pritikin." He turned away and left her standing in the parlor all alone.

Two hours later Marydyth sat across the desk in Moses Pritikin's small office, feeling her heart pound slowly in her own ears.

A thick sheaf of papers had been spread out, examined and read. She stared at the pages feeling numb, confused and *betrayed.*

"But I—don't understand. Why didn't I know about the terms of J.C.'s will before now?" Her voice was a ragged whisper.

"There seemed no need to worry about it at the time, Marydyth. With the trial going on and then the sentencing…" He could no longer meet her gaze. "J.C. loved you, I have no doubt of that, but he never thought of you as capable enough to handle the Hollenbeck holdings."

Capable. The word rolled off Moze's tongue and went straight through her heart like an Apache war lance.

Suddenly all her idyllic memories of J.C. altered, shifted and took shape again. Now she saw things in a different light. Instead of being flattered by his attention, she realized that in some ways he had thought she was weak. Instead of seeing the way he treated her through the eyes of an innocent girl being protected and loved for the first time, Marydyth saw the truth.

J.C. had considered her a lovely woman-child—a trophy more than a helpmate. He had petted and pampered and dressed her in fine clothes, he had built her a mansion and was proud to have her on his arm when they gave lavish dinner parties for the territorial governor. But now she realized that he had never considered her his equal in any way. And he certainly had not considered her competent enough to take care of their daughter's interests. He had left his money and the future of Hollenbeck Corners in Victoria's hands, and now…

"She put it all in Flynn O'Bannion's control?"

"Every red cent, every acre, every mine and lease.

Even the stock wearing the Rafter H brand. Flynn has done a good job of managing it all up to now," Moses explained patiently.

"But—but there is money in my account at the bank— the bank manager and I spoke on my way over here. J.C. must've left me something?" Marydyth had seen the account.

Moses cleared his throat and shifted in his chair. His frosty gaze slid over her face.

"Where did that money come from?" Marydyth asked.

"I am not at liberty to discuss your account at the bank or any more of this." He began to gather and straighten papers. When he had them in one pile he shoved some of them into a battered folder. "I am Victoria's attorney, and according to J.C.'s will that means I handle whatever legal questions Flynn O'Bannion may have. I can't take you on as a client, Marydyth. I have an extra copy of everything for you." He glanced up and handed her a stack of papers. "I hope you understand."

"Perfectly," she said stiffly as she rose from the chair.

"If you feel you need an attorney of your own, there is a new fella from the East who settled in recently. Wainwright Sloan has set up an office over on Fir and State. I would suggest you go retain him—ask him any questions you may have." Moses managed a grim smile. "I'm afraid that's all I can do for you, Marydyth."

She clutched the stack of papers he had shoved toward her. "Thank you, Mr. Pritikin. You've been very informative." She turned toward the door. When her fingers closed around the knob, she paused with her back still to Moses. "Knowing Victoria as I do, I am certain that she did not set up that account for me."

Nothing but the sound of Moses shuffling papers could be heard in the compact office.

Marydyth continued. "That leaves only one person who could have done it."

"I really cannot discuss this, Marydyth."

"There's no need for you to. I intend to ask Flynn O'Bannion why he gave me the money—and just what kind of game he is playing."

Marydyth walked through the kitchen door and found Flynn and Rachel eating oatmeal cookies.

"Aren't you afraid they're laced with arsenic?" she asked acidly.

He looked up at her and frowned darkly. But when he turned to Rachel, his face was bland. "Sugar, would you do me a favor?"

"What, Unca Flynn?" Rachel asked around a mouthful of cookie.

"Would you get a couple of carrots and take them out to Jack?"

She was off the chair in a blur of blue and white gingham. Her shoes clattered on the floor as she raced into the pantry and found a bunch of carrots.

"I'll take him three," she said. Her curls, bright as new pennies, bounced as she skipped to the door.

"Good idea, but you stay on the outside of the stall," Flynn warned.

"I will." Her words were muffled by the slamming of the back door.

As soon as she was gone Marydyth took off her gloves and walked to Flynn. She stared at him for half a minute, then she slapped him hard across the face. "I hate you."

He sat there, feeling the sting of her hand on his face

and the sting of her words on his soul. And then something in him snapped.

He was out of the chair and had both of her hands in his before he even realized what his intentions were. Flynn drove her back until the wall stopped her. With one hand he gathered her wrists together, forcing her breasts to jut out toward him. He could have snapped those bones with no more effort than it took to break a matchstick.

"Do you, Marydyth?" He studied her face from no more than two inches away. "Do you really hate me?"

Before he knew what he was doing his lips were upon hers in a crushing kiss. He wanted to silence her sharp tongue; he wanted to dominate her.

No, he didn't. Because as he felt her body shudder and recognized it as a tiny whimper, something inside of him changed. The kiss became one of desire and hunger. He found himself growing gentle and curious. His tongue traced the outside of her lips, tasting the cool, sweet spice that he had sensed last night.

His blood got thick and heavy inside his veins and his pulse raced. He pressed himself against her.

She stiffened.

It felt good. No, it felt better than good. But then in the midst of his muddled lust he realized who it was he was holding.

He drew back and studied her face. Her eyes were wide and her breasts were rising and falling with each agitated breath.

"Why?" she whispered. "Why didn't you tell me?"

Flynn searched her face and realized that she wasn't questioning him about the kiss. "About what?" His own voice was low and husky with latent passion.

"You bastard!" She jerked her hands, trying to get

away but he held her tighter, bringing her body hard up against his. Heat radiated between them.

"I hate you—I hate you!"

"No, you don't." He kissed her hard and long. And this time he felt her body lose some of its brittle tension. When he released her wrists her hands slid up his shoulders and curled around his neck. Damn it all to hell, she felt good in his arms. Marydyth didn't exactly return his kiss, but she didn't resist it either. Maybe she was hungry for a man's touch after being locked in prison. Whatever the reason, his bruising possession of her mouth was long, sweet and uninterrupted.

She settled back on her feet with a kind of startled sigh. Then she reached up and wiped her mouth with the back of her hand, as if she had only then become aware of what had happened between them.

"Don't ever do that again," she whispered. Impotent rage burned in her eyes. "Do you hear me?"

"I hear you, Marydyth, but I can't say I won't do it again," Flynn replied truthfully. He didn't trust her, but damn it all to hell, he could no longer trust himself either.

In that moment she hated herself almost as much as she hated him. She should have fought him, should have scratched his eyes out. But the kiss...

It filled her with an emotion she didn't want to feel and was hungry to feel again. She was mad and confused, and Flynn only made it worse. All of her notions about J.C. were nothing more than a foolish woman's dreams, and in the midst of all of that Flynn O'Bannion had managed to make her feel like a woman again.

"I do hate you." She spit out the only defense she had.

He backed up and gave her a little space between them. She sighed unconsciously in relief.

"Quit spitting like a she-cat and talk to me."

"I spoke with Moses Pritikin."

"Oh." Flynn watched her draw her wrist close to her body and rub it with her fingers.

Had he hurt her? Was she afraid of him—was that why she kept herself all bristly like a porcupine?

"Is that all you can say?" She looked up at him with unshed tears swimming in her eyes. "Why?"

"Why, what?" The misery in her face sent a hard shaft of pain through his chest.

"Why didn't you tell me about the money?" She inhaled a ragged breath. "Why didn't you let me know that J.C. had left me nothing?" She shuddered, and a sob left her lips.

Flynn had the most overwhelming urge to gather her into his arms.

"Why did you let me think the money in the bank was mine?"

"Damn it, Marydyth, it is yours."

Her features altered and something like wounded pride came into her face. "No it isn't. Moze told me the truth. J.C. left me nothing. You opened that account, didn't you?"

Well, you can lie but it won't do any good.

"Yes."

"Why?" In that moment between her hatred and confusion he wondered why he couldn't think of anything but how pretty she was. And how much he wanted to hold her and tell her that it would be all right.

It was not an observation he was happy to make.

"The money isn't mine—it *is* yours and Rachel's. Spend it all on lawyers taking me into court, go shopping, go to the dressmaker—hell, I don't care if you burn it. It is yours to do with as you want. I never asked for it."

He turned and stomped away before he lost control and kissed her again.

Over the next two days Flynn made a real effort to stay away from Marydyth. But he always managed to keep a watchful eye on her and Rachel. It wasn't difficult. More and more he found himself aware of her in ways that made his skin itch and his belly knot up. He knew when she was near without ever seeing or hearing her. All day long, everyday, she was *there,* battering his senses.

There was some sort of animal connection between them and had been since he kissed her. At night he lay naked staring at the ceiling and all he could think of was *her.*

It sickened him. Never in his life had he been a man to think with anything but the head on his shoulders, and now—well now he was burning from the inside out over a woman he didn't even like.

"Been cooped up too much," he told himself as he adjusted his arm beneath his head. And maybe he had been. Maybe that was all it was, this strange awareness of Marydyth.

But he found himself rising from the bed and pulling on his Levi's. He fastened only the two bottom buttons and stepped out in the hall.

The night was hot, sultry and still as death. He wished there was a breeze to cool the burning of his skin.

"Take more than a summer breeze," he said to himself scornfully, and he knew that it was true.

The reason he was itchy and restless had nothing to do with the weather and everything to do with Marydyth Hollenbeck.

Flynn stepped out onto the porch. The boards felt

rough beneath his bare feet. He leaned against one of the tall posts that supported the little balcony from the second floor.

And then he heard a sound.

He held his breath and listened hard, but he didn't need to. He knew exactly what it was he had heard.

It was Marydyth. She was standing on the balcony right above him.

His pulse quickened and his body hardened, nudging against the half-done-up placket of his Levi's.

Without hearing it, he knew when she inhaled. He could practically feel her thoughts as he stood below her in the night.

Flynn closed his eyes and allowed his mind to wander to her. She would be wearing that gown, the one that skimmed over her body in gentle folds when she moved. Her hair would be hanging in uneven curls around her face.

He gripped the wood on the posts and tried to focus on the sounds of the crickets and katydids but it was useless. His thoughts and his interest were focused on the female above him.

Marydyth could not sleep—rather, she did not want to go to sleep and be trapped with her nightmares.

She stood on the balcony staring out at Hollenbeck Corners. The flickering gas lamps made the main street glow. She heard a gleeful whoop and saw a dark shadow in the street. A rowdy cowboy was enjoying the night—maybe he had just won a hand of poker—maybe Lady Luck had smiled on him.

Marydyth found her thoughts traveling backward in time. She remembered what it had been like to be with Blaine as he dragged her from one riverboat to the next, always sure that his luck would change the next time.

She had been stuck with a no-account uncle because she had no other kin and nobody to care.

She heard a sound and felt something on her bare toes. It was her own tears. She was crying in the dark.

Marydyth turned away from the balcony and went to her bed. She closed her eyes and tried to force herself to sleep, willing her mind to think of something else besides her past.

Flynn was aware of her leaving the balcony. He hadn't heard anything, it was just a feeling of loss. He turned his head upward to the night sky, looking at the wash of stars that seemed close enough to touch.

Marydyth Hollenbeck affected him in a way that he could not understand. It was more than just being aroused—there was some sort of thread that seemed to tie them, and it went beyond the fact that they were bound by Rachel.

He turned, intending to go and put his fevered body in bed when he felt her panic. The short hair on the back of his nape prickled and his breath lodged in his chest. She was frightened—he could feel the cold chill of it.

A soft whimper floated on the night air and he heard her mumble something that he could not make out.

She was dreaming. And, as Flynn stood there beneath the balcony feeling her presence as if she were beside him, he wished that it were he in her dreams.

The morning found Marydyth feeling depressed and empty. She had once again fought the guilt that consumed her at night.

When will it end?

She had suffered within the walls of Yuma—why couldn't she forgive herself for killing Andre?

She went down to the kitchen and found Flynn already

there. His hair was tousled and his eyes red-rimmed, as if he had not slept well either. But the smell of wood smoke was coming from the Monarch and the aroma of coffee filled the room.

"Morning," she managed to say as she eased her body into a chair. She was uncomfortable being in the kitchen where he had kissed her.

He turned to her with his lips parted, but before he spoke Rachel exploded into the kitchen. Her face was wreathed in a happy smile.

"Are you ready, Unca Flynn?" she asked as she scooted up to the table.

"Ready?" He blinked and stared at her.

"You didn't forget, did you?" She eyed him suspiciously.

"Naw, I didn't forget. I just wanted to see if you remembered." He glanced at Marydyth to see if she would challenge his lie but she only averted her eyes.

"Today is the ice-cream social and parade."

Marydyth turned then and pinned him with a gaze. "You have plans?"

He studied her face for a moment, weighing his answer. Then he turned to the pump and filled a pan with water. He stoked the wood inside the Monarch and turned back to Marydyth. "Yes, we both have plans. We are taking Rachel to the ice-cream social and are going to watch the parade together."

Marydyth's eyes widened and she bit her lip. She wanted to go, but the idea of being with Flynn all day filled her with an unease that bordered on panic.

"Please, Mama," Rachel begged.

Her heart melted at the sight of her daughter's face. "All right, sweetheart." She turned to Flynn and frowned at him. "For you."

An hour later Flynn was ushering Marydyth and Rachel out the door of the mansion. The sun beat down on the town, heating up the day. He angled his Stetson and Marydyth adjusted the brim of her straw hat.

Flynn tried not to notice the way the blue-and-white-striped summer frock brought out the color of her eyes or the way the low-cut neck skimmed just off the ridge of her shoulders. Or the way the soft mounds of her breasts showed when she took a deep breath.

He tried not to notice, but he did.

"Are you ready?" he asked them both as they stood on the steps of Hollenbeck House. The boom and trill of the Hollenbeck Corners Brass Band could be heard in the distance.

"It's gonna be fun." Rachel jumped up and down, causing her russet ringlets to bounce.

Marydyth cast a reluctant gaze down the hill to the gathering crowd below.

"I can bring a buggy back for you, if you'd like," Flynn offered.

"No. We can walk." She tilted her head.

Was that fear he saw in her eyes?

"You don't have to do this," he began, "not today—not this soon."

"Yes, I do have to do it." She looked down at Rachel who was almost vibrating with excitement. "For her."

Flynn nodded, and tried to swallow the thick lump that had lodged in his throat. He didn't want to feel compassion for Marydyth—hell, he didn't want to feel anything for her—but how could he not when she looked like spring moonlight and had the courage of a mountain lioness?

They walked side by side down the winding drive. It

was hot and Flynn's shirt was beginning to cling to his back by the time they reached the bottom of the hill.

He glanced over at Marydyth. She looked as cool as a mountain brook, and if she was fearful, she hid it well. She looked to the side and studied every storefront and new house as they entered the town.

"Changed a little, hasn't it?" Flynn's gravelly voice rubbed over Marydyth's skin.

She forced herself to stare straight ahead. "It's a bit bigger."

A woman with two small children in tow nodded when Flynn helped Marydyth and Rachel up onto the boardwalk. There was a clutch of people lining the street in front of Cashion's Bakery. The woman stared for just a moment but Marydyth saw recognition flicker in her eyes.

The woman seemed to melt into the crowd, yet within seconds she returned, pulling a stout woman in a flour-covered smock to the front of the bakery. They pointed in her direction.

Marydyth shivered as they smiled and said something behind their hands.

"In ten minutes, everyone in Hollenbeck Corners will know that I am back," she whispered more to herself than to Flynn.

"I 'spect so if they don't already. I have a notion that Mrs. Young spread the word."

She turned and looked at him, her eyes brimming with emotion.

"There's no painless way to do it—but if you can think of some way to make it easier on Rachel, I'll put in with you."

Marydyth didn't even try to hide the fact that she was

staring at him. He was serious; his face was etched with compassion and concern. And not just for Rachel.

It knocked her off guard that he cared so much for her daughter—and maybe a little for her as well.

"I—I appreciate that." She swallowed hard. She wanted to say more, wanted to admit she was terrified—afraid Rachel would be disappointed in her, afraid to face the townspeople—but those were thoughts she couldn't share with anybody, especially Flynn O'Bannion.

The brass band began a rousing march, and, for the blink of an eye, everyone stopped staring at the trio. Flynn nodded toward a clearing on the board sidewalk. Marydyth picked up her skirt and quickened her step to keep up with Flynn and Rachel.

A little voice in her head told her this was a big mistake. But when Rachel had turned that blue-eyed, angel's face to her and asked, she couldn't have refused her anything.

"Whoa, what's the hurry?" Ted Kelts's voice managed to find Marydyth above the din of the band. She stopped and from the corner of her eye saw Flynn, a few feet away, do the same.

"Ted?" Marydyth tilted her head so she could see him from beneath her straw brim. "How—how are you?"

He smiled and slipped his hand around her waist. "The question is, how are you?" He looked around and made eye contact with a handful of people who were openly watching.

Marydyth refused to give them the satisfaction of seeing her quail before their disapproval. "Fine. I am just fine."

"Where are you headed?" He slipped a careless gaze in Flynn's direction to include him and Rachel in the question.

"To Palson's. Rachel wants a hoarhound stick," Marydyth explained.

"I'll walk with you. Maybe we can talk about my offer again," he said as he urged Marydyth down the boardwalk. "Come on, O'Bannion, let's get the little lady a peppermint."

Flynn felt something tight and burning in his gut when he saw Ted Kelts escorting Marydyth down the boardwalk. It was more than his refusal to take no for an answer about the Lavender Lady—but Flynn wasn't quite sure why he suddenly had the urge to knock Ted Kelts flat.

When they reached Palson's store Flynn took Rachel inside and lifted her to sit on the top of a closed-up pickle barrel. Her legs dangled over the edge of the staved and banded barrel where she kicked her shoes against the wood.

"Hoarhound?" Flynn asked with a lift of his brow.

"Please, Unca Flynn."

He turned to get the candy from the glass jar on the counter and found Ted Kelts with his hand already in it. "Here you go, Rachel." Ted handed her the candy.

Rachel looked at Flynn. He nodded, and she took the candy from Ted Kelts.

"Now, Marydyth, let's talk about the Lavender Lady," Ted said.

Marydyth's breath lodged in her throat. Learning of J.C.'s will had been hard news to take, and the thought of everyone finding out made her stomach lurch. She found her gaze slipping to Flynn while she silently prayed that he would help her.

"Marydyth and I are talking about getting the mine fit to be reopened," Flynn said abruptly. He did not miss the look of relief that flitted across Marydyth's face.

"Marydyth?" Ted mugged a face. "I didn't realize you two were on a first-name basis."

"I owe Flynn a great deal, Ted. He has taken admirable care of Rachel while I—was—gone." She could not bring herself to say the name of Yuma when she was sure the other patrons in the store were listening to every word.

"I see." Ted studied her face for half a minute. "Reopening the Lady, eh?"

"Uh, yes." Marydyth once again looked at Flynn.

"Lot of men have been out of work since the strike. I saw how Tombstone is coming back—the Lavender Lady would help Hollenbeck." Flynn watched Ted's face for a reaction.

Ted shrugged. "I suppose you are right. Actually, I was planning on doing the same thing if you sold her to me." He directed his comments to Marydyth.

"That—that isn't possible, Ted." Marydyth fidgeted, feeling the burn of many pairs of eyes on her back. She had an overwhelming urge to run and hide. She took a step and suddenly found Flynn standing beside her. He lightly touched her arm with his wide, work-worn hand. A flood of determined strength seemed to enter her body.

She glanced up at him.

He winked and grinned.

And suddenly she knew she would not run away. As long as that rough hand was skimming along her arm she knew that she could face the sharp tongues and stares of the town.

"Well, I better get going," Ted said. "The mayor is going to give a speech before we start the picnic. Will you all be staying for the ice-cream social?"

Marydyth hesitated but then she felt a gentle pressure

from Flynn's fingers. "We haven't decided," she said with a smile.

"Best of luck with the Lavender Lady." Ted touched his index finger to the brim of his hat and sauntered away.

Marydyth turned to look up at Flynn. Their hat brims, her straw and his Stetson, shielded them from curious eyes. She took the opportunity to mouth the words. *Thank you.*

"Hurry, Mama," Rachel said over her shoulder.

An hour later Marydyth was struggling to keep up with her energetic daughter. Flynn was there, staying protectively near but far enough away for Marydyth to get to know Rachel.

It was one more thing she felt beholden to him for. It would take time to win her daughter's love and trust completely but today was a good start.

And she owed a big debt to Flynn for the help he had given her. She realized today that he was not heartless. He had helped her when she silently begged him to keep quiet about the humiliation of J.C.'s will—and he had somehow sensed her panic and transferred some of his stubborn strength to her by no more than a touch and a smile. Something strange had happened to her heartbeat when he looked at her with those hard, agate eyes.

They caught up to Rachel and each grabbed one of her hands. Marydyth was glad that Rachel walked in the middle, because even at this distance she could have sworn she felt the sparking heat between her and Flynn.

"Looky, Mama, Unca Flynn got that thumper for the town," Rachel said happily.

Marydyth looked up at the whitewashed building with double doors like a stable. Inside was a shiny brass and red-painted contraption with knobs and hoses protruding from it.

"What did you call it?" she asked Rachel with a smile tickling her lips.

"A thumper...you know, to put out fires." Rachel skipped along, jerking at the ends of their hands.

"She means pumper." Flynn grinned over at Marydyth. "Rachel, honey, it's *pumper*," Flynn gently corrected. Marydyth had the notion it was not the first time.

"That's what I said...a thumper. And you got it for me to be safe."

Marydyth looked at Flynn and frowned. "What does she mean?"

A light stain of color crept up his neck from beneath the collar of his shirt. "There were some fires in Tombstone...a couple of children died." He cleared his throat. "I—I just thought Hollenbeck Corners needed one."

Something like slow honey from a jar poured through Marydyth's middle. Flynn O'Bannion had sides she had never imagined. A hot lump lodged in her throat.

"Thank you, Flynn," she said.

He didn't even look at her but the sound of her voice rubbed over his hide like velvet. His belly contracted and tugged in a way that made him want to squirm. When he finally did glance over at Marydyth, her jagged curls were bouncing beneath the brim of her hat each time Rachel skipped.

Either I'm going crazy or she is getting prettier.

He shook himself. This was a bad sign—a real bad sign. First he kissed her for some damn fool reason he couldn't begin to understand and now he was noticing things about her. Like the way her clothes seemed to fit her better, or the way the skin at the corners of those lovely turquoise eyes crinkled when she smiled at Rachel.

Yep, this was a very bad sign.

Most of the crowd was at the picnic grounds listening to the mayor's speech, but when they turned the corner by Fir Street a small group was gathered.

Marydyth swallowed hard, telling herself that she had to hold her head up and be strong—for Rachel.

Near the butcher shop she forced herself to smile when they encountered a portly woman. The woman was a stranger to her, but evidently Marydyth's reputation had preceded her.

"I never...the nerve." The woman harrumphed loudly and trotted across the street as fast as her short legs would carry her. "Indecent to be living under the same roof. Downright sinful." Her words carried clearly on the dry summer air.

"What was the matter with Mrs. Gerding, Unca Flynn?" Rachel asked as she stopped skipping.

"She...she was just in a hurry, punkin."

"Oh."

Marydyth felt a thickening of her throat. The town would view her as a murderess and a fallen woman. But what could she do? Flynn had the legal right to be in the house—and after spending time with him today she was finding that she was glad he was there—for Rachel.

"Oh, looky, Unca Flynn, it's Mary Wilson and her mama!" Rachel pointed at a slender woman with a line of stair-step children walking behind her. "She has the new baby. Let's go see if she liked my present."

Before Flynn could react, Rachel had jerked her hands free and run ahead to see her friend. Mary and Rachel chattered loudly, looking at the new baby while one of the older girls held the basket steady.

"Mrs. Wilson." Flynn touched the brim of his hat.

"Mr. O'Bannion," Mrs. Wilson greeted him and allowed herself to glance in Marydyth's direction.

"This is Rachel's mother, Marydyth Hollenbeck." Flynn introduced Marydyth.

"I know who she is," Mrs. Wilson snapped. "Come along, children, we can't be standing in the street with...with these *folks*." Her eyes lingered on Marydyth for a moment. Flynn saw Marydyth go pale and a confused look pass between Mary and Rachel. Mrs. Wilson took the basket holding the baby from the older girl and turned away.

But Flynn had no intention of allowing the woman to escape so easily. He reached out and caught the handle of the basket with one hand.

"The baby looks mighty nice, Mrs. Wilson. Isn't that Rachel's baby blanket?" He looked her square in the face. Marydyth didn't envy Mrs. Wilson for being the object of those stony brown eyes.

"That color pink is pretty on her. Rachel was mighty happy you had a girl so she could give some of her things to you." The sound of anger was in his soft-spoken words.

"Uh...yes, it is," Mrs. Wilson said while a stain of color crept up her cheeks. "It was a thoughtful gift."

"Rachel and Marydyth thought it would suit." Flynn lied about Marydyth's having anything to do with it. "They thought you might appreciate it—being neighborly, I mean." He fastened his gaze on her face. "I hope they weren't wrong, Mrs. Wilson."

"I do appreciate—the—kindness," she stammered in a flustered voice. "It was a nice thing to do." Mrs. Wilson turned to face Marydyth. She swallowed hard. "Thank you, Mrs. Hollenbeck."

"It was nothing," Marydyth replied. She had no idea

what was going on, except that Flynn O'Bannion was once again coming to her rescue, forcing a respectable woman to speak to her in public—trying to set the tone of what would be expected when she went out.

Flynn released his hold on the basket and managed a thin smile. Some of the tension surrounding the group seemed to evaporate.

"Perhaps you can bring Mary over to play with Rachel—real soon." His words were pregnant with meaning.

"Perhaps." Mrs. Wilson looked left and right like a cornered rabbit. Marydyth found herself in awe of his intimidating, masculine control. With his quiet voice and an easy smile, Flynn managed to get everyone to do exactly what he wanted.

"Good, we'll be expecting you on Friday this week." His smile widened but it did not warm.

"Friday, Mr. O'Bannion?"

"Uh-huh, Friday is good."

She swallowed and nodded. "Friday. What time?" Mrs. Wilson was caught in his power as surely as if he were a great eagle with talons fastened around her.

"Two o'clock? The children will be ready to nap by then, and you and Marydyth can have a nice visit."

"Two o'clock it is." Mrs. Wilson glanced up the street where a small clutch of women had gathered. They pointed, and Marydyth heard snippets of their conversation.

Black Widow. Murderin' Mary. Living under the same roof without benefit of a preacher. And other bits of whispered accusations.

Marydyth unconsciously squirmed. She felt a modicum of sympathy for Mrs. Wilson. It couldn't do her reputation any good to accept the invitation to Hollenbeck

House. But when Marydyth glanced up at Flynn's hard face and unyielding jawline she knew that Mrs. Wilson had no choice.

"If you will excuse me, Mr. O'Bannion—Mrs. Hollenbeck." Mrs. Wilson stepped back, looking at the group of women down the walk.

"Of course, I am sure you and your...uh...*friends* have a lot to talk about. I hope you will share all the latest gossip with us when you come on Friday."

Mrs. Wilson paled, then she nodded and hurried up the street with her children trailing behind her.

"Why did you do that?" Marydyth whispered. "Why did you force her to talk to us and accept the invitation?"

Those hard eyes sent a chill marching up her spine when he turned. He leaned close enough for her to smell him—a blend of man and Arizona sunshine. "Because Rachel has to live in this town, and I'll be damned if they will shun her—not while there is breath in my body."

In that moment Marydyth knew she could never hate Flynn O'Bannion with the same kind of passion again.

Chapter Nine

Marydyth sat in her room nursing a headache, with a cool damp cloth on her head, trying to forget the humiliating afternoon. Everywhere they had gone, people pointed, stared and whispered.

Until Flynn O'Bannion turned his chilly wrath upon them. He had bullied, intimidated and coerced everyone into behaving themselves—to a point.

Marydyth sighed and tried to erase the whispering voices from her head. She had been so grief-stricken over J.C.'s death and then charged with murder and put on trial, that she had never considered what had happened to the town. Hollenbeck copper mining had brought settlers to this part of the Territory. With J.C.'s death, the mine never reopened after the strike. A lot of men had gone without work. Another sin laid at Marydyth's feet if the whispering of the townspeople could be believed.

But Flynn had taken care of that, too. While they walked through the streets he had let it slip several times that *they* were considering getting the Lavender Lady in shape to be worked again. He was a puzzle.

A knock on the door brought Marydyth to her feet. She held the damp cloth in her hand. "Come in."

She expected to see Rachel's sunny face, but it was Flynn who stood at the door with a tray in his big hands. He looked naked without his Stetson and more than a little uncomfortable to be standing in the doorway of her bedroom.

"Rachel made tea for you. She thought it would help your headache." He looked down at the tray. For the first time Marydyth noticed two cups. "Can I come in?"

She realized that she had never moved since she opened the door. "Yes, come in."

He moved past her with a masculine grace that made her pulse heavy. In seconds he had the tray on the table by the balcony window and was pouring the tea.

"You don't mind if I join you?" He was polite to ask, but it was obvious the answer was unnecessary.

"Be my guest." She left the door open and moved to the balcony window. The sun was dipping low, and at regular intervals the sound of fireworks in Hollenbeck Corners below could be heard.

"What is Rachel doing?" Marydyth asked as she stared out the window.

"Playing with a book of paper dolls." Flynn said with a lopsided grin. "I...well...there are some things I leave her to herself about—paper dolls is one of them."

Marydyth found herself smiling at the mental image she got of rangy ex-marshal Flynn O'Bannion retreating from the scene of a little girl playing with paper dolls.

"Here's your tea." He gestured toward the steaming cup.

"Thanks." Marydyth picked up the cup but she didn't take the chair opposite Flynn by the round marble-topped table. She continued to stare out the window.

"It will be night soon," she heard herself say. There was a thready catch in her voice.

"Marydyth—I—I heard you last night." Flynn concentrated on the cup of tea even when he felt the burn of her eyes upon him.

"I'm sorry that I disturbed you," she finally said, wondering how much he had heard.

"I would be willing to listen—that is, if you want to talk about—anything." He glanced up and met her eyes. "I'm here."

"No. I don't want to talk about it—I don't want to *think* about it. I wish to God I could forget it all." She stared at him for three full heartbeats. "But...thank you."

He shrugged and let his gaze slip away. "It was nothing—just an offer. Sometimes talking things out gets rid of them."

Her face burned with heat. She hated the nightmares and hated it even more that Flynn was aware of them. She felt vulnerable.

"Rachel has nightmares too, but then, you know that, don't you?" he said softly while his finger traced the edge of the delicate china cup. Marydyth stared at his hands. Such big, rough, sun-browned hands, but they touched the china cup with a delicacy that made her shiver involuntarily.

Would his hands feel like that on her skin?

She shook herself to banish the thought. "Has she—has she had them for a long time?"

"Since she started talking." Flynn grimaced as if the memory caused him pain. "I never know what to say or do, so I usually just talk nonsense and wait until it passes."

"That's all you can do," she said softly. "Until the nightmare lets her go she can't hear you anyway."

Flynn looked up. Marydyth was staring out the window at the setting sun. The vermilion streamers turned her blond hair to copper—like Rachel's. Her face was tense with pain. Flynn had the urge to hold her and talk nonsense until the haunted look was erased from her face.

He shoved the desire to the edge of his consciousness and stood up. "I better go downstairs."

"Flynn?" Her voice reached out and touched something deep within him.

"Yes?"

"I was wondering if—well, if you would do me a favor?" She stared at her hands while she spoke.

"Name it."

He didn't even ask what it was.

"It is a lot to ask…but would you help me cut my hair?" She finished the last in a rush before her nerve failed her.

Flynn rocked back on his heels. He had expected her to ask him to leave the house, or that he let Rachel go away with her. But this…

"Cut your hair?" He looked confused, befuddled.

"Yes. This—" she pointed to her hair "—happened when one of the other prisoners…" Marydyth shuddered. "If we're going to have company on Friday I would like to look presentable. I doubt anyone else in town would do it for me."

Flynn studied her for a long time, and then he lifted his hands. "I am big and clumsy as an ox, Marydyth. I know how to dress and skin a deer, but—your hair?"

This time the smile was warmer. "I'll tell you how to do it and watch you in the mirror."

"I might make matters worse."

"I trust you."

I trust you.

The words echoed in Flynn's head. She had gone from

hating him to trusting him in less than a week. He picked up the black-handled dress shears and squeezed his fingers into them.

When he looked down at the looking glass he met Marydyth's reflection.

"I washed and rinsed it. Now just run your fingers through it and hold it up."

Flynn swallowed hard and did as she instructed. He splayed his fingers and laced them through the strands of wet hair. He lifted a tress and looked at her questioningly.

"Like this?"

"Uh-huh. Just cut the ends where they are all ragged."

He put the long, sharp shears against the silken strands and snipped. The hair slid through his grip and tumbled down.

"That's right. Now just do that all over." She gave him what he thought was supposed to be a reassuring smile.

Flynn pulled his gaze away from her reflection and concentrated on her hair. It wasn't easy. The hollow at the nape of her neck kept drawing his attention. He wanted to touch it—to put his lips on it. He wanted to nuzzle the soft spot beneath her ear and see if it felt like velvet.

He wanted...

Flynn forced himself to pick up a strand of hair, hold it up and snip at the ends. Over and over he repeated the procedure while his Levi's got tighter and more confining in the crotch.

The smell of her wet skin, mingled with the musky, subtle odor of *her* swirled around his head. He inhaled deeply and felt himself becoming drunk on the fragrance.

Having Marydyth this close, touching her and holding her, was ecstasy. But when she closed her eyes and leaned her head back against his turgid sex it was pure hell and pure delight. While she was in that position— her head tilted back and her eyes closed—Flynn did something that he knew was loco.

He spread his hands and gently held her slender neck. It was a crazy thing to do; his hands were too big and rough and looked out of place against the creamy white-ness of her flesh but it *felt* right.

He had never touched a woman like this. Oh, he'd bedded so many he couldn't remember their faces. Like any man old enough to shave he had undressed them and explored the mystery of the female body, but this was different.

In some strange way it was almost better.

Maybe it was because she had said she trusted him. But the instant that thought came into his head he drew back and clenched his hands into hard fists like the knot in his gut.

She trusted him, but he couldn't quite trust her.

When he was finished with the cutting he took both of his hands and cupped her head. He wove his fingers into the strands and held them there.

Their eyes locked in the mirror. Hers were wide and questioning. His were hard, and held a trace of suspicion and a full measure of lust.

Flynn couldn't allow himself to lose his judgment with Marydyth. They were immobile, staring at each other in the glass, until the sounds of childish footsteps broke the magical spell that bound them.

"Mama! Unca Flynn! When is dinner? I'm hungry!"

Flynn stepped back and cleared his throat. "I'm going to throw some steaks in a pan and fix some gravy. Too bad there aren't any of Mrs. Young's biscuits."

Marydyth ran her fingers through her hair and smiled up at him. "I'll be happy to help—if you will let me."

His heart nearly stopped.

"I'm sure my belly would be damned grateful," he said around the tightness in his throat.

They shared the kitchen from that moment on. Meals were a hodgepodge of whatever they could whip up together. Flynn and Marydyth would work around each other, occasionally finding their hands on the same knife or picking up the same onion. When that happened they would freeze and stare at each other in silence while a hot ribbon of desire bound them together. There were even times when Flynn found excuses to go into the pantry when he knew she was there, just so he could feel her nearness and let the soft feminine scent of her engulf him. He was playing a dangerous game and his instincts told him that if he didn't stop he would be sorry—they would both be sorry.

But mostly it was good. Flynn noticed that Rachel laughed more often and had fewer nightmares. And he couldn't ignore the way Marydyth's eyes sparkled and danced when she and Rachel sat down opposite each other to eat.

But Marydyth still had her nightmares. They were getting worse, and he wondered if it was because of him.

One night while they were washing and drying dishes he heard his own voice. "It must be hard for you—coming home to find—well, *me* in your house." He shrugged.

"It doesn't matter," Marydyth said. "All that matters to me is Rachel. She loves you and she wants you here." She stopped to look at Flynn but he surprised her by grinning in a boyish lopsided way.

"She's kind of special to me, too."

A strange, itchy feeling rubbed over her flesh. Her gaze focused on the little weathered lines at the corners of his eyes—eyes that were the color of rain-slicked sandstone. He had splashed water on his shirt, causing it to cling to his hard chest and drum-tight belly like a second skin.

She looked away, fighting the emotions that were bubbling and simmering inside her. "I want to thank you for trying to make people accept me."

"They'll learn." His voice was clipped.

"Maybe, but they won't ever stop talking." Marydyth sighed. "And now they have new fodder for the mill—with us living under the same roof. They'll think the worst and say even more than that."

"They will only say it once within my hearing." He scowled.

Unconsciously she reached out and trailed her fingers over his hard jaw. The contact made him stiffen, and her nerves prickled. "I wanted to talk to you about that, Flynn."

Suspicion sizzled through him. "Stop right there. Gossip be damned, Marydyth, you and I are stuck with each other and there isn't a thing either one of us can do about it."

Though she didn't want to believe it, there was a small part of her that was ridiculously happy that he said what he did. There was a strange security in knowing that Flynn O'Bannion was here, would always be here. For Rachel and for her.

"I understand," she said. "And I don't blame you a bit."

His brown eyes searched her face—made her feel hot and itchy beneath his scrutiny. "You do?"

"In your place I am sure I would feel the same way."

She finished drying the plate and put it in a stack. "But that wasn't what I wanted to talk to you about."

All Flynn could do was stand there with his hands submerged in soapy water and wait. He didn't understand a damn thing about Marydyth Hollenbeck, not a single damned thing. And the more time he spent around her the more confused he was getting.

"I've been thinking about the Lavender Lady and—" His face turned to a thundercloud.

"No. I won't put the Lavender Lady up for sale. Ted Kelts is a sidewinder. He thought he could weasel his way round me by warming up and flirting with you."

She wasn't sure when he did it, but he had closed the small distance between them. His fingers grasped her upper arms and bit into her flesh. She could see the shadow of his heavy beard and the gray specks in his brown eyes. A wavy strand of his auburn hair caught the afternoon light spilling through the chintz curtains on the kitchen window.

He was handsome as a morning sunrise.

It had been so very long since she had been in the company of a man who wasn't carrying a club and treating her like an animal. It was only natural that she should be aware of him in that way. Or at least that was what she kept telling herself as her eyes swept over his rock-hard jawline and wide chest.

"Do you hear me, Marydyth? The Lavender Lady is not for sale."

"I don't want to sell it. I wanted to tell you that I'm glad you're going to reopen it," she said with a trembling smile. Strange things were happening to her middle. She felt hot and cold all at once, and an age-old thrumming had started in her veins.

"What?" Flynn released her arms and staggered back an inch or two.

She was sorry he let her go. For one crazy minute she had thought he might kiss her again, and she had wanted it. Oh, she had wanted him to.

"You are? You are in agreement with me?"

She nodded. "If the townspeople see that you—*we*—are trying to restore jobs, maybe it will be enough to make things a little better for Rachel."

Flynn regarded her through narrowed eyes. Beneath her yellow curls and sorrowful blue eyes, there was a quick mind. She wasn't afraid of taking risks for Rachel. Something apart from lust warmed and liquefied inside his chest.

"It will be a big project," he heard himself saying. "I have to see what shape the shafts are in, order new shoring and timbers, hire men." He frowned while he rubbed the pad of his thumb across his jaw. The abrasive, scratchy sound of beard stubble against flesh made her own skin tingle and her heartbeat quicken.

"I would help you. Anything you said would of course be the last word. I wouldn't expect to make any of the decisions," she added quickly when his brows shot upward. "I would be willing to work like a dog to get it up and running again." She twisted her hands together eagerly. "I'd do anything that you say, to help Rachel."

The scowl disappeared as rapidly as sunshine burns through storm clouds. He looked at her with a new approval in his gaze.

She liked it, and she hated herself for feeling that way.

"I'll ride out to the Lady and take a look at the place. If it looks like she has any ore at all left under her skirt, then we'll reopen it." He dried his hands on a clean flour sack and started to leave.

She reached out and touched his shirtsleeve. "There is one more thing." Marydyth stepped in front of him. She took a deep breath and met his gaze without flinching. "I want to go with you to the Lavender Lady."

He studied her face for what seemed like a long time before he narrowed his eyes and expelled a heavy breath.

"All right, Marydyth. We'll leave Rachel with Gertie and we'll both go."

The next morning Marydyth searched through the trunk Flynn had brought from the attic and found her best clothes. She fluffed her blond curls and put a bonnet on her head.

She couldn't go on without having a few questions answered, and she wanted those answers before they went to the Lavender Lady. His words, "you and I are stuck with each other and there isn't a thing either one of us can do about it," had haunted her day and night.

She needed to know exactly what he meant.

Rachel and Flynn were in the barn with Jack when she left the house. She didn't tarry, setting herself a quick pace as she walked down the hill and into Hollenbeck Corners.

As she entered the main business district she was greeted by hostile gazes and whispers. One man even stepped in front of her, barring her way. She had thought he might be moved to violence but—coincidentally?— then Ted Kelts had appeared from nowhere.

"Marydyth, you are looking well." Ted fell into step beside her, and the bully faded away into a nearby alley. "Where are you headed so early?"

"I have an appointment." Marydyth ducked her head and used the bonnet to shield her face as she lied.

"I see, a woman of mystery." He didn't say any more,

just continued walking with her up Fir Street to the corner
of State Street.

"Well, here I am." Marydyth stood in front of a plate-
glass window that had fancy lettering. Ted's eyes
scanned the words.

"Seeing an attorney?" he finally asked.

"Yes, I—I have affairs I need to sort out. You understand." She didn't want to discuss this with Ted—or anyone else for that matter. She gripped her reticule tighter,
thinking of the copy of the will and the other papers that
Moses had given her tucked safely inside.

"I thought Moses Pritikin handled all the Hollenbeck
business?" Ted narrowed his eyes and studied her face.

"Yes, he does." Marydyth smiled. "Thanks for walking me, Ted. Now if you'll excuse me..." She turned
and stepped into the office. When she looked back Ted
Kelts was watching her with a strange expression on his
face.

She heard a sound and turned to see a young man with
pale skin and a quick smile. He was rolling down his
sleeves and pulling on a frock coat all in the same clumsy
motion.

"I was still unpacking. Excuse the mess." He had a
rich, melodious voice that was surprising in one so young
and slight of build.

"Think nothing of it." Marydyth extended her hand.
"I am Marydyth Hollenbeck. I need you to look at some
papers for me."

"Nice to meet you. I'm Wainwright Sloan, and I
would be pleased to help you." He coughed and sneezed
twice, coloring hotly and apologizing for his rudeness.

"Perhaps if you leave the doors ajar some of this dust
will clear out," Marydyth suggested.

"You don't mind?" he asked before another sneeze

exploded from him. He held his kerchief over the bottom part of his face and opened both the front and back doors.

Marydyth took a seat in front of his cluttered desk, and waited for Wainwright to get settled. Over the next hour, Wainwright answered all of her questions. J.C.'s will and the guardianship papers were unbreakable. They bound Flynn to the Hollenbecks as tightly as Marydyth's love for Rachel bound her to Flynn.

"I am sorry I don't have more promising news, madam, but the papers were properly executed." The attorney looked at her over the rim of his spectacles.

She sat back in the chair. A smile curved the edges of her mouth. "I see."

"I must say you are taking it rather well."

"I've had a few days to adjust to the idea," Marydyth said, but inside she felt a secret flare of relief.

"It appears that your mother-in-law made certain that Flynn O'Bannion has total control—with no restrictions."

"And there is no way for this to be revoked?"

"None whatsoever, for as long as he and your daughter live. Now, should they precede you in death—" Wainwright Sloan coughed a little when he read the horror in Marydyth's face "—something I am sure will never happen, but if it should, then the trust would revert to you under the conditions that Mr. O'Bannion insisted upon when he took over the duties as your daughter's guardian."

That information settled uneasily in her brain.

"It was most forward thinking of Mr. O'Bannion but the wording is quite clear. Unless he and Rachel pass on, the fortune and day-to-day operations of all the Hollenbeck properties remain under his control."

"What about Victoria's money?" Marydyth heard herself asking.

"The way I understand it, upon Mrs. Hollenbeck's death, should Mr. O'Bannion be unable to continue in his capacity or precede her in death, her portion of the money goes to a charity in Denver."

She stood up and straightened her skirt. "Thank you, Mr. Sloan, I think I understand now. What do I owe you?"

"I'll send a bill to your home as soon as I get a bit more organized. It was my pleasure to assist you, madam, and let me know if I can do anything else for you."

"Yes, yes I will, and thank you again." Marydyth walked out of his office and into the bright sunshine. Now she was prepared to go to the Lavender Lady with Flynn.

The next two weeks whirled by with the speed of a desert dust devil. Flynn got estimates on timber and freight charges and hired a foreman who would find laborers and oversee the day-to-day refurbishment of the mine if, after his inspection, the Lavender Lady proved to be a viable venture once again. All the while, Marydyth did the cooking and the cleaning, and cared for Rachel. Life at the mansion was settling into an easy routine.

Every day Flynn found himself growing more and more aware of Marydyth. He knew when she laughed and when she cried in her sleep.

Several times he had been on the porch with a cold cigarette in his mouth when he heard her whimper from the room above him.

Once he had even started up the stairs to her part of the house.

He had stopped on the stairs and asked himself what he was doing. She had made it clear she did not want to discuss the past or her dreams with him. Still, he found himself listening for her, wishing that he could go to her, damning himself for wanting to.

It was like walking over cactus needles. *And it scared the bejesus out of him to feel this way about her.*

He had always been a lone wolf. He had ridden alone until Rachel had come into his life. And now Marydyth was nudging her way under his skin whether he liked it or not.

He felt responsible for them both, but it was more than that with Marydyth. He felt a searing attraction to her—an attraction that was eating him alive.

He could go to town and visit a bordello but some nagging little consciousness told him that it just wouldn't be the same.

That worried him even more. What if he bedded a painted cat and found himself thinking of Marydyth, wanting Marydyth? It was a test he didn't want to take for fear of the outcome, so he sat, night after night, and thought of her smooth white skin and her sad blue eyes.

This crazy notion of possessiveness toward Marydyth and Rachel made him a little weak in the knees. And then one night, after he had been contemplating his weakness with two fingers of whiskey and unlit cigarette, he ran into Marydyth on the stairs.

It was well past midnight, and she was the last thing he expected to see.

But there she was, standing on the staircase like a wisp of white smoke. Her nightrail fell softly from her shoulders, only a shade whiter than her skin.

''Marydyth?'' He gripped the smooth wood banister, wondering if he could have gotten drunk on a shot of whiskey or if his mind was making him see what he wished to see.

"Flynn," she said softly.

"Are you all right? Is anything wrong?" His hold on the wood tightened.

She moved. It was only the slightest twitch of her body but it brought the musky attar of her washing over him. His pulse quickened and his blood got heavy and thick with lust.

"I—I couldn't sleep." She shivered. "That's not true. I was afraid to go to sleep."

"The nightmare," he said.

While they stood there on the stairs the air became electric. Flynn was painfully aware of the gentle rise and fall of her breasts. Even in the partial darkness with only the thin, thready light of the moon leaking in windows he fancied that he could see the rosy rings around her nipples. His traitorous body stiffened when his eyes automatically skimmed downward to the faintly darker triangle at the juncture of her legs.

He let out a harsh breath and cursed himself. This was madness. She hated him—or at least she said she did.

So why did he want her so badly that his body ached?

"Flynn?"

"Yes, Marydyth?"

"Could you—would you—sit with me awhile?"

Every shred of common sense he possessed told him to refuse. She was no child to be lulled to sleep, and he was damned sure no nursemaid. Couldn't she see the danger? Wasn't she able to see how damned bad he needed a woman—needed her?

"Sure." Part of him wanted to turn tail and run to the whorehouse and the other part of him wanted to slip his arm beneath her knees and carry her straight to his bed.

It was a hell of a note.

Marydyth was barely able to hold back the sob in her throat. Every time she closed her eyes the terrible images assaulted her. She was exhausted and yet she was afraid to sleep.

But the moment Flynn started moving toward her on the darkened stairs she felt an overwhelming sense of relief. It was as if he could hold back her demons with his strength and his will.

When he was beside her on the stairs she felt herself succumb. She crumpled like a shattered porcelain doll but his strong arms wrapped around her and kept her from falling.

While she was in his arms she was safe—at least for this moment—safe from her past.

After that night when he had sat beside her bed till dawn, Flynn had forced himself to ignore Marydyth. He didn't trust himself around her and he still didn't fully trust her. He couldn't shake the sound of her voice confessing murder to Victoria.

By day he told himself that she was a criminal—that she had admitted it, but by night his conviction wavered. He heard her murmurs of fright and his heart bled a little for her.

Only rarely did Rachel have bad dreams now, but when Marydyth rushed to Rachel's bedside, he held back, watching, waiting, filled with suspicion. He stood in the shadows and observed her with the hardened, experienced eyes of a lawman but his heart didn't want to listen.

And when Ted Kelts came to visit, which he was doing more and more often, Flynn found himself livid with an emotion that was strangely like jealousy. Even when

Kelts shook his hand and said how happy he was that the Lavender Lady might be running again, Flynn could only think of the way Marydyth smiled at him.

So it went until one bright, hot Wednesday afternoon, when Rachel was taken to Victoria's house to be cared for by Gertie and Victoria's nurse. The Hollenbeck mansion was locked up tight. Saddlebags were packed on Jack and a steady line-back dun named Trooper that Flynn had bought from the livery was saddled for Marydyth to ride. In total silence they set out in a southeasterly direction toward their first stop at Brunckow's cabin.

Marydyth felt her palms growing wet with perspiration. She wanted—*needed*—to go with Flynn O'Bannion, but that didn't stop her heart from pounding hard within her chest each time he slid that hard, agate gaze her way.

And the way he looked today. He was wearing a soft buckskin shirt that slipped over his head. The front was cut low and decorated with turquoise beads. He had a wicked-looking blade strapped to his leg.

He looked mean, tough and entirely too appealing. But while they rode out of town he treated her with quiet tolerance. If he was happy she was along, or unhappy, he kept that information to himself.

At the very outskirts of town a small crowd had gathered. There were mean stares and people pointed, but when Flynn looked at them their eyes slid away. She was still a pariah and an outcast.

But opening the Lavender Lady will change all that. She had to believe it. She had to hope that providing jobs at the mine would help people to forget and forgive her.

And then maybe Flynn would be able to forget, too— at least a little about her past. It was something to look forward to, something to cling to. She had hope. If she could make things better for Rachel and stop seeing the cloud of suspicion in Flynn's eyes, it would be enough.

It would have to be enough.

Marydyth caught herself gasping in delight when they rode over a rise and Hollenbeck Corners disappeared behind them. She had been locked up for so many summers. The colors of nature's palette washed over her and she looked at summer on the wild free plain for the first time in three long bleak years.

Barrel cactus were blooming with orangy crowns; short purple verbena was flowering everywhere. A roadrunner darted out from behind a stand of jumping cholla cactus, and a long-eared jackrabbit watched them from the shade provided by a huge cluster of prickly pears while he nibbled at the bright reddish blooms.

"Pretty, ain't it?" Flynn's deep baritone washed over her.

She turned and looked at him. His chiseled face was half in shadow from the brim of his pale hat. Marydyth found herself breathing an unconscious sigh of relief because she couldn't see those probing eyes on her face.

"Yes. I hadn't realized how much of this I had missed." She focused on the trail ahead, unable to stop butterflies from entering her belly each time she looked at Flynn.

They rode over gentle rises and down into a long, rugged cut where the ragged mountains rose up on every side. Brittle brush and Mojave yucca made it necessary to weave and thread their way through a maze of sorts. In the distance Marydyth could see Joshua trees and saguaro reaching toward the sky. Abruptly she pulled up on the reins.

"What?" A note of concern was in Flynn's voice. "What's wrong?"

"Nothing." Marydyth swallowed thickly.

"I can hear it in your voice, Marydyth. Tell me." Flynn reached across the small space separating their horses and touched her hand with his. A diffuse heat twined from that spot to her middle.

"The century plant." She lifted her hand and pointed.

He frowned and followed the line of her finger. There, on the rough ridge of land, was a solitary century plant in bloom.

"There was one on the outside of Yuma's walls. I saw it once. I used to tell myself...all I had to do was hang on until it bloomed."

"But they only bloom once every hundred years, Marydyth." Flynn squeezed her fingers, wishing he could erase some of the misery from her face.

"I know." She laughed but it was a nervous sound that held no joy. "It was a foolish thought, but it kept me going."

"I thought your hatred of me kept you going," he said softly.

She didn't look at him.

He reached out and grasped her chin in his fingers and drew her gently around.

"Is that true? Was it your hatred of me that gave you strength?"

Her eyes misted over. She blinked and searched his face. Was she looking for the answer there? Or was it something else she sought?

"I don't hate you."

The information settled over him like heavy fog. For a moment his heart actually seemed to freeze within his rib cage.

He didn't know what to say. So he said nothing. He cleared his voice and released the hold he had on her chin. But when he kicked Jack, a strange, prickly satisfaction sat in the saddle with him.

She doesn't hate me.

The morning wore on while they rode in silence. By mutual agreement they had decided to skirt around both Millville and Charleston and head straight toward Brunckow's cabin for their first stop. At nearly sundown Flynn saw the dark outline of cabin walls. He drew his pistol and stopped Jack.

"Hold up and wait here," he ordered.

"What's the matter?" Marydyth frowned, feeling her belly sink to her boot tops.

"Probably nothing, but this cabin is a favorite hideout for outlaws and no-goods." Flynn glanced at her and managed a crooked smile. "I'd just as soon not have my hair parted by a bullet while we bed down for the night."

Marydyth nodded. Once again that feeling of safety washed over her. She had always thought he hated her, but perhaps she had been wrong about that as well as how she felt about him. She watched him lope Jack toward the structure, keeping low in the saddle, body tensed and ready for anything.

A hot surge of admiration swept through her. He was a hard man—an unyielding man—but he had provided Rachel a home full of security and acceptance.

For that kindness she would be forever grateful to Flynn O'Bannion.

Within moments she saw Flynn wave his Stetson in the air. She exhaled the breath she had been unconsciously holding and kneed Trooper forward. By the time she reached the cabin, Flynn had a blaze going in the remnant of the fireplace on one partial wall. Coffee was boiling and the smell of frying bacon made her mouth water.

"Need some help?" Marydyth asked.

He looked up and grinned. "What's the matter—afraid I'll poison you?"

For half a heartbeat she stiffened and then a strange thing happened. She found herself chuckling with him.

"Go on. Go unsaddle the horses and I'll do this," she said with a giggle.

He rose to his feet, the smile making his normally rigid mouth full and sensual.

"There's a small stream in back. I'll take the horses down to water." He stood up and slipped the rifle from the scabbard on his saddle. He thrust it toward her.

Marydyth looked up in surprise. She wiped her hands on the front of her Levi's and took the rifle. "What's this for?"

"You know how to use it?" he asked.

"Yes."

"Then you know what it's for," he said with a nod. And while they stood looking at each other, the atmosphere around them shifted and changed. An unspoken truce had finally been reached in the isolated cabin where Frederick Brunckow had thought to find his fortune.

"I'll be back."

"I'll be here—waiting."

Chapter Ten

Marydyth did not dream that night. She rose before dawn and found Flynn already frying bacon and drinking strong black coffee—standard camp fare, but somehow the aroma and the company made it just right.

She pulled herself from her bedroll and stood, stretching the kinks from her back.

"Morning," Flynn said.

"Good morning." She was amazed that the night had gone by so quickly. The last thing she remembered was staring up at velvet black sky studded with diamondlike points of light. Then it was simply morning.

After they ate, they saddled up and started out again. Marydyth felt more rested than she could remember and as the sun rose and beat down on them she found herself happy.

Then when she was feeling drowsy from the dipping disk of the sun in the west and the gentle sway of the horse below, Flynn cleared his throat and pulled Jack to a stop.

"There's the Lavender Lady." He pointed toward an outcrop of rock, gray and black in the dusk.

Marydyth stood up in her stirrups and squinted. The

mine was nothing more than a giant cavern carved into the stone. A weathered sign that had once said Lavender Lady, J.C. Hollenbeck, Owner had cracked in two. The top half was still attached crookedly to a cedar post.

Flynn laughed, and she realized that her expression must have betrayed her.

"It ain't much to look at from the outside, is it?" He dismounted and waited for her to do the same. While she was stretching the stiffness from her legs he took her reins.

"There's a stream about a quarter mile away. I'll take the horses to water so you can have a few minutes of privacy."

"Thanks." She took a step but her legs were weak and shaky. It was years since she had ridden this long, and every muscle in her body ached.

"I'll get a fire going when I get back and then we'll eat," he said over his shoulder as he led the two geldings away.

Flynn was true to his word. Within the hour they ate another portion of bacon, biscuits and washed it all down with strong coffee. Flynn had built a fire near a sheltering overhang of rugged stone. Their upturned saddles would be both pillow and mattress, just as they had been in Brunckow's cabin.

Marydyth tugged off her boots and snuggled down in the blankets, feeling a sense of well-being that she had never known before. She looked forward to another night without nightmares.

That was the thought in her head when she glanced at Flynn one last time, crouched by the fire. Then she closed her eyes and went to sleep, thinking how the future was going to be better than the past.

* * *

Marydyth was alone in her cell. The air was cold, and she was shivering beneath the thin blanket, mourning for her lost baby.

Then the air became heavy, thick and wet. The scent of river, magnolias and the South permeated everything around Marydyth.

She was on the riverboat. It was her wedding night.

Oh God, no.

Andre was drunk, cruel and rough. The kiss he gave her was sloppy and wet. He bruised her lip, made it bleed.

"Come here." His words were slurred.

"Please, Andre, please. Not like this—I'm frightened."

He tore her gown, told her she was sixteen, old enough to take a man. He raked his nails over her breasts as he tore away the last of her clothing. Reddened streaks welled up on her flesh. She struggled in fear.

He grew angry and slapped her. She shoved him.

"Little bitch." He unbuttoned his placket and drew himself out. Gripping his flesh like a weapon, crazy-eyed, reeking of liquor, he advanced upon her and hit her across the mouth with his free hand. "If you will not lie down for me then we'll do this another way." He grabbed her by the hair, forced her head downward...she was gagging, struggling.

Marydyth screamed. She fought to breathe, fought to raise her head from the disgusting thing that he was forcing her to do. But no matter how she struggled, Andre and the dream would not let her go.

Flynn tossed off his blanket and rushed to her. He knelt beside her. "Marydyth. Marydyth, it's Flynn."

She was thrashing wildly, talking out of her head, struggling with someone named Andre.

Andre. Her first husband.

She was lost in the grip of her nightmare. Flynn could not reach her. She didn't seem to know where she was or who he was.

He touched her face, patting gently. He shook her. It did no good. She screamed and kicked and fought him. The horses blew and stomped, frightened by the sound of Marydyth's terror.

"Ah, to hell with it!" Flynn cursed in a low voice.

He drew her near him, just as he had held Rachel during her night terrors. His voice was low and he wasn't sure what he was saying, anything to calm her, anything to slay the demons in her mind.

He stroked her brow, moving a handful of sweat-dampened golden curls from her forehead. Clouds had scudded across the sky and blocked out the stars and most of the moon. The last embers from the fire were glowing, casting a bit of light onto her face and the smooth column of her slender neck. She smelled of fresh air and woman and fear.

"I'm all right now." There were tears in her voice. "You can let me go. I'm—I'm sorry I made such a fool of myself."

He inhaled a ragged breath, determined to ignore the stirring within him. "You don't have to be so strong, Marydyth. It's all right to admit you are not made of stone. You can talk to me about this."

No, I can't talk to anybody. I can't let anybody know what happened and why I murdered Andre.

She pulled away from him enough to look up. He could barely make out her eyes from the dim glow of the dying fire. "I don't want to talk about it."

She doesn't trust me any more than I trust her, not down deep, not where it really counts.

"Then you don't have to, Marydyth. It's all right, I understand."

"Don't be nice to me, please, please don't."

"You deserve to have somebody be nice to you." He dragged his index finger down her cheek. His turgid body was straining against the two bottom buttons, the only ones that were fastened on his Levi's.

She shuddered. "Flynn, if you are nice to me, I'll cry."

"Then start crying, honey." He dipped his head low. "'Cause I am going to be nice to you." Flynn pulled her fully up onto his lap. Her weight settled firmly on his throbbing groin.

"Flynn?"

"Yes, Marydyth?"

"Would you—I mean—could you—?"

"Could I what?" His pulse had settled into a heavy thud in his ears.

"Could you kiss me…please?"

The kiss he gave her was full of sparks and hot burning desire, and Marydyth leaned willingly into his embrace. It had been so long since she had felt like a desirable woman, even longer since she had known the touch of a man like Flynn O'Bannion.

She probably never had.

He was different. He was unique, both complicated and simple in a way that made her blood burn and her heart beat fast. He was a hard man, but nobody could argue that Flynn O'Bannion was anything but *all* man.

She could feel the sinewy muscles in his arms contract as he held her close. When she slipped her hand up around his neck she touched corded tendons and raw strength. As she drew in a deep breath, never breaking the kiss, she inhaled the scent of desert and ashes, the scent of his buckskin shirt—of Flynn himself.

He squeezed her tighter and probed deep with his tongue. And when she thought his kiss would crush the very life from her, he turned gentle and teasing, drawing her bottom lip into his mouth to tenderly nip at it.

"God, you're like honeysuckle nectar." He nuzzled her neck and nipped bits of her flesh as he roamed over her face in his own private exploration.

She rubbed her palms along his collarbones, sculpted them down the front of his chest beneath the turquoise beads at the front of his buckskin shirt. Her nails scraped along the slender channel of hair that grew down the center toward his belly. He was warm, hard and soft and all sexy.

"It has been a long time," she murmured. "So long."

He slipped his hand inside the shirt she had borrowed from him for the trip. Under the soft, lacy camisole he cupped her breast. Gently, but with a definite purpose in mind, he rubbed his open hand across it, lingering on her nipple, rubbing his rough warm palm in a circular motion, lifting her, drawing her out, making her hotter. Her breasts grew heavy with wanting. There was a drawing sensation that went all the way to her groin when he grasped her nipple between his index finger and thumb.

She shivered.

He bent his head and kissed her again, exploring the inside of her mouth with his tongue, plunging and withdrawing in hard, rapid strokes. Flynn shifted slightly, turning his head without ever breaking the contact of his warm mouth.

Her heart beat faster and her hands slipped lower, over his ribs, across his drum-tight belly, to the half-buttoned placket of his Levi's.

"I want you, Marydyth." His breathing had grown harsh.

"Then take me," she said as she rubbed her flattened palm across the hard bulge that jerked in response.

He stared at her for a moment. She could barely make out his eyes in the shadow of the night, but she felt the heat of them on her face.

"Are you sure?" His voice was deep and husky with desire. "I want you to be sure—I mean...it's me."

"I know who you are," she whispered as she pressed her hand harder against him. "I could never forget."

"No, I guess you couldn't." He pulled away and raked his fingers through his tousled hair. "I don't know what got into me," he said gruffly.

She reached out to him, grabbing his shirt on either side where it hung open, feeling the hard edges of the beading against her palms.

"You don't understand, Flynn." She tilted her head. "I know who you are—what you are—and what I want." She pulled him close and kissed him. She explored his mouth with her tongue.

"Marydyth, are you sure?" His breath was coming ragged and fast. "We can stop now...."

"No. I want you, Flynn. I *need* you. Make me remember what it is to be a woman."

He groaned and pulled her to him. With expert hands and care he drew her beneath him on the bedroll. He popped open the front of her shirt and shoved down the top of her camisole. Fire and ice skipped along her body as he deposited kisses to her breasts. His stubbly beard scratched her skin, and his lips were soft and gentle as the petals of a rose while he stimulated every nerve ending. Then, when the ache in her middle had become a steady hungry throb, he licked one nipple and drew it into his mouth. Liquid fire poured through her veins and she found her pelvis arching up to meet him.

"Oh, Flynn…"

"I know, sugar, I know." He deftly opened the placket on her Levi's and shoved them down to her knees as she squirmed and lifted her bottom to help him. Finally she was free of the trousers. Then he slipped his hand inside her drawers and touched her.

A searing path of wanton desire arched from that point and flared throughout her body. A hundred lonely nights, a million shattered dreams, fell away, and there was only Flynn. Only Flynn, with his sensual mouth, Flynn, with his talented hands, Flynn, whose hard sex nudged against her.

Marydyth's heart and body sang as she welcomed him inside her. While the darkness of night folded over them and more clouds gathered, he demonstrated every way he knew of giving her pleasure.

Flynn was still awake when the sky turned pink in the east. After he had taken Marydyth in every way a man could take a woman, his senses had returned. Now he was plagued by guilt.

He had taken advantage of her.

She had been frightened and vulnerable after her nightmare and he had behaved like a horny billy goat.

It sickened him to think of what he had done. Flynn had never been a saint, not by a long country mile, but he had never in his life taken advantage of a woman.

Until now.

It didn't sit well with him, and he vowed not to repeat his mistake. He intended to apologize and let Marydyth know that as soon as possible.

She woke while he was building a fire for coffee. Her

curls were tousled and she had the heavy-lidded look of a woman well pleasured.

A current of conflicting feelings roared through him. He didn't want to notice how the lacy camisole tightened over her breasts when she breathed. He didn't want to remember how her soft breasts exactly fit inside his palms as though they had been made just for him or the way her flesh had tightened around him until he thought he would pass out from the pleasure.

"Morning," she said softly.

"Morning." He stood up with the empty pot in his hand. "I'm going down to get us some water. It'll give you a few minutes...." He felt awkward and tongue-tied in the light of day. "You'll be all right?"

"Um-hmm. I've got the rifle." She nodded in the direction of the rifle he had left with her yesterday.

He didn't want *Marydyth,* for God's sake.

He couldn't.

Flynn climbed over the scattered boulders and stood aside for the horses to follow him up. He could see the shimmering thread of the stream below. Sunlight made a string of diamonds sparkle on the water's surface, occasionally blinding him with their brightness. He started to put the coffeepot in his other hand, but it slipped and clattered to the rocks.

"Damn it." He bent over to pick it up and the report of the rifle smacked by him, sending rock shards splintering into his thigh. He felt as if he had been peppered with rock salt. Another shot rang out, and Trooper squealed and toppled over backward.

Flynn crouched low and let Jack's reins slip through his fingers. He pulled his gun from his holster and peered at the emptiness around him.

The smell of blood engulfed Flynn. He looked at the gelding, which was still, and clearly dead. Flynn could see a black bullet hole in the horse's head and a trickle of blood running onto the rocks.

Beads of sweat popped up beneath his hat and along the nape of his neck while he scanned the rocky horizon.

He was being watched. He could feel it in his bones. As he stared at the dead horse, the chilling knowledge washed over him.

Somebody was trying to kill him.

Curiosity had driven her. Now Marydyth had her head just inside the mouth of the mine shaft when she heard a funny noise. A sinuous shape moved within the shadows. She realized it was a snake, when it coiled up and lifted its head.

She inhaled and pulled the trigger. The smell of gunpowder drifted around her head while the snake uncoiled and slithered into a crevice. The mine seemed to sigh and shudder beneath her feet, and then everything went quiet.

Marydyth put one hand on the side of the craggy wall and peered into the darkness. If there was anything to see, she couldn't see it, and she certainly wasn't going to go into the Stygian, damp interior. While she looked at the yawning cavern, her flesh crawled, and she was suddenly transported back in time. Back to Yuma where sunlight was cut off by walls five feet thick, where she was captive, where the sunlight never reached her.

Marydyth swallowed down her terror and turned, blinded by the sun pouring into the mouth of the black pit. She stood there frozen, blinking at the disks of white that obscured her vision. Then, suddenly, her rifle was ripped away and she felt the bite of fingers on one arm.

"What in the hell are you doing?" Flynn's voice was stern as Judgment Day.

Marydyth blinked, trying to clear her vision, but all she could see was his tall, broad outline against the sun. His fingers tightened on her arm. It was hard to believe this was the same man who had held her and pleasured her in the dark.

"Answer me, woman! What the hell are you doing?" Flynn could smell the cordite. The rifle, *his* rifle, had been fired.

Anger, mistrust and fury that he had been so careless as to give a firearm to the Black Widow coursed through him.

What the hell had he been thinking? He never should have turned his back on her.

"You need to practice your aim," he said bitterly.

"You're hurting me." She jerked her arm but his grip was powerful and sure. "Let me go."

"Tell me what you're doing in here." His words grated over her like a rough-edged stone.

"I went inside the mine to look."

"And while you were in there you decided to shoot me?"

"What?" She blinked and squinted. "I don't know what you're talking about."

She could make out his features now, shadowed under the brim of his hat. His eyes were darker than midnight in their anger. "What are you saying?"

"Somebody tried to kill me." He finally let go and shoved her away from him, bringing the rifle up. He sniffed it and his lips tightened. He was a savage beast, a hound on the scent of prey and ready to spill blood.

Her blood.

The realization hit Marydyth. Flynn thought she had

tried to kill him. Wainwright Sloan's words rang in her
ears.

*You will never control Hollenbeck money or property
as long as Flynn O'Bannion or your daughter are alive.*

"I shot at a snake," she said.

"A two-legged snake, one who's in your way?" he
asked while he glared at her.

"It was a rattler." She pointed toward the mouth of
the mine. "Right over there."

He looked. "There's nothing there now, if there ever
was." He raised his brows. "You really expect me to
believe you took a shot at a snake, inside a mine? Nobody, not even you, could be that stupid."

She recoiled as if he had slapped her. His suspicion
was like a living thing. She should have been used to it;
she had faced it often enough, but after last night it cut
her deep.

"Where is my horse? I want to go home." She turned
away, ready to go, but only Jack was standing nearby.

"Your horse—" his lip curled up in distaste "—is
lying dead with a bullet between his eyes."

"Oh, my God." She gasped and brought her knuckles
up to her mouth. "And you—you think I did it?"

He looked her straight in the eye. "You seem to be
the only one around, and the smell of gunpowder is still
clinging to your clothes. The evidence is pretty damning,
Marydyth."

"It always is, Flynn."

Flynn guided Jack through a maze of cactus and into
the sparse shade of a paloverde. Every step of the way
he had been aware of two things: Marydyth's hands
around his waist and the nagging voice of guilt and reason that would not let him be.

Without a word he pulled up on Jack's reins.

Marydyth slid off the back of the saddle before he could say anything. It was pretty damned obvious she didn't want to give Flynn any excuse to touch her.

And he didn't much blame her.

But once again fate had thrown them together. With one horse there was no question that they would be riding double and stopping frequently to rest Jack.

A quail darted by them and Flynn drew his pistol and dropped it. Bright red blood oozed into the dry soil near an ocotillo.

Marydyth nearly vomited. The sight of the blood, the memory of Trooper's body and the suspicion in Flynn's eyes were becoming too much for her.

She felt more alone than she ever had. She hadn't tried to shoot Flynn—so somebody else had. She scanned the horizon with squinted eyes, expecting the person to make another attempt.

She shivered involuntarily.

Flynn must have felt her fear because he turned around and looked at her. She could feel the burn of accusation and betrayal in his eyes.

It was as bad as being locked in Yuma to see that disapproval in his eyes, but she had learned long ago that denying guilt did little good.

They mounted and started out again. Flynn tried hard to ignore her but he couldn't.

He could not ignore the fact that she was behind him with her legs spread. It brought visions of last night, and the memory of their sweat-slicked skin. He tightened his jaw but he could not dispel the way she felt, the way she sounded.

Dear Lord.

She was a sweet poison, and he had drunk deeply from

her. Now she was in his blood, deadly and addictive. And no matter how much Flynn distrusted her, no matter that he had heard her confess with her own sweet lips to doing murder, his body throbbed and pulsed with wanting her. And that made him fight the attraction all the more.

Chapter Eleven

"We can't make Brunckow's cabin tonight." Flynn's words were clipped and hard. "We'll have to camp here and ride into Millville tomorrow and buy a horse for you." He pulled up on the reins.

Marydyth was more than happy to get off the horse and away from Flynn for a few hours. She awkwardly slid from her perch behind Flynn as soon as she could manage. He had stopped near a small outcrop of rock. While she walked toward that raw shelter she kept him in sight.

In a strained silence they made camp, tended Jack and ate a cold meal. When the stars filled the sky they went to opposite sides of the campfire to bed down.

Marydyth stared into the flames, thinking. When she was alone under her blanket, would her body ache to be held? Would she dream of Flynn's firm, sensual lips on hers? Would the blood in her veins thrum with wanting his large body over hers and his turgid flesh filling her again?

Would the nightmare come now that he was no longer willing to hold it back?

She looked at him from the corner of her eye and felt a wave of sadness wash over her. He had her daughter's love and respect and now he had a part of her that she didn't seem to be able to reclaim.

"What have you decided about the Lavender Lady?" she heard herself ask abruptly. She wished she could think of something besides the way the soft buckskin shirt drew taut across his wide shoulders. Or the way his work-roughened hand grasped the saddle when he positioned it for his bed.

Flynn looked at her sideways, searing her with the look in his eyes. "I haven't."

She told herself it didn't matter. Besides, he had only been in the mine for a couple of minutes when he put Trooper's saddle inside. She doubted that even those lightning-fast eyes of his could have seen much ore—if there was any copper ore to see.

It had been a foolish idea, she decided. A silly pipe dream that the mine could be reopened and people would begin to forgive and forget.

She wished she had not talked to him about it. She wished that she had not come with him. But then a tendril of panic flashed through her. What if he had been shot? What if he had come alone and been killed?

The memory of his big, muscled body over hers crept into her mind and shoved everything else aside.

She closed her eyes and let it wash over her, hot and breathtaking. Now there was another memory to haunt her dreams—but at least it would be a memory that was more pleasant than the one she had of Andre and her wedding night.

She shoved the thoughts aside, determined to sleep the

night through without nightmares of prison or specters from her past disturbing her.

Flynn sipped the last of his cold coffee and stared at Marydyth from the corner of his eye. His belly had been one big knot since he jerked the still smoking rifle from her hand.

She had tried to kill him.

The thought nibbled at the edge of his mind like a great beast. He didn't want to believe it, but…the evidence.

Still, there was something that nagged at him. There was a look in her eye that shouted her innocence. He had seen that look before. He had also seen the eyes of the guilty.

And no matter how damning the evidence was, he just didn't believe, deep down in his gut, that Marydyth had tried to shoot him.

He tossed the dregs into the dust and set the tin cup aside. Using his saddle as a headrest, he tugged the blanket up over his shoulders. The fire was low and he could clearly see Marydyth's outline across the flames.

Sensations of last night crept into his mind. Lying with Marydyth had been a powerful thing, a humbling experience. She had touched him in a deep, secret place that made him feel vulnerable and not in control.

He could not ever remember a woman doing that to him.

She had been like parched soil, eager and ready to soak up all the passion and desire he could give her.

And lying with her had shown him just how much passion he had dammed up.

At first he thought it was just because he hadn't been sporting for a while, but as the night continued and he slaked his lust in her more than once, he had to face the truth.

Something about Marydyth Hollenbeck got to him. She was under his skin, making him itch and burn.

With that thought nipping at him like a chigger, he turned over and pulled his hat down over his eyes. Tonight the clouds played hide-and-seek with the tiniest sliver of a moon, but there was enough light to make him aware of her across the dying embers. There was more than enough light for him to want to rub his hands over the outline of her hip, to touch her breasts, to bury himself deep and have her hot and panting beneath him.

Marydyth heard the sound of laughter from on deck. She wanted to scream for help but Andre slapped her hard across the mouth and shoved her back onto the bed.

His eyes were glazed over. He looked like a man possessed.

Marydyth screamed. She screamed and kept on screaming, praying that somebody above would hear and come to help her....

Flynn was out of his blankets and across the dead fire before the scream died in her throat. Jack snorted and sidestepped wildly, startled by the sound that echoed through the desert night.

"Please, Andre, ple—ease!" she begged.

Flynn grabbed Marydyth's shoulders and dragged her up. She fought him, throwing her weight from side to side in an effort to break his grip. Great wet tears hit him in the face each time she moved.

"Marydyth. Wake up."

She tried to shove the cotton in her head aside but she

was trapped. Andre laughed, a cruel, thin sound that chilled her soul.

"Marydyth, it's Flynn. Wake up." Flynn shook her gently, trying to rouse her from the nightmare. "Marydyth, honey?"

Her eyes fluttered open. She saw Flynn's face only inches from hers. His eyes were gentle and filled with compassion. There was no accusation or suspicion in his expression.

"Oh, Flynn, hold me." She sobbed into his strong shoulder. "Please, please, don't let me go." She rested her face against the softness of his buckskin shirt.

A sound like a great beast growling rumbled beneath her cheek. He was real and solid and strong enough to hold back her terror.

"I will hold you, Marydyth, I will hold you till the sun comes up," he said softly. "And long beyond that."

The minute his strong warm lips touched hers, Marydyth leaned into him. She clung to Flynn as if she could physically draw upon his strength.

"Marydyth, I want..." Flynn said raggedly.

"Hold me." She kissed his jaw, his neck and slipped her hands around his neck to draw him nearer. "It doesn't matter what you believe, just hold me and keep me safe tonight."

"Oh, honey." He expelled a heavy breath. Then he slid his hand down to the small of her back. "I don't trust you—but I can't get you out of my mind." He pulled her along the length of his body and rolled. When he stopped she was on top of him. She stared down into his face.

"I don't have the answers you want, Flynn."

They looked at each other for what seemed a long time. The only sound was their own breathing.

"I know you don't. This is one of those things I have to answer for myself." Then he moaned, as if giving up a great battle, and drew her mouth down to his.

Her heart beat faster as he slipped one hand around to the front of her Levi's. He had them unbuttoned and shoved down in seconds. Then he cupped her bottom in his wide, rough hands. She could feel the hard bulge of him against her. He rubbed his pelvis along hers, creating heat and friction so deep inside her that she nearly screamed with wanting him.

"Let me." She broke the hungry, savage kiss long enough to slip her own hands down the length of him. She unbuttoned his pants and freed him. He was hot and silky smooth, throbbing and jerking when she grasped him.

"Take me, Flynn. Hold back the night," she whispered. And then he lifted her up and impaled her on his flesh. Marydyth drew in a ragged breath and settled herself on him, allowing him to pump against her. He lifted her buttocks with his hands and shoved her down on him with each upward thrust.

Her body melted around him and she shuddered, her climax shattering through her. It drained what little sense she still possessed and scattered her thoughts like dried leaves in the wind.

She thought she might have murmured his name as she collapsed against him. Then she slept.

The sound of Jack pawing woke Flynn while it was still fully dark. He started to turn over, to take a look at the horse, but a weight kept him in place.

"What the hell?" He stirred himself and opened his

eyes. Marydyth's silky yellow curls were splayed across his chin. One arm and thigh were draped across his chest. He had held her against him all through the night.

The realization rocked him.

She inhaled and shifted slightly and he realized that he was still between her legs. He felt himself growing hard. His flesh nudged against the curls between her legs. He felt heat and a soft, answering warmth.

He was inside her.

Her breathing changed. She stiffened but she did not move. He knew the very instant that she came fully awake.

Marydyth put her palms against Flynn's chest and pushed herself up into a sitting position, never breaking the intimate connection between them.

His body filled hers, pulsing, pushing.

The silvery shaft of moonlight cascaded over their bodies, locked together, mating almost against their own will, against their own common sense.

Marydyth swallowed hard. She searched his face, looking, for what she was not sure.

A muscle in the side of his jaw jumped.

He was a hard man, unforgiving and strong. And yet she had seen his gentleness with Rachel, had felt his compassion during her own nightmares. Had tasted his desire.

Marydyth shifted her hips and ground them down against him. His jaw tightened more and his eyes narrowed down to predatory slits.

She continued to stare at his emotionless face while she raised her pelvis away from him slightly, then slid back down the rigid shaft.

A stifled groan left his lips.

Once again she raised her body and ground herself down against him, slowly.

"Marydyth."

He grabbed her buttocks in his hands and pushed her hard against him. Then he rolled and pinned her beneath him, holding his weight above her on his knees and elbows.

"Damn you, Marydyth Hollenbeck, you are in my blood," he said as he began to pound himself against her. Harder and faster with each thrust, as if he could drive her from him.

But Marydyth clung to him greedily, determined to have the solace of his body, if only for this one night.

The next morning they rose, drank coffee and mounted up without a word about what had passed between them. Flynn wasn't sure what to say. Hell, he didn't even know how he *felt* about what had happened.

Twice now he had tasted Marydyth and yet it was not enough. Each time her tiny fist tightened at his waist while Jack picked his way through the cholla and yucca, he felt himself growing hot and aroused. She was close enough for him to feel the whisper of her breath along the back of his neck.

With Marydyth at his back and his conscience hollering inside his head, it was a damned uncomfortable way to ride.

The sun peaked, then headed toward the western horizon before Flynn saw the outline of Brunckow's cabin. It was a mighty welcome sight, not just because they were an easy ride from Millville, where he could buy another horse, but because he had made a decision.

He was going to tell Marydyth that he had flown off

the handle. He was going to tell her that he *knew* she hadn't tried to shoot him.

All he had to do was find the right way to tell her that he had been a royal jackass.

Camp was set, Jack was tended to and their meal was eaten—and still Flynn could not choke out the apology.

Hoping to dredge up his gumption, he pulled the tobacco from his pocket and rolled himself a smoke.

"Why do you do that?" Marydyth asked.

"Do what?" Her voice rubbed over his skin and made him itch to hold her.

"Roll them but never light them. I have never seen you smoke, and I've never found an ash anywhere in the house."

Flynn caught himself grinning as he rotated the cigarette between his thumb and forefinger. "I haven't smoked one in years."

"Why?" she prompted.

"Doctor told me it wasn't good for children."

"So...you quit for Rachel." It was a statement, not a question.

"There isn't much I wouldn't do for her," he said softly.

"I understand," Marydyth said. He looked up and their gazes locked.

Tell her, you damned fool. Open up your mouth and tell her that you jumped the gun—tell her that you are a dunderheaded fool. Tell her now.

Flynn stuck the unlit cigarette in his mouth and got to his feet. The words were just not going to come. Maybe if he took a walk, then he would be able to find the courage to say it.

Twilight cast long fingers of shadow across the landscape, before Flynn stopped. How far had he come? A tall, rocky outcrop of stone silhouetted itself against the setting sun, and it was in that place that Flynn found himself a niche to sit and think.

What is it about her that makes me go mute?

Is it her sad blue eyes? Or the way the sunshine and moonlight play along her yellow curls? Or maybe it's the way she squints her eyes when she thinks nobody is looking—or the way she sighs in her sleep after being loved.

He jerked his mind away from that line of thinking.

Using all his willpower he forced himself to think about the shot that killed Trooper. Somebody had tried to kill him—and it hadn't been Marydyth. But he had seen no sign or indication that they were being followed.

A coyote yipped. Several answered in the distance. Flynn toyed with his unlit cigarette. He rose to his feet just as he heard a rumble, as if a great thunderstorm was coming. He climbed from the crevice in the rocky face and looked up, searching the pewter-gray sky for thunderclouds. But as he watched the side of the mountain, the outcrop of rock shifted, tilted and fell away.

The spray of giant boulders gathered speed and momentum as they crashed toward Flynn. He turned to flee, and caught just a glimpse of someone running away before the first stone hit him.

Marydyth heard the sound, smelled the thick odor of dust in the air at the same moment Jack snorted and shied away from his picket line.

"What is it, boy?" She touched the gelding's neck, trying to calm him as she had seen Flynn do. The sound

ended as abruptly as it started but the thick taste of dirt
hung in the air.

Marydyth stood by the horse, scratching his neck, talking to him, unwilling to break contact with another living
thing. But as the minutes stretched on, her panic began
to grow.

Flynn should have returned by now. He would not
leave her alone for this long—unless something terrible
had happened.

Marydyth swallowed hard and picked up the canteen
from the ground. The sun was almost completely gone,
but she could make out the firm and definite print of
Flynn's tracks in the sand.

"I promise I'll be back, Jack," she said as she turned
and started walking.

She hoped she was able to keep her promise.

Chapter Eleven

Marydyth tried to make a little noise while she walked, in case Flynn was out here somewhere just wanting a little privacy. After the incident at the Lavender Lady, she sure didn't want him to accuse her of sneaking up on him.

As she walked the odor of dust in the air grew stronger. There had been no wind, and she wondered why the air was thick with it. She swallowed and tasted it heavy on her tongue; Arizona soil, gritty and pungent.

Then she reached an area where dust hung in the air like a thick curtain. It turned the air a dirty, brownish color. The only time she had ever seen dust like that was when J.C. had taken her to one of the smaller mines and a blast had been set off. Dust and dirt had belched from the hole.

Marydyth stumbled over something. She looked down, squinting through the dirt in the dim twilight.

She blinked, not believing what she saw. It was an arm—Flynn's arm—protruding from a pile of stones.

Marydyth fell upon the pile like a madwoman. The rocks cut her hands and she knew her fingertips were bleeding, but she didn't care. She focused only on digging Flynn free from the rocks.

"He can't be dead—oh please, God, don't let him be dead," she murmured over and over, like a religious chant, as she removed the stones from his body.

When she had them off she leaned down to check if he was still breathing. Yes, thank God—he was still alive. But then she saw the back of his buckskin shirt, dark with drying blood. Miraculously his face was unmarked, but there was a lump on the back of his head the size of a turkey egg. Marydyth rolled him over and gingerly peeled up the shirt to see how badly he was hurt.

Flynn felt consciousness returning with a searing streak down his shoulder and back. The second thing he became aware of was Marydyth's frantic whispers.

"I wanted him out of Rachel's life, but not like this, not like this. Oh, please, God, oh please, don't let him die."

"Am I that bad off?" he asked as he opened one eye. He did not miss the way her body stiffened.

"You're alive," she said in a breathy whisper.

"Don't sound so damned happy about it," he growled and tried to get up.

"You're hurt," she said.

"You think I don't know that?" he snapped.

"Then stop trying to get up. What happened?"

"You tell me," he said while he pushed himself up off his belly, fighting the nauseating wave of pain that went with each excruciating movement.

"How would I know what happened?" She sat back on her heels and watched him slowly rise.

His head was swimming and his vision was a little blurry but he managed to push himself up into a sitting position. "I saw someone running away after the slide."

"Yes?" Marydyth asked.

"I thought it was you." His voice fell with the impact of a hammer on an anvil.

Blunt, direct and straight to her heart. She drew in a breath and stood up.

"Damn you, Flynn O'Bannion. Damn you to hell. What do you want from me?" Her voice rose. "You have my home, my daughter… Do you want my sanity as well?"

"Sanity? What the hell is that supposed to mean?" He rubbed the back of his head with one palm. There was a hard lump beneath his hand.

"I'm beginning to think you're doing all of this to make me think I'm crazy," she said. "Well, I am not crazy!"

Her voice rang out while she stood there with her feet braced apart, hands on her hips, glaring down at him. Looking up at her made his head throb more. "If I wanted you dead I could've put a knife between your ribs while you were otherwise occupied last night."

She clamped her luscious lips together and defied him to deny it.

He blinked and stared at her. It was a sobering thought to consider that he could easily have been murdered while they were locked together in passion.

"Damn you—I didn't try to shoot you—I didn't cause these rocks to fall on you, but you won't believe that, will you? No, you won't believe it because I have killed before and 'once a murderess, always a murderess'— right?"

She turned on her heel and stomped away. He wanted to call her back, to tell her that he didn't believe that she shot him, but once again her words echoed in his aching head.

He sat there mute and watched her until she was nearly out of sight. The throbbing in his head grew harder while her words echoed through his brain.

Because I have killed before. Once a murderess, always a murderess.

They rode into Millville a few hours later. Flynn had chewed the inside of his mouth raw while he fought off the waves of dizziness and nausea that accompanied every mile. A knot had formed in the pit of his stomach, but it was not due to the injury—it was because of his doubts about Marydyth.

He knew she was innocent of the shot that killed Trooper, and doubted that she could have been responsible for the rock slide. But damn it, how could he discount her own words?

"There's the doctor's office," Marydyth said flatly, pointing to a wooden sign hanging from a second-story balcony.

"Thanks." Flynn guided Jack toward the hitching post and waited until Marydyth had slid off the saddle before he tried to move.

When he swung his leg over the cantle, a line of pain scorched its way down his back. He felt the warm, sticky ooze of blood clinging to the back of his shirt and the waistband of his pants.

"I'll get another shirt from your sleeping bag," Marydyth offered.

All he could do was nod. He stood, holding on to the saddle horn and the cantle, drawing in deep breaths, trying to accustom himself to the pain.

Her lips were compressed into a thin straight line—well, as thin as those lush soft lips could ever be—and her eyes were like blue flames each time she looked at him.

Flynn did not recall ever seeing Marydyth so damned mad. During the trial when she had been charged with J.C.'s murder he had seen her go from disbelief to shock and finally into mute misery, but he had never seen her mad. And through it all she had never defended herself of the charge. It was almost as if she were resigned to her punishment, as if she welcomed the sentence that consigned her to Yuma.

His gut and his heart told him that Marydyth was telling the truth, that she never would harm him. But if Marydyth was telling the truth, then she *was* a murderer by her own admission.

A wave of dizziness washed over him while he tried to make sense of the puzzle. Flynn rolled his eyes upward and looked at the noonday sky. Why was it growing so dark in the middle of the day?

Marydyth stood frozen while Flynn seemed to crumple. It was incomprehensible to her that the rock-hard, unyielding brute could ever have a weak moment. But his eyes rolled back in his head and his face lost some of the tension.

She rushed to him and managed to get his arm over her shoulder. But he was too heavy for her to hold. She felt herself being crushed toward the earth by his masculine weight.

"Hey, you need some help, ma'am?" A toothy man in typical miner's garb stepped up and slipped Flynn's other arm over his shoulder, hitching some of his weight from Marydyth just before her own knees buckled.

She took a deep breath and pulled herself up, determined to shoulder at least half his weight. "Yes, we need the doctor."

"Doc's office is on the second story. We'll never drag

this big galoot up those stairs. Not without help, we won't."

Marydyth scanned the street, cursing her wayward curls for falling in her eyes and obscuring her vision.

"Marv? Joe?" the miner called out. Within seconds Flynn was being hauled—none too gently it seemed—up the stairs by three brawny men. Marydyth trotted behind them, murmuring to be careful, not to jerk him like that, to watch out for the railing, but they didn't seem to hear her.

Flynn regained consciousness while the physician was working on his back.

"You are a very lucky man," declared a voice from above and behind him. Then he saw a capable right hand, which was missing the two middle fingers, bring a white strip of bandage around to the front.

"Sit up," the voice ordered.

The doctor tied the last strip of bandage in place and stepped around so Flynn could see his face. It was plain and deeply lined, like most country physicians.

"You have a pair of cracked lower ribs and a lot of torn-up flesh, but nothing was truly broken—only bent a mite," the doctor said with a wink and a humorless smile.

"Can I ride?" Flynn asked.

"Would it make a difference if I said no?" The doctor never even looked at Flynn, but went on adjusting the bandage.

"Not a bit."

"You've got a fine little nurse here." The doctor smiled at Marydyth. "I think your wife can tend what needs tending."

Wife.

Flynn and Marydyth locked uncomfortable gazes. The word hung between them like a dark veil.

"Try to take it easy when you get home. No heavy lifting—a little common sense—and you should be right as rain in a few weeks."

"How much do I owe you?" Flynn dug into his pocket, ignoring the pinch of his ribs when he swiveled.

"Two dollars."

Flynn stood up, a little shaky but on his own two feet. He picked up the clean twill shirt that Marydyth had brought, noticing his buckskin was ragged and filled with little stone cuts. The dark smear of his blood stained the back. He put one arm in a sleeve of the fresh shirt but when he went to rotate his shoulders and slip a hand in the other one, a knife blade of pain shot through him. He gritted his teeth and sucked in a breath, then he tried again.

"Oh, for pity sake!" Marydyth snapped. "Would it kill you to ask for help?"

She strode to the table where he was leaning and pulled the shirt up to help him slip his hand inside. She brought the front together and started buttoning it. Her nearness was impossible to ignore. She smelled like sunshine, leather and *her*.

Each time she drew in an agitated breath, her breasts rose and fell enough for him to get a heartwarming glimpse of them within his own baggy shirt that she had borrowed. She licked her lips, and he remembered what it had felt like to kiss her.

"There now, you are done," she said. But she lingered close and looked up at him.

For a moment time was like slow honey being poured from a jar. Everything lay suspended while they searched each other's eyes.

He felt...something that he could not name.

"You two ride easy." The doctor's gravelly voice cut through the strange bewitchment.

In silence Flynn slowly maneuvered down the steep stairs to where Jack was still standing with his reins hanging loose in front of him. They found a livery, bought a horse and a beat-up saddle and headed for Hollenbeck Corners.

Even though he didn't complain of pain, by evening, Marydyth could tell Flynn was hurting. Each step Jack took made him stiffen and hold his breath for an instant.

She rode alongside him, wanting to reach out and touch him, to give him some comfort.

During their ride to Millville she had felt his flat belly beneath her hands with each step. It had made her squirm in an itchy, aroused sort of way. Now, each time she looked at him she silently wished that she was still riding double, still sitting behind him feeling the heat and strength of his body in front of her.

"How much farther?" she asked.

"'Bout an hour, I'd guess." Flynn had taken a slightly different route home. It was a little faster and he hoped they would arrive soon so Rachel would not worry.

"I'm as anxious as you are, Marydyth."

His voice was low and thick, and she knew he was fighting to keep control while he was suffering.

"We—we could stop for a bit," she finally said.

He pulled up on the reins and turned his upper body to face her. They stared at each other across the gulf between their horses.

"I'm not going to die on you, Marydyth. I've been banged up before—I'll heal up and hair over." He gave her a lopsided, boyish grin.

Something happened to Marydyth at that particular moment. Something insidious and frightening. Her heart thumped so loud in her chest she was sure he could hear it.

Dear Lord, I am falling in love with Flynn O'Bannion.
She couldn't—she *wouldn't*.

"I only thought you might want to rest a minute—but if not, then let's go." Marydyth kicked her mount and stared straight ahead. There was no way in hell she was going to allow herself to care for a man who didn't trust her—no matter what her heart said.

Rachel was halfway through Victoria's hall and headed straight for Flynn's cracked ribs when Marydyth stepped in front of her and intercepted the bone-crushing hug.

"I missed you, sweet pea," Marydyth said as she took the momentum of Rachel's weight into her arms and spun her around. She staggered a bit but she held her feet.

When Marydyth finally looked at him he mouthed one word—*thanks*.

She nodded, and her cheeks colored a little. Then she turned back to Rachel, who was chattering a mile a minute about making cookies with Gertie and the big calico barn cat out back who had delivered a litter of kittens, and could she have one if she was really, really good—could she please?

A warm, tickly feeling entered Flynn's chest. His back hurt, his flesh stung—he couldn't even take a deep breath without black spots dancing in front of his eyes—but by all that was holy, seeing Marydyth and Rachel together made him happy.

Happy.

He felt connected to them both, linked in a way that made him proud, happy and humble, and it all scared him more than an Apache raiding party ever had been able to. And that, he thought wryly, was a hell of a note.

The trio returned to Hollenbeck House with Rachel happily filling them in on all her activities. She had extracted the promise from Flynn and Marydyth that as soon as the kittens were weaned she could have her pick. The news brought a glorious smile to her young face.

Once they reached Hollenbeck House, Marydyth insisted on helping Flynn unsaddle the horses. When she bent over, pulled by the weight of his big saddle, her rump had strained prettily against the denim fabric. He caught himself smiling more than once. When Marydyth finally left and went in to to get Rachel ready for bed he saw the stub of a half-smoked cigarette, and by it a scrap of paper.

He picked it up and read the careful printing.

If you try to open the Lavender Lady, you will die.

Marydyth could feel Flynn's gaze on her every step into Hollenbeck House. Knowing he was watching her gave her a mingled sense of excitement and dread.

She didn't want him to scrutinize her so closely. She lived with the fear that eventually he would see the truth about her. That his probing eyes would find the rotten core of her soul and know her for what she was.

When they stepped inside the kitchen she got the largest pots she could find and put water on to boil. Flynn watched her from beneath his thick lashes for a few minutes before turning and walking stiffly away.

She was both glad and bereft to have him gone.

Flynn went into the front parlor and eased himself into a chair. His body ached and his mind was not much better off. Every time he looked at Marydyth he wanted to drag her into his arms. He wanted to kiss her and make her feel safe.

Mostly, he wanted her to trust him enough to tell him what she dreamed.

But the one thing he didn't want to do was tell her about the note he had found.

Flynn must have dozed because when he woke the shadows angling through the windows were gone. The room was dim, but then a golden flare drew his attention to a round side table. Marydyth was lighting one of the lamps.

She didn't even have to look at him to know when he became aware of her.

"Feeling better?" she asked.

The room seemed to crackle with the strong emotions that sparked between them. She found herself feeling shy and insecure when his dark gaze turned in her direction.

Flynn wanted to inhale her scent, to taste her essence on the back of his tongue, but the bandage around his ribs prevented him from doing that.

He answered her with a grunt, more because he was frustrated with himself than for anything she had done.

Marydyth turned around and frowned at him. For a moment he thought he was going to get the rough side of her tongue but then Rachel came running into the library sucking on a fresh hoarhound stick.

"Where did you get that, Rachel?" Marydyth squatted beside her daughter, pushing back a strand of copper-colored hair from her face.

"That man who wanted me to call him Unca…he brought it to me."

Marydyth straightened up and met Flynn's gaze. Her face was taut.

"Where did you see him, Rachel?" he asked.

"He was in the front parlor," Rachel said between licks on the sugar tit. "He was waiting for Mama."

Flynn's expression darkened. "Ted Kelts is here?" His voice was an indignant rumble. He awkwardly levered himself forward in the chair.

"Uh-huh." Rachel nodded. "He said he wants to talk to Mama in pri-private." She stumbled over the word.

Flynn's brows pinched closer together. "Do you know anything about this, Marydyth?"

Each time he looked at her she felt hot and cold inside. One part of her longed to be taken in his arms and the other part of her wanted to hide from his perceptive gaze.

"No, I don't know anything about it," she answered softly. "Ted coming here is as much a surprise to me as it is to you." She bent down and pulled Rachel near. "Rachel, did you let him in?"

"Uh-huh. He gave this to me." Rachel held up the candy stick.

"That's fine, sweetie, but from now on, you let Uncle Flynn or me open the door. Understand?"

"Uh-huh." Rachel nodded and continued to suck on the hoarhound. Marydyth looked up at Flynn. There was something wary in the way he looked at her, something dark and wintry that broke her heart.

"Marydyth, you had better go see to your *guest*," Flynn said with a reserved control in his deep voice.

His tone stung her soul. Why had she allowed herself to be so vulnerable around him? Like a fool, she had opened her heart and let him in.

"Come on, punkin, you stay here and keep me company. I'll tell you a story." Flynn grimaced when Rachel scrambled up in his lap but he never said a word as Marydyth turned and walked away.

Ted Kelts was staring at her portrait when she walked into the parlor J.C. had used as an office. He turned to her and smiled. "You are a mighty handsome woman, Marydyth."

"That was done a long time ago. There's been a lot of water under the bridge since then."

"And over the dam." He finished the old saw. "For both of us." He smiled warmly, and for a moment she felt the relief of being accepted for just who she was.

If only Flynn would treat her this way.

Even though they had shared each other's bodies, there was a barrier between her and Flynn. She knew what it was, of course: they didn't trust each other. He didn't believe in her, and she didn't trust him enough to unburden herself about the past.

"I stopped by to make you another offer on the Lavender Lady," Ted said as they sat down side by side on the lemon-yellow settee. "I thought perhaps Flynn wasn't making the decisions anymore."

A chilled finger traced its way up Marydyth's back. There was something about the way Ted wouldn't meet her gaze....

No. That was silly. He just assumed that she would have found a way to regain control of the estate. It was a natural enough assumption. She had thought the same thing—that it was a matter of having a few papers signed. Nobody but Moses Pritikin, Wainwright Sloan and Flynn knew the terms of the will and trust.

"Flynn is still making the business decisions, Ted." She twisted her fingers together in her lap.

His face fell.

"But I thought—that is..."

"What, Kelts?" Flynn walked into the room. "What did you think?"

"O'Bannion." Ted's eyes widened. There was a strange tautness in the lines that bracketed his mouth.

"You act surprised to see me, Ted." Flynn narrowed his eyes. "I live here, remember? Or would there be another reason why you look so surprised?"

"Uh, I heard about your accident. I thought you'd still be in bed." Ted flashed a friendly smile at Marydyth.

Something red-hot surged though Flynn's blood when she smiled back.

Jealousy?

"It takes a lot to keep me in bed." His involuntary gaze slid to Marydyth. She colored slightly.

"Anyway, it wasn't that bad." Flynn sat down in the chair facing the settee and crossed his long legs. "How'd you hear about the—accident, Ted?"

For a moment Ted frowned, then the smile returned. "Uh, I saw Moze Pritikin."

"Really?" Flynn toyed with the stitching at the top of his boot. "Moze told you, did he?"

"I'm glad to see you're not seriously injured." Ted rose to his feet. "I had thought you might be laid up and could use some help to get the Lavender Lady up and running. I am real anxious to see her spitting out ore again—be real good for business."

"I mend quick," Flynn said with a cheerless smile.

"How did it happen?" Ted asked Marydyth.

"We were—" Marydyth began.

"I slipped and fell on some rocks—damned clumsy of me," Flynn said with a casual shrug.

Marydyth glared at Flynn. He silently willed her to go along with him.

"Really? You fell?" Ted asked, with a note of doubt ringing in his voice.

"Yep, I'm just glad we were already finished looking at the Lavender Lady when it happened." Flynn studied Ted's face as he spoke. "If things go according to plan we'll be able to reopen it in a month."

Ted's eyes narrowed. "You went inside the mine?"

Flynn tilted his head. "I got enough of a look to decide it would be in Hollenbeck Corners' best interests to see it running again."

Marydyth sucked in a breath and stiffened. Up until this moment Flynn had said nothing, given her no indication he thought it would be profitable to reopen the mine. A feeling of relief coursed through her.

"I see. Well, if you have everything under control and don't need any help...I should be going." Ted shifted his attention from Flynn to Marydyth. "Take care, Marydyth, and I'll be talking to you again soon." She escorted him to the front door, and said goodbye quickly, determined to get back to Flynn and find out just what was going on.

"Why didn't you tell me that you found copper in the mine?"

"I didn't," Flynn said with an arched brow.

"But you just told Ted..." She frowned, trying to understand.

"I told Ted I thought it would be in everyone's interest to reopen. And that is true, whether there's enough ore or not."

"But if it doesn't make a profit?"

"Hollenbeck's other mines near Bisbee can more than absorb the loss for a while. I agree with you, Marydyth, it will be good for Rachel if the mine is open and men are back to work."

She felt a hot, thick lump in the back of her throat. He agreed with her. He had considered what she thought and decided her opinion had merit.

It was all for Rachel, of course. It had nothing to do with her. But still it made her feel good, feel worthwhile, that he agreed with her. Perhaps he was beginning to trust her, at least a little.

The next few weeks passed uneventfully. Flynn did what the doctor had suggested and took life easy. He slept late and spent time with Rachel while Marydyth busied herself with running the huge house and doing all the cooking.

During that time Flynn had never been able to find the right words to tell Marydyth that he trusted her. It nipped at the edges of his mind every day. It made him mean and grumpy, but, try as he might, he couldn't swallow his pride.

Then, one night as Flynn was lying in his bed trying to form the words to tell Marydyth he felt like a damned fool, he heard her scream.

He sat up in bed, feeling the twinge of pain. She screamed again, and the pit of his stomach contracted. He ignored the dull throb in his ribs while he raced to her room, wearing only his drawers. The cool air washed against his bare legs while he ran through the maze of corridors. He burst through her door and found her, twined in the sheet, grappling with her invisible demons. It tore at his heart to see her suffering.

"Marydyth, it's Flynn." He yanked the sheet away from her body. A tearing sound filled the room. He realized that he had accidentally pulled her gown too. Her breasts were bare in the moonlight.

Her eyes flew open but they were misty and unfocused.

"Oh, please Andre, not like this, please, please..." She grasped at Flynn's arms, her nails digging into his flesh.

"Marydyth." Flynn grabbed her shoulders and stared into eyes that did not see him. "Marydyth, honey," he said gently.

She blinked and her expression shifted. It was like a cloud passing over the sun. He knew the moment she realized it was him.

"Flynn, thank God you are here." She collapsed against his bare chest, unmindful of the effect her own silky flesh against his was having on him.

His heart skipped a beat when she nuzzled into him.

"I—I had a nightmare," she whispered, as if saying it too loudly could bring the terror back.

"Yes, I heard you." He stroked her head, feeling the slip of her silken hair beneath his palm.

She stiffened beneath his hand. "Oh, my God, do you think Rachel heard me? I don't want her to see me like this." She started gathering the blanket to her, trying to straighten her ripped gown, struggling to restore her shattered composure.

"Honey, stop." Flynn stilled her hands. "It's all right. She slept right through it. I passed by her room getting here. It was quiet."

She slumped against him in relief. "Thank God. Oh, thank God."

"Marydyth, I think it's time you told me what it is that terrifies you so."

She tilted her head and looked up at him.

He could feel the blood surging through his veins, felt himself tighten and harden while she looked at him. She licked her lips and her eyes roamed over his face as if she were looking for something there in his eyes.

"Flynn?"

"Yes, darling, I'm right here."

"I don't want you to know—I don't want you to see what I am...really like inside. If you knew, then you would hate me."

"I could never hate you." He brought his mouth down to hers for a soft grazing kiss.

"But you don't trust me now. It would be worse if I— if I told you."

"Honey, I trust you." He took as deep a breath as his bandage would allow and gazed up at the formless ceiling. "I've been trying to find the words to tell you." He expelled a heavy breath. "I acted like a real bastard, Marydyth. I know you didn't shoot me."

She was still in his arms. For what seemed an eternity to Flynn she just sat there, unmoving, barely breathing. He expected her to slap his face and order him from her room.

He deserved it.

"Oh, Flynn." She shuddered. "You don't know what that means to me. You, more than anybody on this earth, know the kind of life I led before."

"I know you had it rough, but I don't know the particulars."

"Maybe it's time I told somebody what happened. Maybe it is time I told you why I have bad dreams."

He released his hold on her. She lay back on the bed. There was a full moon tonight, its silver shaft spilling into the room and across the bed. It turned her yellow hair to ashy silver and made her blue eyes luminous.

"Come and lie beside me, Flynn," she said softly. "I want to feel you near me—it will give me strength."

Flynn stripped off his drawers and slid into the bed beside her. Her fingers played along the white bandage bisecting his ribs.

"Does it hurt much?"

"Not enough to keep me from you. I've missed you, Marydyth," he admitted as he bent his head and kissed her. She was sweet and warm and he drew her bottom lip into his mouth.

Marydyth's heart sang when Flynn kissed her. She told herself that his trust and approval did not really matter, but it was a lie. His was the only opinion that really *did* matter.

He kissed her and she sighed. She shifted her body and helped him slide above her, mindful of his ribs. "But, Flynn—I want to tell you."

"And you will, darling, you will...later." He positioned himself between her thighs and slid into her with a heavy sigh.

"This feels like coming home, darling," he murmured. "You feel like home."

A sigh of pure pleasure escaped her lips, and she realized with a tug on her heart that she had lost the battle not to love him.

Chapter Thirteen

Flynn woke to the rhythmic sound of thumping. He opened one eye and discovered a bright shaft of noonday sun blazing through Marydyth's bedroom window. It was hot and his skin was sticky with a sheen of sweat. The window was open and a wisp of a breeze carried fresh, warm air into the room.

Flynn glanced around the room, searching the tangle of blankets as he tried to locate his drawers. Finally he spotted them, beneath the ruins of Marydyth's nightgown.

An involuntary smile curled the corners of his mouth. They had tasted a passion last night that was all the sweeter for their spoken truce.

He eased himself out of bed, suddenly aware of the new ache in his ribs. A chuckle escaped him when he wondered if the doctor would consider hot sweaty love-making "taking it easy."

Flynn opened Marydyth's bedroom door and peered out into the long hallway. He could see nothing. The dull thump grew louder and seemed to be coming nearer.

"What in hell can that be?" he muttered as he followed the sound. After leaving the hallway and negotiating a series of turns and stairs, Flynn finally discovered the source of the noise.

It was Marydyth. She had her back to him, her firm, rounded rump swaying prettily beneath her day dress each time she tugged the huge trunk down another stair.

Jerk, thump, sway. Jerk, thump, sway.

Her progress was loud, slow and too damn sexy for words.

"Need any help?" Flynn leaned against the wall and leered at her. He wanted to give her more than help.

She whirled around, wide-eyed and startled. "Oh, you scared the life out of me."

He grinned and drew her near him to claim a kiss. "Why didn't you wake me?"

"After last night I thought you might need your rest. Lord knows I don't want to be the cause of your death."

As her words registered on both of them, their smiles faded. An awkward moment passed between them, then Flynn finally grinned.

"We both need to stop being so sensitive about things like that. That was funny. There ain't a thing in the world wrong with us laughing about it."

So they did.

"You mean it?" she asked as he looped a big arm around her and pulled her near once again. "You don't think I tried to kill you?"

"If you say you shot at a rattler, then you shot at a rattler." He nuzzled her earlobe.

"And the rock slide?"

"A quirk of nature." He nipped her chin playfully.

"And the person you saw running away—the one you thought was me?"

"I was hit on the head. I couldn't have been thinking clearly. I haven't had a clear thought since I met you."

She smiled at him. It was a golden image that burned into his heart. Then she laughed and the sound trickled over his skin like sweet rainwater.

"I am glad you finally believe me but I still have some things to tell you."

"Later. Hell, we have all the time in the world. Where is Rachel?" he asked as he molded her buttocks against his groin and rubbed against her.

"She's stirring up gingerbread makings."

"Mmm, my favorite. I don't suppose we have time for another one of my favorites right now?" He rubbed against her suggestively.

"Not right now, but there is always tonight." Marydyth grinned and kissed him.

"Honey?"

"Mmm?" She was occupied kissing his collarbone and trailing her fingers along the edge of his bandage.

"What in the hell are you trying to do with this old trunk?"

She stopped kissing him and turned. She looked at the dome-topped trunk, balanced between one stair and another, and shrugged.

"I need more clothes. This one has several dresses and other things I could use."

"Frilly things?" He waggled his brows. "Soft woman things, the kind that are so much fun to take off?"

"You are insatiable!"

"I hope so." He swatted her behind playfully. "Now tell me where you want this thing and get out of the way. If I have to listen to any more of those thumps I'll have a headache tonight."

"In my room." She leaned against the wall and folded her arms beneath her bosom.

"Now, may I make a suggestion?" She didn't wait for

his reply. "Will you put on a few more clothes before you join Rachel and me for lunch?" She glanced down at his drawers where the evidence of his passion strained against the fabric in the front. Then she scurried away before he could swat her again.

The trill of her happy laughter echoed over her shoulder as she ran down the stairs toward the kitchen.

Flynn picked up the trunk, ignoring the dull ache in his ribs as he strode down the hallway to Marydyth's room. But he underestimated his injury and overestimated his strength. By the time he reached her door, one side of his ribs was burning like liquid fire and his breath was coming in short, pain-filled gasps. He bent to put the trunk down but a sharp pain grabbed him and he dropped it hard to the floor.

The unlocked latch opened. The top opened, spilling the contents of the trunk and the tray on top at his feet.

He picked up a handful of lacy embroidered fluff, rubbing it against his cheek as he imagined how it would look on Marydyth.

Then he froze with the fabric still clutched in his hand.

A small lap secretary had broken open. A dried-up ink bottle, a pen and some paper were at his bare feet.

Flynn dropped to one knee and picked up the paper. He held it to the light and felt his breath catch in the back of his throat.

There was a distinctive watermark on the page. The exact same mark that had been on the letter that had caused him to see Marydyth's sentence commuted.

He stood up, staring at the paper in his hand as if it were alive. The letter—the confession—that had freed Marydyth had been written on her own stationery. The letter was old, so old it could have been written before

Marydyth went to Yuma. It would have been an easy matter to pay an accomplice to write and post it.

A sickening feeling gripped him. Her whispers of innocence faded away and were once again replaced by dark shadows of doubt.

The moon was high when Flynn settled down in the front parlor with his unlit cigarette, two fingers of brandy and the letter. He had sent Marydyth on to bed, telling her that his ribs were bothering him too much tonight.

What a lie.

He held the paper up to the lantern and examined the watermark, comparing it to the piece of stationery he had taken from Marydyth's trunk.

That trunk, like all the others, had been packed away before he ever moved into Hollenbeck House. Whatever was inside any of them had been there for more than three years.

Flynn rubbed his finger over the scrawling script and the signature. The writing was nothing like Marydyth's— he had seen her signature on papers at Moze's. But then, if she had somehow figured a way to concoct a fake confession, she probably wouldn't have used her own hand. The notion she might have paid someone to do this once again came to mind.

But why wait so long?

Hell, if she had managed to forge the letter, using the mysterious Blaine as the scapegoat, then why had she not done it right away? Serving three years in Yuma couldn't have been a picnic. Nobody in their right mind would delay if they had a choice. But, then again, Moses had said it looked as if the letter had travelled a lot of miles and years!

He knocked back the whiskey and closed his eyes. It

burned a path to his gut. As if he could feel her eyes upon him, he found his gaze traveling upward to the portrait.

Marydyth. Beautiful passionate Marydyth.

He crumpled both pieces of stationery in his hands and dropped them on the side table. Suspicion warred with trust and swirled around his thoughts like a cold mist.

He was faced with a choice. He could either believe what his eyes told him, or he could believe his heart.

Flynn's life had always been black and white, right or wrong. Never before had he been faced with so many shades of gray.

"No, by God. I don't believe it. I refuse to believe that Marydyth Hollenbeck is a killer or that she carefully plotted and planned the confession to get her release." His voice echoed through the empty room until Marydyth's scream drowned it out.

The fine hair on the nape of Flynn's neck prickled. He took the stairs two at a time, knowing what he would find when he reached her room.

Just as before she was covered with a sheen of sweat, thrashing and twisting in the bed, crying out in terror.

"Marydyth, darling, it's Flynn."

She latched on to him as a drowning man grabs a lifeline. She was trembling so hard that her teeth kept knocking together.

"Honey, what is it?" He stroked the damp hair back from her face. "Can you tell me?" He rubbed her back, feeling the delicate bones beneath his hand, feeling his own arousal rear to life.

"Are you sure you won't hate me?"

"I am sure. You can trust me, Marydyth."

She stilled for a moment, hiccuping loudly. "Trust

you?'' Her voice was a husky whisper. It rubbed along his skin and made him itch to be naked with her.

"That's what this is all about, isn't it? You can trust me now. I know I've been slow to trust you.'' He gave life to his own thoughts and flung the last shred of doubt away. "But I trust you now, Marydyth. Do you hear me, Marydyth? I...trust...you.''

She drew away from him and studied his face in the half-light of the moon. Tears glistened on her cheek; her hair was wild. She looked like a woodcut from one of Rachel's fairy books.

"In spite of all the evidence and my past?''

"I mean it.'' He grinned. "I trust you, Marydyth Hollenbeck—as God is my witness.''

His words sang through her like light through the darkness. Something cold and dark that had gripped her heart was released. She inhaled deeply, savoring the feeling of having someone's faith.

No, not just someone's faith—Flynn's faith.

A heavy burden rose from her shoulders, and for the first time in many years she felt whole and alive. There were no more shackles on her heart.

"Flynn, I'd like a glass of brandy.''

He chuckled. "Sure, sugar, I'll have one with you.''

"Good, let's go downstairs and when we've finished our drink, there is something I have to tell you. Something I *need* to tell you.''

Downstairs, Marydyth settled herself in the big leather chair. She looked small and very young, with her white gown tucked around her bare toes.

Flynn sloshed brandy into two glasses and handed her one. She didn't sip, instead tipped the glass and swallowed awkwardly, sputtering and coughing as the brandy went down.

"Want another?" His brows were arched in surprise. He didn't think she was much of a drinker so she must have been looking for courage in the bottom of her glass.

"Please." She coughed. "I've never...talked about this before. I wish I could forget it." She shuddered. "But you deserve to know the truth—about me."

Something thick and tight formed in his throat, knowing that Marydyth had finally crossed the same bridge that he had. They had both decided to ignore old wounds and hurts. Come hell or high water they were laying open their hearts and trusting for the first time.

He refilled the glass and handed it to Marydyth. Then he went and opened a tall window that faced the back garden. It was hot, with no breeze to stir the heavy air.

She just started talking, in a low soft voice. He had to listen hard to hear her.

"My family died of river fever when I was seven." A ghost of a smile flitted across her face. "Uncle Blaine was my only living relative—a bachelor, a gambler—not the sort of person who should raise a child. But to give him credit, he took me. He was Mama's baby brother and a good deal younger than she was."

Blaine is real. A happy voice shouted inside Flynn's head.

She took a sip of the brandy and then leaned her head back and shut her eyes. Her throat was smooth and slender and Flynn could see the thrum of her pulse beneath her flesh.

"At first it was a great adventure, staying up late, going places with my uncle, but then it changed. I suppose it had something to do with how Blaine's luck was running—or not running. I began to hate it."

Flynn studied the curve of her jaw, the delicate bones of her shoulders. Her hair spilled against the dark leather of the chair. She looked like an angel, a sad, tormented angel.

"We went from one riverboat to another. And eventually I grew up." She opened her eyes and looked at Flynn. "When I was sixteen Blaine had a particularly bad streak of luck. He owed a tremendous amount of money. There was a man—he owned part of the riverboat we were on. His name was Andre Levesque."

Her first husband.

"One night Blaine came to my room, more drunk than sober." Her eyes filled with unshed tears. "He told me that he had no choice—he was sorry—but I would be taken care of."

Her hand was shaking so badly that brandy was sloshing from the glass onto the front of her gown. An amber stain began to spread on the snowy-white material. As the fabric grew wet it plastered it to her breasts. Flynn reached out to fold his own hand over hers as if to reassure her.

"You don't have to tell me any more, Marydyth. I said I trust you and I believe you. You don't have to go through this."

"Yes, yes I do." She shivered and drew herself up. "I want to tell you—I *have* to tell you."

"All right. I'll listen, but if you can't do it I'll understand."

She looked at him and smiled. "Thank you." She let out a long breath, then she looked at the wall, focusing on the past.

"Andre was at least willing to marry me, I suppose that is something I should've been grateful for. Anyway, all Uncle Blaine's debts were to be cleared by Andre, and he was going to give Blaine a stake so he could go to San Francisco. All I had to do was get married."

Flynn tightened his jaw until it pinched. *The bastard had sold her. She was only sixteen and he sold her like a damned common whore.* He clenched his hands into fists, fighting the rage inside him.

"The wedding was quick, Uncle Blaine the only witness. We had supper, lots of champagne and then it was—it was—" Her voice cracked and broke. She took a great gulp of brandy and choked.

"Marydyth, honey, don't put yourself through this." Flynn felt helpless watching her suffer and knowing there was nothing he could do to help.

"I have to—I can't live with the ghosts any longer."

"Marydyth." He said just her name but she inhaled deeply and smiled.

"I was young, inexperienced. I knew nothing of men and women. I was frightened of what was going to happen. Andre didn't care. I tried to explain but he became furious. He hit me and he forced me to—to—do things."

Flynn tasted bile in his throat. He clenched his hands tighter, wishing he could have been there—wishing there were some way he could turn back the clock and reckon with the bastards who had mistreated her.

"I—I—was crying and then he—he—he hurt me."

Her cheeks were flushed, her eyes were wide and haunted. With a tenderness he didn't know he possessed he pushed back a cluster of yellow curls and stroked her face.

"It's over now, honey. You told me. Now you don't have to think of it again."

"No. No." She shook her head from side to side. "That is not the worst part." She shoved him back, dislodging his hand. "You don't understand. He was going to—to...do it again. He was coming at me and I was so sc-sc-scared. I picked up the lamp and I hit him. I hit him, and then I ran.'' She was near hysterics.

Flynn grasped her shoulders, trying to calm her. "Honey, it's all right.''

"I ran and I ran. Blaine told me that I should. I worked hard, got on my feet. But then each time I would try to forget and start a new life, Blaine would come, wanting money.'' She was trembling. "I would have to run again.''

"Why didn't you just stop, honey? Why didn't you tell Blaine to go to hell?''

"I believed it was God's punishment. He was judging me since man couldn't. I deserved to be punished. Don't you see? I deserved to be punished for what I did.'' Her eyes were wet with tears. She was sobbing and clutching at Flynn.

"No, honey, you didn't deserve to be punished.''

"I did. And when—when J.C. was murdered, I thought—I thought that was God's way of seeing that I was punished.''

Flynn frowned at her. "Do you mean you didn't defend yourself during the trial because you thought God was punishing you?''

"Yes! He was. Don't you see? I had gotten away with murder before but he made sure that I paid for my sins.''

Flynn frowned at her, trying to make sense of what she was saying. A hard knot formed in the pit of his stomach as he started to understand. "Marydyth, honey? Do you believe that you killed Andre Levesque?''

"Yes, yes, yes. I killed him. I murdered Andre. Dear God, I murdered him.'' Her voice was high and tight with horror. "And when I was sent to Yuma...the nightmares began.''

Flynn's mind was racing. Blaine was real. Blaine had

written the letter. Blaine confessed to killing Andre and robbing him. But Marydyth didn't know that? Marydyth really thought she had killed her first husband? How could she have not known that Blaine did the killing? Unless... With a jolt, Flynn realized Marydyth knew nothing about the letter.

"Marydyth, listen to me. You did not kill Andre."

"I did—that was why my face was on the Wanted posters. I killed him and I ran, but Blaine followed me wherever I went—even after J.C. married me."

"No, Marydyth. Blaine killed Andre," he said gently.

"You don't know what you're talking about." She was shaking her head; her golden curls were flying. "I did it." Her voice was high and tight with misery. "I did it, God forgive me, please, I did it."

"Marydyth, listen to me. Blaine did it—he confessed."

Her eyes grew wide and round. She stared at Flynn and he wasn't sure if she had drunk so much brandy that her thinking was fuzzy or if she simply could not believe it. "What?"

"Marydyth, it's time you learned the truth about what happened," Flynn said as he picked her up and folded her into his arms. "There are things you don't know about your past—things it seems that only I can tell you."

Chapter Fourteen

He folded himself into the chair with her in his arms. "Haven't you wondered how you got released from Yuma?"

"I didn't care. I was free to be with Rachel."

He smiled at that and pushed one strand of hair back from her forehead. "Marydyth, I received a letter."

Flynn looked at the crumpled paper lying on the side table. With one hand he reached out and snatched it up. He smoothed it out as best he could and handed it to Marydyth.

She was still trembling, shaking like a leaf in his arms. "This is Blaine's handwriting."

"Uh-huh. I think it was written some time ago by the look of it, but I only got it this spring," Flynn explained.

She searched his face and then she lowered her eyes and read. All the color drained from her face. "Oh, my God. Could it be true?" she whispered. "All those years of running…"

"You didn't do it, sweetheart." All Flynn wanted to do now was free Marydyth from the ghosts that haunted her. "There is no reason for you to keep hating yourself. You didn't do it."

"But—but Blaine told me I killed Andre. He found me when I was headed back to my cabin. He told me Andre was dead. He helped me get off the riverboat." She clung to the page.

"I'd guess that Blaine found Andre after you left. They probably got into a fight—maybe over the way Andre had treated you."

"More likely it would've been over money," she whispered. "It was always money." She shivered, as if the truth were still too hard to comprehend.

"If I ever get my hands on Blaine..." Flynn swore.

"My whole life—my entire life—has been based on lies. I have been running from my guilt, thinking I didn't deserve happiness. How could my own flesh and blood let me suffer like that?"

"I don't know, honey. If only he had come forward during the trial here."

"But then he would have had to face a jury for J.C.'s murder. I guess he didn't have that kind of courage."

Flynn remembered how Marydyth had sat in stony silence throughout the proceedings, saying only that she was innocent of killing J.C. and nothing more. He had wondered at the time. Now he understood. She had a deep sense of morality and justice. A part of her felt as if she had gotten away with murder after Andre's death. A part of her wanted to be punished for that crime.

"Flynn?"

He rubbed his chin on the top of her head. "Yes, honey?"

"There's something wrong with this confession." Marydyth frowned and read the paper again.

"What?" Flynn squinted and followed the line of her vision.

"Blaine admits to killing Andre—but J.C...."

"Yes?"

"He doesn't actually say he stabbed J.C."

"It doesn't matter now, sweetheart." Flynn had been haunted by that question for months, but now it just didn't matter. He was sure she was innocent.

"I don't want you to have any more doubts."

"I believe you, Marydyth. I believe *in* you."

"But Blaine should have admitted it. It doesn't make any sense, Flynn. If he was driven to write this because of his conscience, then why didn't he confess to J.C.'s murder?"

"I don't know, honey." Flynn reluctantly allowed himself to wonder also. It didn't make any sense. A man driven to confess one bad deed would not omit the other.

Unless he didn't do the killing.

A chill ran up Flynn's spine. His old instincts prickled.

If Blaine hadn't done the killing, then a murderer had gotten away. A murderer who might still be in Hollenbeck Corners.

"We've got to do something." Marydyth drew herself up. Her eyes were wide. "We have to investigate and find proof."

"No!" The sharpness of Flynn's voice shocked them both. "We aren't going to do a damned thing, Marydyth."

"But the truth…J.C.'s killer…"

"Leave it alone, Marydyth, just leave it the hell alone. I don't want you doing anything that will put you in danger."

Flynn was sprawled in a big leather chair in the library, sipping a whiskey. Worry and fear had been two emotions he had little experience with.

Until now. Now he was paralyzed with fear for Marydyth.

The notion of Marydyth stirring up the past terrified him. If she brought attention to the confession, the one that Flynn had used to get the governor to release her, it might get the wrong kind of attention.

There was a chance she might end up back in Yuma.

"Rachel couldn't survive that...and neither could I," he admitted to the darkness surrounding him.

He didn't want to worry Marydyth with his suspicions, but now Flynn saw some things clearly that he had never noticed before. He intended to find the killer, but he was going to do it his way. And unfortunately that meant keeping Marydyth out of it for her own safety.

Marydyth was innocent. Of that he had no doubt. And, like her, he didn't believe that Blaine would confess to one murder and deny another. The only thing that made any sense was that somebody else had killed J.C. That led Flynn down a frightening path because the murderer might be among them.

Flynn frowned and rubbed his forehead. Somebody had taken a shot at him. And somebody had started that rock slide.

Why? What did anybody have to gain by killing him?

Not a damn thing. He didn't have anything that anybody would want.

Except control of the Hollenbeck fortune. A shiver ran through Flynn as he pondered that possibility. Because if Flynn died, the fortune remained in trust in Rachel's name.

Unless she died, too.

If the killer was trying to get to the Hollenbeck fortune, then Flynn and Rachel were standing right in the way.

Marydyth tossed and turned, trying to understand Flynn O'Bannion. He said he trusted her. He said he believed her. But he didn't act like it. She shoved her fist into her pillow. If he did, then he would help her find J.C.'s killer.

Flynn O'Bannion was an ex-lawman and a man who had a thirst for the truth.

So why didn't he want to find out the truth about J.C.?

She knew the answer. Because he still had some doubts about her. Marydyth sighed. It hurt her to admit it, but it was the only possible explanation.

Yet she needed to know, to find out, for J.C. and for Rachel.

She flopped over on her back and stared up into the darkness. Her bedroom window was open. She never slept with the window shut now. After so many nights in Yuma where she couldn't see the stars, couldn't smell the air, having a welcome breeze wafting over her body was close to heaven.

Marydyth lay there, with only her thin cotton gown covering her body, and tried to figure out some way of getting to the truth.

She couldn't go to Moses Pritikin. He had made it abundantly clear that he was Victoria's man.

Wainwright Sloan might help her, she thought, picturing her lawyer's pale face. But for this she needed a man who had the ability to ferret out things, not a greener who sneezed at a room full of dust. She needed somebody who could talk to everyone in Hollenbeck. *Ted Kelts.*

Ted had always stood beside her. Since her return he was one of the few people who even spoke to her. Yes, she decided. As soon as the sun came up, she would pay Ted a visit.

The next morning Marydyth rose early and after breakfast she dressed Rachel in her best frock of blue and green plaid. The copper curls shone like a newly minted penny as Marydyth fastened a blue bonnet over them.

"Where are you two headed?" Flynn asked over his first cup of coffee.

"I'm taking Rachel to visit with Victoria for the day."

A slow smile bloomed across Flynn's lean craggy face. "That's mighty big of you, Marydyth." He wished he were better with words so he could tell her how much he thought of her—how much he admired the way she had acted since she returned. A lot of men wouldn't have carried off their return half so well as this little slip of a female. "It takes a big person to forgive and forget." He wanted to tell her that he was proud of her but the words stuck in his throat. There were a dozen things he wanted to tell her but all he said was, "Have fun, you two."

Marydyth left Rachel playing with Gertie while Victoria sat in silence watching her granddaughter. A tendril of guilt wound around her heart when she remembered how easily Flynn had accepted the lie.

But it couldn't be helped.

The familiar chill of guilt nipped at the corners of her mind as she walked down the streets toward Ted Kelts's home at the edge of town.

Ted's house was not as large as Hollenbeck House, but it had traces of opulence in unexpected places. A black wrought-iron fence separated it from the street, and a matching railing ran around the entire second floor. A huge brass knocker waited to be thumped in the middle of a massive set of double doors. And wooden scrolls and curlicues decorated every square angle and window from top floor to well-tended flower gardens.

Marydyth gripped the brass and heard the hollow echo

as the knocker announced her presence. Almost instantly the door was opened by Ted himself.

"Why, Marydyth." He leaned out to see if she was alone. "What are you doing here?"

"I came to visit," she said, while twisting the strings of her reticule in her hand. "Is this a bad time?"

"No, not at all." Ted was coatless, wearing a starched pale blue shirt and string tie. "Come in. I was just having a cup of coffee."

The house was the usual Arizona Territory combination of adobe and brick. It was cool and quiet. Tall, narrow windows lined the front of the house, but Ted led her to the back and out into a Spanish-style courtyard. One cup sat on a table beside a spreading rosebush.

"Can I get you a cup?"

"That would be nice." She sat down and loosened the ribbon holding her bonnet. Now that she was here she didn't know where to begin.

Ted returned with another cup and saucer. He poured coffee from a fancy silver service and sat down.

"Is this a social call or have you come to accept my offer on the Lavender Lady?" He sounded cheerful, almost expectant.

Marydyth sipped the strong hot coffee and tried to organize her thoughts. "I need your help."

"What can I do for you?"

"I want you to help me find J.C.'s murderer."

Ted Kelts dropped his china cup on the stones of the patio. Hot coffee splashed on her skirt.

"I'm sorry, Marydyth," Ted said, as he dabbed at the stain with his clean handkerchief. "I thought you asked me to help you find J.C.'s murderer."

"I did, Ted," Marydyth said evenly.

"But, Marydyth..."

"I didn't kill him, Ted, if that's what you are thinking."

"Never. I never thought it for a minute." He diligently wiped at the stain and shook his head in denial.

"Well, I didn't do it, and I thank you for believing in me. If you will help me, I'd like to find out who did."

"But your Uncle Blaine...?"

"Didn't do it either. I know that now." Marydyth set her cup on the table and leaned forward. "Please, Ted, you were once J.C.'s partner. You would know if he had enemies—somebody he might've hurt in a business deal perhaps."

"Yes, of course. I would know things that somebody else wouldn't." Ted rubbed his chin with the pad of his thumb. "What about Flynn O'Bannion?"

"I don't want him to know anything about this." She sat up straighter.

Ted's smile beamed at that news. "I knew you would see the light soon enough. I have no great affection for O'Bannion, never understood why Victoria gave him control...." He frowned and grew quiet. "Sure, I'll help you, Marydyth, and maybe when Flynn is out of the picture, you and I can come to an...understanding."

Marydyth looked up and frowned. "I can't think of anything right now except finding out who killed J.C."

"I understand." He scooted back into his chair and patted her hand. "I can be patient. When I want something I can be very patient."

"Thanks, Ted. I've been thinking a lot about what happened three years ago. The strike that shut down the Lavender Lady caused a lot of hard feelings on both sides."

Ted studied her face. "I suppose you are right."

Marydyth sighed heavily. "Do you think I am grasping at straws?"

Ted smiled. "Not at all. Let me ask a few questions, see what I can find out. How soon do you think the Lady will be ready to open?"

"I'm not sure. Flynn takes care of all of that. Soon I guess," she said absently.

"Things are going that well?"

"He said he should be able to take a load of new timbers to the mine at the end of the week," she said with a sigh. The last thing Marydyth was worried about was the Lavender Lady.

"It will be nice to have the old girl producing again—if there is any copper ore down there."

"I suppose, but Flynn is opening it for other reasons besides copper ore," Marydyth said without thinking.

Ted stiffened. "Is that right?"

"Yes. Well I want you to know that I appreciate your help, Ted."

"No problem at all, Marydyth. I enjoy your company, I always have. I want you to know you can rely on me."

Marydyth was humming when she and Rachel opened the front door and stepped inside the cool, dim mansion. It had felt good to sit and talk with Ted. She felt a sense of relief knowing that he was going to be searching for answers on her behalf.

"Unca Flynn!" Rachel said as he stepped out of the library. She launched herself at him so quickly that Marydyth didn't have time to deflect her momentum. Rachel hit him full force, driving the air from his body in a painful grunt.

"How's my girl?" Flynn asked as he knelt beside her. His healing ribs would not allow him to pick her up yet.

"I had fun today, Unca Flynn," she said as she put her hands on either side of his face.

"Really? What did you do?"

"Gertie and I made a cake and some biscuits. I pounded them all by myself." She leaned close. "And my kitten is growing real fast."

Flynn slanted a look up at Marydyth. "And what was Mama doing all this time? Did she help make biscuits or did she visit with Grandma?"

"Oh, no. Mama wasn't there," Rachel said quickly.

Flynn and Marydyth locked gazes. His brows furrowed together. "No?"

"Uh-huh. Mama left."

Flynn stood up. Worry over Marydyth and Rachel folded over him and constricted his breath. He didn't want to act like Marydyth's jailer but he couldn't shake the idea that they all might be targets of the faceless, nameless killer.

"Marydyth, where did you go?" He saw her flinch and immediately regretted his tone.

She narrowed her eyes. "Since you ask me in that tone, Flynn, I don't think it is any of your business." She turned as if to walk away.

He grasped her arm and held her in place. His voice was low and controlled. He didn't want Rachel to see them fighting. "It damned well is my business. Now where were you?"

"Enjoying myself," she snapped.

Flynn searched her face. He could explain himself to her—make her understand that he was worried about her—but he had never explained his actions and decisions to anyone in his life, and he damned sure wasn't going to start now.

"Don't ever go off like that again. Do you hear, Marydyth? From now on I want to know where you are going and who you are with—every minute of the day."

Her mouth fell open in shock. Then her lovely, lush lips curled up at the corners. She leaned close and whispered in his ear, "When hell freezes over." Then she jerked her arm free. "Come on, Rachel, let's go change our clothes and start dinner."

Flynn could only stare after her, wanting to call her back, to explain, to apologize. But he had too much pride to do either.

Over the course of the next week Marydyth ignored Flynn, and he, in turn, tried to act as if he didn't care.

She felt he said what he did because he didn't fully trust her, and he wanted her to trust him enough to let him know where she had been and what she had been doing.

It was like a dog biting its own tail. Neither one would give in and so the silent feud continued. Because of their discord, Marydyth had stopped sleeping with Flynn.

He told himself it didn't matter. But it did. He thought of her every waking minute. When he was climbing the stairs he fancied he could smell her skin, fragrant from being scrubbed with hard-milled French soap. And when he was lying in his bed, hard as a post, he could almost feel her body near him.

He had it bad, and that made him angry at himself. He had never needed a woman before—not like this. This went beyond physical need, it was deeper, more intense.

And that shook Flynn.

He had always been a lone wolf. He told himself that he could do without her—he had certainly survived before without a woman. And so, as if to prove it to himself, he went to the bordello in search of Annabelle, the whore who had captured Moze's regard.

The sound of plinky piano music, the scent of cheap toilet water and cheaper cigars followed Flynn inside the cathouse. And when Flynn found the woman, he searched her face, looking, for what he did not know. But the one thing he did know was that the painted lips and rouged cheeks were not Marydyth's.

Her hair didn't catch the lamplight and shimmer like a skein of gold; the eyes held no shadow of pain and regret. And when he looked deep into those eyes he didn't feel as if he were falling down a dry well. He touched her skin, but his fingers didn't burn as if he had touched hot embers.

In the end he sighed in disgust and went back to Hollenbeck House, determined to be man enough to find a way to heal the rift that had come between him and Marydyth—the woman he swore he didn't want or need.

Chapter Fifteen

Flynn rented a buggy and horse from the livery. He drove it to the Blue Belle Restaurant and left it outside while he ordered three full meals at two bits apiece. Then he went to the Mercantile on Fir Street and bought a basket to pack it all in.

"Looks like somebody is goin' a-sparkin'," the robust cook quipped as she carefully wrapped up half an apple pie.

Flynn smiled sheepishly. He had wrestled with his pride and his feelings for Marydyth for two days after his harebrained trip to the bordello. Now it was time to face facts and do something about it.

Marydyth had a right to be angry. He had followed her around like some sort of hunting dog, sniffing the air for danger, growing more grumpy and surly by the minute. And never once had it occurred to him to simply tell her what was wrong.

All he succeeded in doing was making the gulf between him and Marydyth grow wider.

And that was not good for Rachel, he justified to himself. It was true that he missed seeing Marydyth smile at him upon waking in the morning. And it was a fact that each time she walked by and he caught a whiff of her spring-flower-fresh hair he ached to pull her into his arms. But he was doing this—planning a surprise drive in the country and picnic—mostly for Rachel.

A half hour later, Flynn returned to Hollenbeck House. He passed Amos Clark and his milk delivery wagon as he turned the last curve in the hill.

"Morning, Amos."

"Mr. O'Bannion." Amos touched his forehead and clicked to the steady roan mare that pulled the wagon.

Flynn watched him until he was out of sight, then he walked to the kitchen door. Marydyth and Rachel were sitting at the small kitchen table. They each had a bowl of oatmeal and a glass of milk in front of them.

"Did Amos leave some buttermilk for me?" he asked with a grin.

"In the pitcher," Marydyth said without looking at him. He was hungry for her eyes, her body—for every part of her.

"I have a surprise for you two," he said as he poured himself a glass of buttermilk. He put a pinch of salt and a pinch of pepper in it and then tipped it up. The cool, tangy liquid slid down his throat.

"What surprise, Unca Flynn?" Rachel was out of her chair and climbing on the top of his boot.

"A nice surprise." He scooped her up in his arms and crossed the room, enjoying this simple act now that his ribs had healed.

"I hired a buggy and got us some lunch. I'd like to take you two on a picnic. Sort of my way of apologizing for being so cussed hard to live with."

Marydyth turned and looked up at him. "Do you mean it?"

"I mean it. I hope you can forgive me," he said softly,

while his eyes soaked up the look of her, all fresh-scrubbed and beautiful. Her hair had grown out enough that she could pull it all up and capture it in a ribbon. One or two wayward strands hung around her face and at the delicate nape of her neck.

He wanted to kiss the sweet, inviting hollow but instead he said, "I'm no bargain, Marydyth, I know that, but I'd like to start over—I'd like for us to start fresh."

She smiled and rose on tiptoe to kiss the side of his face and he took that as an acceptance of his awkward apology.

When Rachel and Marydyth were dressed and bonneted, Flynn helped them into the buggy. Marydyth sat next to Flynn with Rachel on her other side. "So I can see bestest," Rachel had explained.

He wrapped his hands around the leathers and directed the buggy in a northeasterly direction to Watervale. The breeze was cool and sweet, the conversation easy.

Marydyth had never been to Watervale and only knew of the place as the water source for Tombstone. The drive was mostly uphill through rugged country. At one stretch the path grew narrow and treacherous as it switched back upon itself and continued to climb. She gripped the supports of the buggy and put her faith in Flynn, confident that he would let no harm befall them.

Suddenly the terrain flattened out and turned into a panorama of colors. The yellow of brittle brush, the purple verbena and the golden poppies ran together in a wild slash, as if a rainbow had fallen to earth and painted the prairie.

Rachel was giddy. Her happiness was contagious, and Marydyth soon found she was delighted to get out, to enjoy this day of quiet with Rachel—and Flynn.

The summer sunshine beat down on them but there was a strong breeze so it was not oppressively hot. Flynn had insisted on bringing three full canteens of water, and whatever goodies he had in the basket tucked beneath the seat that she wasn't supposed to know about.

It was a wonderful day.

A dust devil swirled and made a revolution across the road in front of them, carrying twigs and dirt and a dried jumping cholla in its gritty funnel.

"Looky, Unca Flynn," Rachel said. She marveled at everything, and through her young eyes, Marydyth received the gift of wonder.

A jackrabbit hopped by and Rachel laughed. She wanted to touch every critter, sniff every bloom, see every cactus up close. Flynn patiently halted the horse and let her do so almost every time she asked, although the rabbits were faster than Rachel. While Marydyth watched her scamper from hedgehog cactus to ocotillo, being careful not to touch the thorns, Flynn watered the horse.

They made many stops before they reached Watervale. The area around the natural spring was lush with grass and wildflowers. A sturdy stone building held the mill wheel, turning beneath the gentle persuasion of the water that eventually went to slake the thirst of those in Tombstone.

"This is lovely," Marydyth said as she allowed Flynn to pick her up by the waist and lift her from the buggy. His hands lingered a moment after he had deposited her on her feet.

"I had no idea the spring would be so large."

Roadrunners, crows and meadowlarks lined the banks, poking their beaks downward, drinking and searching for grubs.

"It is nice." Flynn's deep voice rumbled over her. "But not as pretty as you." She looked up and found him studying her with a hungry look in his eyes.

"Thank you for today," she said, suddenly feeling shy beneath his gaze. It was strange. They had shared each other's bodies, given each other their passion, but in many ways they were little more than strangers. She knew virtually nothing about his life before he came to help with the mining strike. Now she was curious about this hard, solitary man.

"After we eat and Rachel goes down for a little nap, would you—have a talk with me, Marydyth?" Flynn managed to choke the invitation out. He was a man of few words, and speaking to Marydyth was somehow harder than facing down a band of outlaws.

"I'd be pleased to, Flynn."

They walked and explored and laughed. Rachel was allowed to take off her shoes and stockings and wade in the shallow end of the pool while Flynn lay on his back in the shade, watching her from under hooded eyes.

He seemed relaxed, but Marydyth wondered if that was an act. Was his body tightly wound, ready to spring at the slightest noise, or was he calm in the middle of nowhere, with the clear spring and sounds of wildlife all around them?

Marydyth sat on the grassy bank with her own toes curling into the cool foliage. She tucked the edges of her skirt around her legs and drew up her knees as a rest for her chin.

Sunlight danced on Flynn's dark auburn hair. His deep baritone voice and laughter made chills march up her spine as he chatted with Rachel.

Rachel giggled and squealed in mock fear as Flynn

scooped her up and made a show of tossing her into the water.

Marydyth felt something hot and liquid expand in her chest. She could learn to like this. She could learn to *want* this. If she let down her defenses for even a minute she could fall head over heels in love with Flynn and long to build a family and a life with him.

Today had been wonderful, but it was a special day. Marydyth was sure that when they returned home Flynn would watch her like a hawk, unwilling or unable to let her and Rachel out of his sight.

Flynn glanced at Marydyth and felt his heart thud against his ribs. She was so beautiful with her golden curls spilling from the ribbon, coming to rest beside her cheeks on her knees.

He wanted her.

But more importantly he wanted to keep her and Rachel safe. It was the only thing he thought of day and night. Somebody was out there, somebody who would not stop at murder. It was high time he let Marydyth in on his fear—but he was loath to see the smile fade from her lips. Tomorrow, he told himself. He would tell her tomorrow.

He clenched his jaw and scanned the horizon. All day long he had kept a watchful eye on his back. But now as the sun was hanging like a ripe apple in the western sky, he allowed himself to ease up his vigil.

Rachel was sleeping soundly and safely beneath the shade of a cottonwood when Flynn stood and reached out to take Marydyth by the hand.

"I want you... I've missed you," he said as he pulled her to her feet and against his body.

The hard length of him against her made her breath catch. Damn it all, she had missed him. She had missed his kisses and caresses and she had missed the way his body covered her.

She hated herself for missing all that and the way he made her bones feel like melted wax with little more than a glance. She yielded to him now, molding her body to his form, sighing when he cupped her buttocks and lifted her slightly for a better fit against his groin.

"Lord, Marydyth, you make me dizzy with wanting you," he murmured.

"We can't—not here." She looked down at her sleeping daughter.

"Then let's take a walk up to the top of the mill." Flynn glanced at the livery horse, who was tied firmly and munching on tender grass. "We'll be nearby if Rachel wakes."

"I'll walk with you, Flynn." Marydyth wanted him as much as he wanted her but...

Flynn swallowed hard. He understood what she had not said. He couldn't blame her. Hell, he had been acting like a domineering bastard. But he had to keep her and Rachel safe. He was a man and a man was supposed to keep his family safe.

His family. Was that how he had come to think of them?

He realized with a sobering jolt that it was. But he couldn't tell Marydyth that he had come to think of her and Rachel as his, couldn't do anything about it until he had found J.C.'s murderer and put the past to rest.

Many hours later Flynn hitched up the horse and wedged the much lighter basket beneath the seat.

"I'm sleepy, Unca Flynn." Rachel yawned and leaned her head against his shoulder as he helped Marydyth into the buggy. When she was settled he handed Rachel to her.

"I know, sugar. You walked about a hundred miles today. Chasing butterflies is hard work for a little girl," Flynn said with a grin.

"I had a lovely time, Flynn, thank you," Marydyth said softly when he sat down beside her and gathered the reins.

"I'm glad, and I hope that we have many more like it." He turned and looked at her with an expression of tenderness that made her belly drop to her shoe tops. Something in his eyes spoke of tomorrow.

She wanted that. She wanted tomorrow with *this* man. If only Flynn would remain Flynn and not become her stern-faced jailer when they returned home.

Dusk turned the desert to a mauve landscape as the livery horse plodded toward home. Long shadows reached for the rising moon and Marydyth saw the flicker and flash of wild eyes out in the coming darkness.

Flynn clucked his tongue to encourage the horse to move a little faster. They were trotting along at a comfortable clip when they reached the winding switchbacks. Marydyth held Rachel with one hand and grasped the buggy support with the other. She was glad it was Flynn's strong hands on the reins as the trail narrowed and twisted, falling away sharply on her side. She could not see it, but she heard the pelting of falling rocks as the wheels passed over a particularly narrow spot.

"We'll be on the flat in a bit," Flynn said reassuringly, as if he could sense her terror in the dusk.

"I'm all right. I know you'll keep us safe."

Her words flowed over him like summer rain. That was all he wanted—to keep her and Rachel safe.

As the horse pulled the buggy around the last curve in

the trail, a loud crack broke the silence. Flynn felt the buggy sway, heard the sickening snap of the tongue and knew immediately what had happened.

"Marydyth—when I tell you, jump. Rachel, I want you to hold on to your mother's hand and jump, too. Roll with me and try to keep on rolling to break your fall." His voice was flat, calm. Hearing that made Marydyth resolve to be calm too. She gathered Rachel close and held herself ready, waiting for Flynn to tell her what to do.

"Jump!"

Flynn pulled on the leathers as hard as he could, then he jumped. The horse thundered away, leaving the buggy to careen in a different direction, borne by its own momentum. He landed on his back. The hard-packed earth drove the air from his lungs.

Marydyth and Rachel both screamed as they rolled and rolled. Dirt flew up in their faces, cactus needles poked into their shoulders, but they kept rolling at a dizzying speed until finally they slammed up against a rock next to Flynn.

A dull pain radiated from Flynn's left arm above the wrist. He drew in a breath and fought waves of nausea.

"Are you hurt, Rachel, Marydyth?"

A few seconds elapsed while they did an inventory of limbs. "No, no, we seem to be all right."

"Good, good." Flynn exhaled slowly, thankful that they were not harmed.

Marydyth and Rachel managed to untangle themselves from him and the ribbons of their torn skirts. Slowly they stood up and began to dust themselves off. Flynn managed to shift his weight to his right side and used that hand to steady himself as he climbed to his feet.

"Oh my God, your arm," Marydyth said.

Flynn looked at the source of his throbbing agony for the first time. A piece of bone poked out of a ragged hole on his sleeve about four inches above the wrist. It hurt like the devil but there was only a little blood staining the fabric.

"Could be worse, might've been our necks." He chuckled but his observation was still a grim one.

"Oh, my." Marydyth turned to Rachel. "Honey, see if you can find me some sticks."

Marydyth flipped up her skirt and tugged off her white petticoat. The lace and embroidery had been damaged in the fall.

"What are you doing?" Flynn asked.

She started tearing the six-inch-wide ruffle from the bottom. "I am going to set that arm."

"I was afraid you were going to say that," Flynn said dryly.

A half hour later Marydyth gulped down her dread and looked at the assembled supplies. She had torn a half dozen bandages from her petticoat and Rachel had found some dried and hollow organ-pipe cactus that was straight enough to use for splints. Flynn had explained to Rachel that a part of the wagon had broken.

"Are you ready?" Marydyth asked Flynn, trying to ignore the way her stomach fluttered each time she looked at him.

"The question is, are you ready to do this?"

"I can do this, I can," she said under her breath as if to reassure herself and not him.

"Take hold of my hand and pull until the bone goes back into place." He extended his left arm toward her, ignoring the ugly gash and the nauseating pain it brought. "Tell me if it hurts too much."

"Just pull, Marydyth, and don't worry about me." His deep, gravelly voice rubbed over her skin and made her throat tight and thick.

"Ready?"

"Do it."

She did as she was told, grabbing hold of his wide wrist with both of her hands. She bit her lip and made sure not to jerk but to apply firm, even pressure.

The bone moved. Flynn made a husky sound in the back of his throat at the moment the bone ground into place.

She tried not to feel his agony, but strangely she did. It didn't help matters that she was the one who was causing his pain.

She never wanted to cause him pain.

"Keep pulling. You have to keep the pressure steady while you wrap it." The tone of his voice was different, lower and taut. She knew he was fighting to control his reaction to the pain—for her and for Rachel.

She loved him for it.

"There." Quickly she grabbed the splints from Rachel's ready hands and put them on top and bottom of Flynn's arm. Then she began to wrap the bandages.

"Not too tight," he instructed.

"I know." Her breath was coming quick and shallow. It had been one of the worst things she had ever had to do, but it was nearly over.

When she tied the last cotton strip into place, she sighed. "There."

Flynn swallowed hard and gingerly moved his left arm. The splint was irregular and way too long but it was keeping the bone from moving.

"You did a fine job, ladies," he said with a weak smile. "I am a lucky man to have you two."

Marydyth shoved her hair out of her eyes and locked gazes with him. And in that electric moment she prayed hard for Ted Kelts to find a clue about J.C.'s murderer because she yearned to have a future with this man.

Next they retrieved the canteens and a few items from the splintered picnic basket. When Flynn picked it up he looked at the bottom, or what was left of it. There was a small piece of paper with familiar careful block printing.

You've been warned. Stop trying to open the mine—or die.

The question ripped through Flynn's mind. At which stop in Hollenbeck Corners had someone slipped the note in the basket?

Walking would have been an easy journey on the road, but within an hour Flynn suggested that they stop and set up a camp. The sun was fully down now and it was starting to get cool as the dry desert soil gave up the warmth of the sun. And he didn't want to be out in the open like a sitting duck in case whoever had written the note decided to come and make a fight of it.

"I've got some matches in my pocket. I'll build us a fire," he told Rachel as he settled their backs against a sheltering outcrop of rough stone. "Would you like that, honey?"

"Yes, Unca Flynn, 'cause I am real tired," she said between yawns.

"Fine. Marydyth, why don't you wrap her up in that checked blanket we brought?"

She nodded, and folded it—and her arms—around Rachel. It felt so good to hold her daughter—even though they were miles from home, tired and shaken up by the crash. It felt good to be alone with Flynn and Rachel.

"A penny for your thoughts." His rough voice jarred her from her musings.

"I was just thinking what a nice day this has been."

He laughed. Hearty deep rumbles of amusement. "Yeah, I'd do this again for certain." He shook his head and awkwardly maneuvered his broken arm while he got a roaring fire going. "Only next time I'd tuck my arm."

"I—I don't mean that. It's just that I feel—so…content."

He looked at her, the fire highlighting the rugged planes of his cheekbones and the deep hollows of his probing eyes. "I know, Marydyth."

Something hot and liquid seemed to pass between them.

"Unca Flynn, I'm cold," Rachel said in a sleepy voice.

"Then you two come over here and let me hold you." Flynn positioned his body on the ground, straddle-legged, and opened his arms. Marydyth sat down with Rachel in her lap and leaned back against his wide strong chest. He engulfed them both in his embrace.

Marydyth knew in her heart it couldn't get any better than this.

Chapter Sixteen

The group of men who had organized the search found them an hour after sunrise. Just as Flynn had predicted, the moment the livery horse showed up in Hollenbeck Corners without its buggy and passengers an alarm had been raised. The pumper company had called out all the fire-fighting crew and had followed the very plain tracks right to Flynn, Rachel and Marydyth.

"Hey, where is breakfast?" Flynn quipped when the men thundered up.

"Got some biscuits and bacon, right here," exclaimed Fritz Handleman, a portly German who ran one of the butcher shops. He lumbered off his enormous horse and passed his kit to Marydyth. She burrowed into it and found still warm biscuits and crispy bacon, which she combined and handed to Rachel first, then Flynn.

"What happened to you?" Fritz asked.

"Tongue on the wagon broke," Flynn said with a shrug. "My fault, I should've checked it better. I feel like a damned fool but I guess this will teach me." He raised his broken arm a bit to show them what he meant.

"That ain't exactly true, Flynn," the livery owner said as he dismounted. His brow was furrowed when he came nearer. He cast a warning eye toward Marydyth and Rachel, who were close by.

Flynn understood and stepped a few feet away so they would not overhear. "What do you mean?"

"That tongue had been tampered with. I checked what was left dragging behind the horse. It was battered some but still easy to see that it had been sawed near in half."

An icy finger skipped up Flynn's spine. He had wanted to believe that the accident was just that. First the shot, then the landslide and now this. And this time Marydyth and Rachel were at risk—not just him.

Anger flowed through him like a hot, turbulent river. Whoever was doing this had taken the wrong step this time. Because now Flynn was more than angry. Now the threat was too personal and too damned close to his heart.

Whoever was behind this had risked hurting the two people he loved most in the world.

As soon as Flynn had Marydyth and Rachel settled at the house he went to the doctor to get a proper splint. Then he headed straight to Moses Pritikin's office with the threatening notes in his pocket.

He felt like a lawman again, only this time he didn't have his oath to bind him to do what was right and proper and *legal*. When he found the snake responsible for this, he could exact his own justice.

The bell over Moze's door rang as Flynn entered. He strode right on into Moze's private office.

"Wheee, I'd hate to be the galoot that put that expression on your face." Moses leaned back in his chair and regarded Flynn with raised brows, his gaze pausing briefly on the sling around his arm. "What the devil happened to your arm? You're getting to be downright accident-prone."

Flynn ignored the question and tossed the notes on the desk. Moses leaned forward and unfolded one, read it quickly, then picked up another.

"Whatever happened to the men who organized the mining strike back in '86?" Flynn asked as he lowered his body into the single chair facing the desk.

Moses frowned and rubbed his bony chin. "Leffert got shot, I heard. Tommy Dade went up around Cripple Creek—if the rumors are to be believed." He tapped the threatening notes. "You think they have something to do with this?"

"Dunno. But it looks like somebody is hell-bent on making sure the Lavender Lady doesn't reopen." Flynn swept off his hat and ran his fingers through his hair. "I damned well intend to find out who."

Moses leaned back and laced his fingers behind his head. "Are the notes your only lead?"

"Right at the moment. I was hoping you could tell me if there has been anything unusual going on regarding copper mines and the like."

Moses shrugged. "Not really. Papers have been full of all the hullabaloo about the proposed silver purchase act, but that would have no bearing on a copper mine." He unlaced his fingers and tipped his chair back down with a thud. "I know you well enough to know that you have a plan. What're you going to do, Flynn?"

"I am going to set an irresistible trap," Flynn said.

"What is going to be so damned irresistible about it?"

"Because I am going to use myself as the bait." He grinned wolfishly.

Marydyth sighed and scooted farther down in the hot tub of water. She soaped her skin and slowly scrubbed, feeling the strain dwindle away, along with the dust and grime. Rachel had been bathed and fed and was sleeping like a little angel in her room down the hall.

The sound of a closing door drew Marydyth up in the tub. Flynn must be returning, she thought. The notion filled her with a strange kind of contentment. She eased herself back down into the water, sloshing some over the edge as she did so.

"Flynn—I'm up here, in the tub," she called out, sure that he would come and find her.

But when five minutes had passed and he still had not come she became uneasy. The house seemed quiet. Certainly too quiet for a brawny cowboy to be clomping around in.

A shiver of wariness slithered up her back. She sat upright, listening hard to the sounds of the house.

A sizzling instinct of alarm burst through her. Marydyth stood up in the tub, sloshing water on the floor as she grabbed for her robe. She yanked it on over skin that was still sheeted in water. She ran down the hall to Rachel's room.

Rachel was sleeping.

Marydyth sagged against the doorjamb in relief. Her heart was beating fast and her mouth was dry as tinder. She closed her eyes and told herself that she was acting silly; nothing had been wrong.

Rachel had her hand drawn into a fist resting against her chin. She was safe and well.

Determined to put her fear to rest, Marydyth crept down the stairs on tiptoe, careful to make no sound. First she checked the kitchen and found it empty.

The library was also unoccupied, as well as the front parlor. She heard the rustling sound of drapery blowing in the wind coming from the formal parlor. When she entered the room she discovered one of the tall windows open. A hot, dry breeze fluttered the curtains and a leaf of paper.

It was stuck in the center of the wooden mantel. Marydyth stopped in her tracks. The paper was secured to the mantel by the tip of a hunting knife.

When Flynn walked in a few minutes later, Marydyth was still frozen with fear, staring at the paper on the mantel.

"What the hell is going on?" Flynn took one look at her and strode past her. He jerked the knife from the wall. Then he opened the paper and read it.

"Who would do such a thing?" Marydyth managed to croak out. She had read the vile words and felt her blood turn to ice.

"Somebody who doesn't want to get any older," Flynn snarled.

"Oh, Flynn." Her throat was thick and tight.

"Marydyth, honey." Flynn drew her into his arms and felt her sag against his chest. "I swear to you, Marydyth, I won't let anybody hurt Rachel or you."

But even Flynn's strong voice could not erase the horrible threat from her mind. She could see the words each time she shut her eyes, felt their sting in her heart.

Open the Lavender Lady and Rachel Hollenbeck will die.

Flynn strode down the main street of Hollenbeck Corners with Rachel and Marydyth at his side. He looked neither right nor left but every nerve in his body was tuned for danger.

"Are you sure about this?" Marydyth asked softly as the Hollenbeck *Herald* came into view.

"I'm sure." Flynn stopped walking and turned to her. His jaw looked as if it had been hewn out of stone but his eyes were soft and full of concern. "Do you trust me, Marydyth?"

"With my life."

A ghost of a smile softened his expression for just a moment and he laid a loving hand on top of Rachel's soft, rusty golden curls. "I'll keep both of you safe. From now on you'll stay with me day and night."

"That won't be a hardship," Marydyth said. She wished she could banish the terrible specter of danger that seemed to be with them day and night.

"Glad you feel that way." He gazed at Marydyth. "I have to do this. We have to set a trap."

"If you say it will be all right, then we are with you." Marydyth looked down at her daughter. Rachel smiled and gripped her finger. Mercifully, Rachel was too young to know she was in danger.

"Good, then let's go talk to the foreman and set a trap to catch a skunk."

Marydyth put the bowl of mashed potatoes on the table and turned to open the oven door on the Monarch stove. The inside of the kitchen felt about the same temperature as hell on a busy day. She felt a tendril of sweat snake from her hairline to her neck.

"Something smells wonderful," Flynn said as he walked into the kitchen with Rachel on his shoulders. He winked at Marydyth and she felt her cheeks grow hotter, if that were possible.

"You know how to feed a man, Marydyth. Steak and potatoes is my favorite." He awkwardly set Rachel on her feet as she giggled.

"How about you, honey? Do you like steak?"

"No, Unca Flynn! Only 'tatoes for me." She laughed and climbed into the chair.

Marydyth was about to sit down opposite Flynn when there came a knock on the back door.

Flynn's eyes narrowed and his entire posture changed. He went from laughing and teasing Rachel to the serious, cautious behavior of a lawman. His fingers hovered near the gun strapped on his lean hip as he strode across the room. Marydyth drew Rachel from the chair and moved her to a secure spot near the hand pump, out of sight of the window and away from the door.

"Who is it?" Flynn stood a little to the side, determined to make himself a hard target.

"What's the matter, Mama?" Rachel asked.

"Shh, honey, we are playing a game," Marydyth whispered. She tried to smile but it felt as if her face would crack from the effort.

"Oh." Rachel's Cupid's-bow mouth made a little O.

"It's Ted Kelts," a voice on the other side of the door announced. Marydyth felt all the tension drain from her body. She moved away from her place of safety. "It's only Ted. Invite him in, Flynn. He can eat with us."

Flynn cast Marydyth a withering gaze but he opened the door and let Ted inside.

"Mmm. Something smells mighty good, Marydyth." Ted leaned over the table and inhaled the aroma.

"Pull up a chair and join us," Marydyth invited.

"Are you sure it's all right? I mean I don't want to intrude. Even though your good cooking is making my mouth water."

Flynn snorted but he remained silent as he sat down. He watched Ted from the corner of his eye. He didn't like the man and he knew the reason why. Ted Kelts was entirely too *interested* in Marydyth.

"Tell me how you've been, Marydyth?" Ted grinned

at her as he heaped potatoes on his plate. "I haven't seen you since we had morning coffee together."

Flynn locked gazes with Marydyth over the table.

"Oops. Did I tell tales out of school?" Ted said with a contrite expression. "I assure you it was completely proper, Flynn."

"Marydyth is a grown woman," Flynn said sharply. "She doesn't owe me any explanations."

"Good." Ted smiled at Marydyth. "Because I have always had a tender spot for this lady."

Marydyth felt her face flushing. She wanted to explain to Flynn but she had kept her meeting with Ted secret, hoping against hope that he could unearth some clue about who was making the threats. When she met his gaze he shook his head almost imperceptibly.

"What have you two been up to lately? Rumors are circulating all over town about the Lavender Lady," Ted said casually as he forked a thick steak onto his plate.

"Well, Flynn and I had—"

Flynn kicked Marydyth's shin with the toe of his boot.

"Ouch!"

"Sorry, my boot slipped," he lied. He gave her a series of meaningful glances. She realized that he wanted her to keep their difficulties quiet.

"You had a what?" Ted asked.

"A little accident with the buggy on a picnic, but we're all fine," Flynn finished quickly before Marydyth could say anything.

Ted Kelts glanced at Flynn. "Yeah, I heard about that. Too bad about your arm. Actually, that's why I am here. I'd be willing to take the Lavender Lady off your hands and get it up and running if you're not up to it."

Flynn wasn't sure what rankled him more—Ted Kelts's implication that he wasn't man enough to do what needed to be done, or the man's continued efforts to spend time with Marydyth.

"Are you sure you're interested in seeing the mine reopen?" Flynn asked. He didn't miss the incredulous stare that Marydyth gave him.

"Why do you think I've been wanting to buy it? Another mine working in the area could do wonders for the economy. I am a businessman, Flynn, and I like profit."

Flynn scowled as he viciously cut the steak on his plate. He grudgingly admitted to himself that he would have been pleased as punch to find out Ted Kelts was the sidewinder behind all the trouble. But if Ted actually wanted to see the Lavender Lady open, then it had to be somebody else since all the clues pointed to someone who didn't want to see it running again. Somebody who Flynn hoped would take the bait he and Marydyth had so painstakingly put into both Hollenbeck Corners's newspapers.

The evening passed pleasantly enough. Ted Kelts made small talk, gossiping mostly about other businessmen, and letting Flynn know that Mrs. Young had packed up and left town "rather than live in a town with *that* woman."

As the moon was chasing the sun across the sky, Flynn sat down in the big chair and rolled himself a smoke.

"Would you like a light?" Ted asked as he pulled a box of stick matches from his shirt pocket.

"Naw, I never light 'em," Flynn admitted gruffly.

"Oh." Ted barely suppressed his laughter. After a few more minutes of small talk he finally stood up and straightened his vest over his belly. "Fine meal, Marydyth, and I thank you. I had better get going. Marydyth,

I hope you'll come with me to the Blue Belle for dinner real soon and let me return the favor.''

Flynn gave her a look that would curdle milk.

"Why thank you, Ted, I'd like that," Marydyth replied as she rose from her chair to walk Ted to the door. When she returned to the parlor Flynn's dark eyes held all the wrath of an indignant warrior.

"I don't want you to spend any more time with Ted Kelts," he grated out.

"Oh, and why is that?" Marydyth asked mildly as she swished by him and flopped down in his favorite chair. She kind of liked to think that he might be a little jealous.

"Because you are my woman and I don't want him or any other man in this town getting the wrong idea." He jerked her up from the chair with his good arm. Then he kissed her long and deep.

Chapter Seventeen

Flynn read the full-page ads he had put in the *Herald* and the *Chronicle*. A wicked grin broke across his face. If their stalker was the kind of cowardly man who would make threats against a little girl, then this gaudy display would be more than irresistible.

"What on earth are you scowling about?" Marydyth folded her feet under and sat down at Flynn's feet in the library. It was late and Rachel was sleeping but the house was still hot. Even the open window did little to help.

Marydyth opened the top three buttons on her dress, blowing a cooling breath down her cleavage. The relief was minor and fleeting.

"I'd be happy to do that for you," Flynn said as he peered over the top of the newspaper page, ignoring her earlier question.

"Don't try to change the subject," she said, while trying to steel herself against the magnetic appeal of his brown eyes. "Now tell me what you were frowning about."

"I was just thinking how happy it is going to make me when I get my hands on the bastard behind this." His voice had all the warmth of an icy wind.

"Do you really think he'll come to the dedication of the mine?" Marydyth shivered in spite of the heat. "It seems awfully public, not to mention a big risk."

"He has to be one of the miners who were behind the big strike. I can't imagine they could miss such an opportunity."

"So you believe it's an outsider?" she asked. "Not somebody right here in Hollenbeck?"

"I can't think of anything else. Of course, maybe I've just gotten rusty. It's been a long time since I had to track a man down."

"You could call on the sheriff over in Cochise County," Marydyth suggested.

"John Slaughter has his own cats to skin. I can handle this, Marydyth. You need not worry for yourself or Rachel." There was a tone of injured defiance in his voice.

She laid her hand on his hard-muscled thigh. "I didn't mean to imply that I had no confidence in your ability— I only thought you might like some help."

"I wouldn't."

They stared into each other's eyes for a moment, and his anger turned to desire. A shimmering kind of heat arced between them. He scooted forward on the chair until he could reach her. His warm hand cupped the back of her head and drew her forward for a kiss. His tongue explored her mouth, questing, teasing, licking her into a stimulated fervor.

"I want you, Marydyth. I want you beneath me, beside me and around me." His deep voice vibrated through her like the purring of a cat.

He slipped farther forward until he was on his knees beside her. "Let me show you how much I want you, Marydyth."

"Yes, do it now," she murmured, lost in her own exploration of his wide chest and the whorls of sweat-dampened hair.

"I want to bury myself in you. I want to hear you whimper my name." He gently eased her down and shoved up her skirts with his good hand. Her thighs were warm but the juncture of her thighs was hot and moist.

Flynn shrugged out of his Levi's. Marydyth helped him ease out of the shirt, tugging it gently when it got hung on the splint.

With one hand he unlaced the top of Marydyth's petticoat. Soon she was left with only the frilly lace of her sweat-dampened chemise. The swell of her breasts strained against the lightweight lawn, teasing him with a tantalizing glimpse of her creamy flesh.

He felt his own sex harden and rear.

He wanted her, and he would show her just how much.

The next two days passed quickly as Flynn made all the final arrangements for the dedication ceremony of the Lavender Lady. The mine was not really ready to be open, but only he, the foreman and Marydyth knew that. As far as anybody else knew, the Lavender Lady had been retimbered and made safe. Flynn was tired of playing cat and mouse. He wanted to be done with this business as soon as possible.

The day dawned strangely cloudy, with winds that whipped up dust devils and pelted flesh with stinging sand. Flynn rolled his eyes heavenward and prayed that he had made the right decision.

Marydyth woke with a feeling of dread. She opened one eye but immediately closed it and tried to shut out the emotion. She chided herself under her breath as she dragged herself from between the sheets.

"Are you all right?" Flynn's husky voice came from

the opposite side of the bed. They had chosen to lie together, neither finishing the sentence with the words "one last time," though each of them had certainly thought it. There was a risk in what he had planned.

"I am worried...about today." Marydyth poured water into the washbowl and dipped a cloth in it. She scrubbed hard at her face, as if the action could banish her fears.

"I can't leave you here alone, Marydyth." Flynn levered himself up on his one arm. The sheet fell away from his bare chest. Marydyth squinted one eye from under the edge of the cloth.

"I know you can't. I'll be all right. Rachel and I will be with you every minute today."

"And when we get to the Lavender Lady, I want you by my side. I'm not giving these bastards any opportunity to get to either one of you." Flynn tossed back the sheet and rose from the bed. The first glow of sunrise capered along the firm round cheeks of his rump, slanting downward on heavily muscled thighs generously covered with dark coarse curly hair.

She sidled up to him. "Rachel will sleep for at least another hour."

He turned, and she saw him, fully erect. "Only an hour?" He grinned wickedly. "That may not be enough time."

He scooped her up, a little off balance since he favored his splinted arm. In three long strides he had her pressed down into the softness of the bed, where they used the hour as well as they knew how.

Flynn hadn't expected such a procession en route to the Lavender Lady. The entire pumper company and most of the merchants had organized a caravan of sorts. There had even been talk of bringing Victoria in an invalid's chair until Moses Pritikin, concerned for her welfare, squelched the idea. Victoria's whole world was inside her mansion, as it had been for three years.

Flynn was gratified to see that Marydyth's notion about the townspeople being more forgiving was correct. Everyone, including those pious women who had not wished to be seen talking to Marydyth a few months back, now clamored to be one of her confidantes as they prepared to leave Hollenbeck Corners.

She gazed at Flynn with a somewhat bewildered look in her blue eyes as each new wave of well-wishers descended upon her and Rachel.

Although Flynn was nervous about letting her stray, he told himself that nobody but a fool would make an attempt to get at them through the crowd.

But when Flynn watched the men also give her warm smiles as they rode beside the wagon in which she sat, a heaviness lodged in his chest.

He told himself he wasn't jealous. He wasn't stupid enough to think that what he and Marydyth shared was love—it wasn't. Hell, it couldn't be. But each time a man smiled at Marydyth, that heaviness turned to pain and Flynn wondered if he was fooling himself.

The first leg of the trip was easy. There were plenty of laughter and frequent stops for the call of nature and sips of lemonade brought in oak casks. Flynn, however, could not relax, for the closer they came to the Lavender Lady, the closer he knew he was bringing Rachel to possible danger.

He had bought a horse for Marydyth but several of the women, including the preacher's wife, insisted that she and Rachel ride with them in a buckboard that had been specially modified with a canopy over the top. The wagon contained bedrolls, blankets—everything the needed to camp—since the distance to the mine was too great to travel in one day.

He rode behind them, keeping a sharp eye on them and the horizon. Flynn was watchful for the flash of sunlight on metal, feeling almost as edgy as he had during the height of the Indian trouble. Just then a slow dawning of truth settled over him.

Marydyth's voice kept nudging at the edges of his consciousness. He remembered a conversation where she told him that the townspeople would always talk, and that by living together under the same roof they were giving them more fodder.

A cold, hard knot formed in his gut. He watched Marydyth and those same sharp-nosed women laughing and talking, and he realized what she had been trying to tell him.

She didn't want to be the object of gossip. She wanted to pick up the pieces of her life and become just another respectable woman in Hollenbeck Corners.

But she could never do that as long as she lived with him in Hollenbeck House.

And he had given her no real choice in the matter. For as long as he was Rachel's guardian and held all the cards, Marydyth would surely stay.

A clammy sort of disgust at himself seeped into his bones. She had called him bastard—many times—and right now that was what he felt like. As much as Flynn didn't want to think about it, he wondered if Marydyth was only sharing his bed because she longed to be a real mother to Rachel.

A short while later he was damned unhappy. Not only had he examined his motives a bit too close, but he had had a bellyful of the young cockerels of Hollenbeck Corners paying court to Marydyth. But the more he denied being mad about it, the more melancholy he became.

He had jeopardized her reputation by laying down the rules that they would live by. Because of him she had no chance to wipe away the stain of her past. His selfish need to have control, and then his desire to be with her, had put her in a hell of a compromising position.

He remembered how indignant he had been with his own father when Bellami had been brought to care for Trace. Even though his blinded brother had needed a nurse, Flynn had never forgotten about Bellami's reputation. Why hadn't he shown the same kind of concern for Marydyth?

Because she's a widow and...because she's done time in Yuma.

The truth was a bitter taste in his mouth, but he forced himself to acknowledge it. And by the time camp was set for the night, Flynn O'Bannion didn't like himself very much at all.

Throughout the night Flynn made sure he was close enough to protect both her and Rachel during the night. It was a sweet hell that he had consigned himself to endure, because now he knew he didn't deserve to be a part of Marydyth's world. But he saw no way to sever the ties that bound them.

During the night Marydyth slipped away to heed the call of nature. As she was returning to her bed beneath the wagon, Flynn was suddenly there. She reached out to him, but he stepped back, a cool reserve about him.

A hard lump lodged in her throat and her heart ached. She was stunned by the intensity of her feelings. Had she truly lost the battle in trying to resist falling in love with him?

She prayed not. In all the time they had been intimat

he had never once said he loved her. Marydyth was mature enough and realistic enough not to read more into their relationship than there was. They were two lonely people, available and vulnerable to physical attraction. No more, no less. But could she continue this liaison and not involve her heart?

If she did succumb to his dark temptation it would be a disaster. She knew she should not risk her heart. It would only set her up for sorrow because he would surely tire of her. And he was Rachel's guardian until she reached her majority. He was too responsible to leave her, and she knew Flynn loved Rachel. So they would be doomed to continue living in the same house until the heartbreaking time when he finally fell in love with someone.

Marydyth grieved because that someone would not be her. No, it would be madness to fall in love with him, but could she prevent it? Could Marydyth continue this dalliance without risking her heart?

Marydyth glanced toward the rows of sleeping people. It was quiet, except for the mayor's snoring. "Where are you sleeping?" she heard herself whisper. She wanted to deny the ache she felt, being so near him yet knowing that he did not love her.

"I'll be close by, right there in the dark. All you have to do is whisper my name and I'll be there."

I'll be there. He made the promise so easily, but, she realized with a painful tug on her heart, she wanted him to be there forever and always, and in more ways than just physically.

Marydyth nearly cried when she finally acknowledged the fact that she had lost the fight. She was in love with Flynn O'Bannion.

Flynn was reluctant to let Marydyth go. He held her

hand too tightly. He was afraid of losing her—but knew in his heart he had never really had her.

He had backed her into a corner and left her no choice. By telling her that he and Rachel were a package deal, he had held all the cards.

When Flynn thought of all the passionate nights and searing kisses they had shared, a strange melancholy filled him. Those moments now were tainted. He cursed himself for being such a stupid man, and he cursed the nameless person who was out there somewhere, threatening all he held dear. He cursed tomorrow, fearful of what would happen when this was all over and he would have to make a decision that would free Marydyth from the hold he had on her.

He had seen with his own eyes that the townspeople were on the road to forgiving and forgetting. Soon men would come calling, of that he had no doubt. But because of the guardianship, he would be there, in the house, condemned to watch as she was courted and wooed. And eventually she would fall in love.

How would he handle that day? Could he let her go? Could he stop her?

Night passed with Flynn sleeping little as he kept watch over Marydyth and Rachel, who was curled within her arms. It was not the unseen danger that robbed him of sleep, it was the nagging voice that kept asking what he was going to do when this was over.

Even though deep inside he knew that he could never shirk his responsibility as guardian to Rachel, he couldn't imagine another man living at Hollenbeck House without feeling a hot tide of rage sweep over him.

Rachel and Marydyth were his. Not exactly.

Images of another man touching Marydyth's sweet soft skin assaulted him. He flung back the rough saddle blanket and rose from his bedroll. The idea made his blood burn hot and bitter in his veins. If he went so far as to allow himself to envision Marydyth beneath another man while he pumped inside her...he knew it was beyond jealousy. He refused to think it, refused to consider it.

No, by God, I am not in love with Marydyth Hollenbeck.

Chapter Eighteen

"**Y**our little daughter is just lovely," one of the church ladies said within Flynn's hearing. "It is just amazing, considering that she has spent so much time in the company of a rough man."

The chill went all the way to his bones. As he watched the woman with Marydyth his earlier feelings returned.

He was the reason they had talked. He was the reason they had turned a chilly shoulder to Marydyth. He was causing Rachel and Marydyth to live with the stain of gossip.

Marydyth looked at Flynn over the top of the other woman's head. Was that anger she saw flit through his brown eyes, or was it the same distant reserve she felt last night?

"Mr. O'Bannion has done an admirable job of caring for Rachel in every way," Marydyth said clearly. "I will forever be in his debt." Marydyth kept her gaze fixed on his face.

Gratitude. There it was, laid out on the table plain as day. She was grateful, beholden. *In his debt.*

Flynn felt the cold shadow of self-doubt roll over him.

Had Marydyth shared his bed, endured his touch *only* because she was grateful?

He bit down hard on the idea. It was not an easy thing for any man to admit. To have a woman take a man into her bed for passion was something Flynn could understand. But if she had done it because she felt beholden to him...

A bitter taste filled his mouth. He turned away on his boot heel, the rowels of his spurs digging deep into the dry earth. He had to put some distance between himself and Marydyth. He needed to be alone to think about what he was going to do.

Flynn was adjusting the cinch on Jack's saddle at one of their rest stops when he heard footsteps behind him. He turned and drew his side arm in one smooth motion.

Ted Kelts stared at him with owlish eyes. "A bit jumpy, aren't you?"

Flynn slammed the gun back into the leather holster. "Kelts. I haven't seen you much on this trip."

Ted grinned. "I've been around. I think you probably would've seen me if you hadn't been just a little preoccupied with Marydyth."

"And?" Flynn questioned, never one to beat about the bush.

"And, I was just wondering if you two have any kind of understanding?" Kelts asked, grinning. "You and Marydyth, I mean."

"Understanding? What kind of an understanding?" Flynn's belly knotted up, and he tasted that bitterness in his mouth again.

"An arrangement of the personal kind." Kelts lifted both brows. "If I'm not cutting in on your time, then I thought I might begin courting the lady."

The words hit Flynn square between the eyes. So, it was beginning already. And it wasn't some faceless interloper who was going to be horning in, it was Ted Kelts. It didn't help matters that Flynn had no use for him, but then, he thought sourly, no man would have been the right man.

"I'm not the marrying kind, Kelts." Flynn detected a note of sadness in his own truthful words. "I ride alone."

"Glad to hear it." He extended his hand.

Flynn stared at it as if it were a diamondback.

After a moment, Kelts withdrew it. "Well, if you'll excuse me I'm going to ask Marydyth if she will let me escort her when we reach the mine and have the dedication ceremony."

"Yeah, why don't you go do that?" Flynn turned and mounted Jack, suddenly wishing that he could just ride out and forget he had ever heard of Hollenbeck Corners.

The sun climbed higher into the sky as the Hollenbeck townsfolk got a little closer to the Lavender Lady. At noon they stopped for lunch. After a short break they started out again at a pace that grated on Flynn's nerves. He was anxious to get to the mine and spring his trap.

Finally, in the afternoon, they had all reached the mine.

Flynn rode on ahead, wanting to make sure that his deception looked convincing enough. The foreman had hired men from Bisbee to retimber the front of the mine and an area about fifty yards into it. From that point on the timbers were rotting and debris covered the floor, left from when the miners had gone on strike. The workers had gone back home, so there was no risk they might have told anyone. Flynn stared at the colorful bunting that stretched across the mouth of the mine. It fluttered in the breeze, catching for a moment on the grip of the craggy rocks that surrounded the Lady.

It looked very festive. Flynn hoped it was convincing enough to fool whoever was behind the threats.

The wagons arrived and preparations began for the ceremony at four o'clock. The church ladies had brought baskets of chilled food, which they began to lay out as soon as the men had erected plank tables. Then, by some mutually decided order, the women began to disappear in small, whispering groups to change their clothes.

Flynn gnawed the inside of his lip. Worry engulfed him. He had little fear that anything would happen to Marydyth or Rachel when they were in a cluster of gossiping hens. But now, as the group dispersed and went into the cover of Joshua trees and the pale green yellow of paloverde, he felt the grip of fear.

How was he going to keep an eye on Rachel and Marydyth without attracting unwanted attention to them all? But then a large-boned widow named Harriet Bessmer took care of the dilemma for him. She stepped into the clearing that was ringed by wagons moving and buzzing with the construction of plank tables and a speaking platform. Then she cleared her throat in a way that halted every hammer and got every man jack's attention.

"Most of you polecats know me, but for those who don't, I am the widow of Harry Bessmer, and this here is Sam Colt." She held up a pistol. Sunlight shimmered along the cool blue barrel. "The ladies will be a-changing clothes now and just so's you randy bucks will understand plain, I will be a-keepin' watch. I am kind of old and cranky and I don't see real good anymore but my hearin' is fine—better'n an old hound's. If'n I hear so much as a twig snap, I'll be a-shootin'."

There were a couple of whoops and catcalls.

"And make no mistake, I'll be aiming jest about crotch

high.'' She squinted one eye and leveled the gun at the appropriate height.

The laughter stopped. Flynn swallowed hard and so did a few other men. But he was also thanking God for Harriet Bessmer because she had solved his problem of how to keep Marydyth and Rachel safe.

An hour later as the sun drifted farther into the west, a wide slice of shade formed in the shadow of the rocky outcrops around the Lavender Lady.

The dozen men who wore bright red coats and hats with black bills made up the marching band of Hollenbeck Corners. They all buttoned their coats and started to practice. After hitting a couple of sour notes they did a passable rendition of a high-stepping march. It took a few minutes for the photographer the *Epitaph* had sent over from Tombstone to get set up, but he finally managed to take a couple of photos of the band and the mayor, promising to share the tintypes with the reporters from the *Chronicle* and the *Herald*.

Flynn watched everything with his hand hovering near his side arm.

Any time now he expected the miners to tip their hand. And in the back of his mind was the constant question of what he was going to do when it was all over.

A condemning voice told him that he could not continue as he had. It was unfair to Marydyth and Rachel. But Flynn shoved those thoughts aside and concentrated on the throng of people.

Flynn circled the outside edge of the crowd, listening to the various businessmen drone on. They had asked him to make a speech but he had refused, partly because he had to be free to watch and observe, and partly because he wasn't used to putting that many words together in a year, much less in front of a gawking group of people.

Marydyth laughed at something Ted Kelts said. A red-hot anger swelled inside Flynn as he looked at her and Rachel, standing with Kelts, sharing a cup of lemonade.

Damn it, he thought to himself. *I don't care what she does. She is free and over twenty-one.* But the hell of it was, he did care. It was eating him up inside to see her with Kelts and making him damned near crazy to admit it.

He clenched his jaw tight and forced the thoughts from his mind. This was no time to get moonstruck. If he let down his guard, harm could come to Rachel and Marydyth.

"Would you like a plate?" Harriet Bessmer nudged Flynn in the ribs and showed him a plate heaped with potato salad, ham and a slice of four-layer white cake.

"No, thanks, Harriet." Flynn smiled. "I'm not hungry." It wasn't a lie. His appetite had left him when Marydyth gave Ted that first smile.

"Better eat. You're just wastin' away." Harriet regarded him from beneath the rim of her faded calico bonnet.

"Maybe later. I appreciate the thought."

Flynn moved away, keeping Marydyth and Rachel in sight as he drifted toward the mine. The bunting fluttered in the breeze. A clutch of women engulfed Marydyth and Rachel. It was impossible to distinguish one voice from another, or to tell one bonnet from the next, but Flynn was relieved to know they were in the center of the crowd.

A shout and the sound of gunfire had Flynn running. He came upon two fuzzy-cheeked youths rolling in the dirt. A crowd had begun to gather around them.

Flynn shook his head, feeling the strain flow from his body. It was nothing—just a typical fight among cocky boys itching to become men. Nearby, some other damned fools were having a good time taking shots at a jackrabbit.

Marydyth mingled with the womenfolk and tried to pay attention to what they were saying. It wasn't easy. All day long her attention had shifted from Rachel to Flynn and back again.

She looked up and frowned. Rachel was no longer at her side. Turning, she scanned the area for sight of her daughter's coppery curls. Terror gripped her. She started to call out to Flynn but she felt an insistent tug on her skirts. Thinking it was Rachel, she turned, smiling, to find herself staring into the freckled face of a boy about six years old.

"Ma'am, I have a…" His voice trailed off as he thrust a folded piece of paper at Marydyth.

"A note?" she asked.

"Uh-huh." He nodded. As soon as her fingers closed over the paper he scurried away, lost amid the tangle of skirts.

Marydyth unfolded the note and felt an immediate sense of relief. It was neatly lettered, printed in a careful block style.

I have taken Rachel to see the mine. Don't worry.

F.

She felt the smile curving her lips and brought the note close to her face. Unconsciously, she rubbed it against her cheek and froze.

Marydyth felt the cold fist of terror squeezing her heart. She put the paper under her nose and inhaled deeply.

It reeked of tobacco smoke. *Tobacco smoke...*

Marydyth ran toward the mine. The townspeople were all grouped around the makeshift podium where the mayor and various businessmen were giving speeches. She had looked for Flynn but didn't see him and was not going to waste a single second searching for him.

Whatever happened now she was going to save her daughter.

When she reached the mouth of the mine, her courage nearly left her. Nobody was around, and the bunting that had been stretched over the opening lay in a crumpled heap in the dirt.

She swallowed hard and forced herself to step inside. Instantly she was engulfed by the darkness. Memories of Yuma and the airless nights threatened to choke her, but she put her hand on the rough, cold wall of stone and drew in a deep breath.

Rachel needed her.

Flynn finally worked his way out of the wall of men. He looked around for Marydyth and Rachel but didn't see them. However the clutch of women was still there, moving like a single creature toward the food table.

They were all right.

Marydyth took a step and froze at the too loud sound of gravel crunching beneath her feet. She swallowed her fear and kept on walking, but this time on the toes of her shoes.

Farther into the yawning blackness the smell of tobacco smoke engulfed her head. Fear, so thick and dark, nearly choked her.

Somebody was in the mine and it wasn't Flynn.

She continued on with her hand against the wall to

find her way until she came to a fork. One side was dark as pitch, but the other had a faint glow, as if a lantern were lit somewhere deep inside.

Marydyth moved cautiously forward. She heard a voice. It was muffled and distorted from the echo in the mine but something about it was vaguely familiar. She inched closer, holding her breath.

Then she recognized the voice. It was Ted Kelts.

Anger and a sense of betrayal wiped any semblance of common sense from Marydyth's mind. She ran toward the light.

Ted turned toward her with a shocked look on his face. The lantern beside his toe gleamed on the gun he was pointing—at Rachel.

"Oh, Marydyth, I wish you hadn't come here," he said in a voice that was too calm, too even.

Marydyth wrapped her arms around Rachel, then shoved her behind her body. If he was going to shoot, then his bullet would find her first.

"Ted, have you gone mad? What are you doing with Rachel…here in the mine?"

He tilted his head and looked at her with a quivering smile on his face. "I thought, finally, you and I…" Then he gestured with the gun barrel. "Why'd you have to come now? In a few minutes it would've been over and *she* would've been out of the way."

His words rippled over Marydyth, chilling her to the bone. "You were going to kill—my daughter?"

He shrugged. "She's in the way, Marydyth. Don't you see? Once she is gone, Flynn O'Bannion will leave. He doesn't give a damn about the money or the mines. Once she is out of the way it can be you and me—the way I have always intended." He frowned and stared at Marydyth. "I've waited a long time for you, you know."

"What are you saying?" Marydyth's eyes scanned the mine, looking for some weapon, some way to save Rachel. There was nothing but stone.

"J.C. was too old for you."

"I loved J.C.," Marydyth said softly.

"You loved his money. But if he had just sold me the Lavender Lady, then I would've had much more money than he."

"Is copper selling so well?" Marydyth asked with a twist of her lips.

"Copper? Do you think this has all been about copper?" He gestured wildly with the gun. "You have no more vision than J.C. did—or that silly uncle of yours."

Blaine?

Then a flash of previous memory sizzled through Marydyth's head. She remembered having coffee with Ted at his house. He had called Blaine by name on that morning. But Ted never knew Blaine—or so she thought—and she had never told anybody about him, either. No one but Flynn even knew his name.

"You were there the night J.C. was killed...." Her voice was shaking but she held a firm hand against Rachel's shoulder, keeping her safely behind her.

"Of course," Ted said with a note of pride. "I had gone there to try and persuade J.C. to sell me the mine, but we were interrupted by your bungling uncle. They had quite a little discussion. Blaine tried to blackmail J.C. by telling him about your past, but J.C. already knew."

Marydyth gasped.

"Ah, so you didn't know that J.C. had a private investigator check you out before he married you, eh?"

She shook her head in denial.

"Well, he did." Ted laughed. "And poor, stupid Blaine...but he came out all right, I suppose. J.C. gave him all your jewelry—stuffed it into his pockets like it was trash—and sent him on his way.'' Ted laughed again but it was a flat sound. ''All but the silver letter opener that dropped. I picked that up.''

Marydyth nearly swooned. The truth hit her like a rock. Blaine had not killed J.C.—Ted had.

''You—you murdered him,'' she said.

''Don't get so all-fired indignant. I was there. I heard what your uncle told J.C. He knew all the dirt about you, Marydyth, he knew you had killed your first husband and so do I. But I still want you.''

Marydyth heard a tiny sound behind her. From the corner of her eye, she saw a quiver of movement.

''I don't want to force you, Marydyth. I'd like you to come with me willingly. We could go to San Francisco, London, wherever you want.''

''I wouldn't go anywhere with you.'' She spit the words at him.

''Are you sure? I mean, I could find Blaine—I could have him testify against you in the murder of your first husband. You don't want to go back to Yuma, do you?''

''Go to hell, you son of a bitch,'' she hissed.

''Then you leave me no choice, Marydyth. The accident that is going to kill your daughter will kill you too. Once you're both dead, O'Bannion will sell. He doesn' care about Hollenbeck Corners enough to stay.'' He took a step. ''Are you sure you don't want to reconsider? mean, after all, you have lived with what you did all thes years—''

''But she didn't kill her husband, Ted. Blaine did that Then he lied about it.'' Flynn's hard voice cut throug Marydyth's panic.

She looked at him, standing there as still and rigid a an avenging angel sent by the Lord, and she knew tha she loved him. Whether it was a smart thing or not, he had captured her heart.

"You!" Ted's eyes bugged out. "Every time I turn around you're in the way."

Flynn heard a warning rattle and turned, seeing a diamondback coiled in a cranny.

Rachel screamed behind Marydyth. Ted Kelts trembled and fired his gun. A burst of flame seemed to come from the barrel and Marydyth crumpled in the dirt like a broken doll. Blood trickled from her temple.

"Marydyth! You son of a bitch, I'll kill you with my bare hands." Flynn took a step but Kelts's gun barrel came up and was trained directly at Rachel.

"Don't take another step, O'Bannion, or I will shoot the girl. And don't think they can hear this shot outside, because they can't. I've checked."

Flynn narrowed his eyes. "Are you sure you want to do this? There is no way out—but even if you manage it I'll track you down and kill you. You know I will."

"No, you won't, because you're going to be dead."

"What can you hope to gain, Kelts?"

"Money, power, prestige." He laughed. "I will admit that I had planned on having Marydyth, too, but I'll find another woman. Her kind are a dime a dozen."

White rage blazed through Flynn.

"O'Bannion, if you will sign this paper, I promise to kill the little girl quickly." Ted Kelts pulled a paper from his coat pocket.

"What is that?" Flynn asked, stalling for time as his eyes flicked around, looking for a way to save them all.

"It is power of attorney. Victoria Hollenbeck won't live much longer—one way or the other. Then Moses Pritikin will be taking orders from me."

"Sorry, Kelts, I don't seem to have a pen on me," Flynn said with a sneer.

Marydyth moaned and Rachel started to cry.

"Sign it or I'll shoot the little girl."

Flynn squatted down, never dropping the barrel of his gun from the position it held, pointed straight at Kelts's heart, and snatched the paper. He held it up so he could see it in line with Kelts.

"No need to read it, just sign."

"Un-Unca Flynn!" Rachel sobbed, and the sound of it knifed right through Flynn's heart. "I'm scared."

"It'll be okay, honey. You be my brave girl for just a little bit." He managed a smile. "Can you do that?"

"Yes, you be a real good girl, Rachel," Kelts mimicked. Then he laughed. "Too bad your mama didn't listen. She wouldn't have got hurt."

A stone dropped somewhere in the darkness, and Kelts jumped. "You and Marydyth should've taken my offer to buy the Lavender Lady."

"You dirty bastard..." Marydyth whispered as she managed to pull herself up into a sitting position. Blood ran down the side of her face and stained the front of her dress.

"I'm going to kill you slow, Kelts," Flynn growled.

"I don't think you're going to kill anybody. Now sign the paper. Sign it or I'm going to put a slug in the kid' head."

Rachel's eyes grew round and tears ran down her cheeks, but she was brave. It nearly crushed Flynn's heart to see how she held her chin high and looked at him with trusting eyes.

"Go to hell, you bastard," he said. "If you hurt her you'll get a bullet in your own head."

"Sign it." There was a note of hysteria in his voice

"No." Flynn held his position, never moving.

"Is that why you killed J.C.?" Marydyth asked in a ragged whisper.

Ted Kelts's gaze slipped to her and he blinked. Then his mouth jerked. "I didn't intend to. I picked up the letter opener and was looking at it. J.C. was going to throw me out—toss me out on the doorstep like some penny-ante shyster."

"So you drove the letter opener into his chest," Flynn supplied.

"Yes. I thought I'd be able to deal with Marydyth—I mean, being a widow and all she would be lonely. But then she was indicted for murder and wouldn't even defend herself. Later, I hoped that Victoria would deal, but she had those strokes and named you her beneficiary." Ted's eyes were glazed and wild.

"Just for money?" Marydyth choked on her question.

"You all are so stupid. Flynn, you are the stupidest of all. Don't you know one of the richest silver veins in Arizona is right here, and all I have to do is pull it out of the ground and the government will buy it? Buy it all." Ted laughed, and it was the sound of a madman. "And you, Flynn, you thought you were so smart, acting like you were going to reopen the mine, but I knew it was a trap. If you had really retimbered it, then you would've found what I found. You would've seen the vein of silver."

Kelts glanced at the ceiling and the walls, mesmerized by the fortune he had felt was right at his fingertips.

Flynn lunged forward at the same instant Ted fired. The bullet went wild, ricocheting off the rock walls, ringing and echoing through the mine. They grappled in the dirt until Kelts squirmed free. Flynn stood up, hatred burning in his gut. Afraid to fire, Flynn swung but missed, as his boot slid on the rocks.

"You bastard, you'll be sorry you did that." Kelts leveled his gun at Flynn, but suddenly there was a keening sound from behind him. Marydyth was up and moving quickly toward Kelts as if she were possessed. Flynn grabbed her and rolled, slamming them into Rachel and ending up against the rough wall of the mine.

Kelts fired again. The smell of cordite hung in the air. Then there was a rumble from deep beneath them. Flynn glanced up. A shelf of stone more than ten feet wide was crumbling behind the timbers. Gravel and pea-sized rocks rained down. The air was thick with dust.

"Quick, Marydyth, Rachel, come with me!" Flynn slammed his gun into his holster and started running, pulling them along, one on each side. When he reached the fork in the tunnel he pushed them against the rock wall.

"Stay behind me," he said, choking. Rocks were falling all around them. Stones rained down on Flynn's ha and struck his shoulders with burning force. Rachel wa: coughing and choking on the dirt in the air.

And then they reached the mouth of the mine.

They stumbled out into the startled crowd, but Flynn didn't stop. He kept tugging them forward away from th cavern. Women's screams and men's shouts mingle with the sound.

And then a great cloud of dirt, debris and dust spewe from the mine as it belched its last, and collapsed befor their eyes.

Chapter Nineteen

Flynn bathed Marydyth's head with his wet bandanna.

"Is Mama going to be all right, Unca Flynn?" Rachel asked as she rubbed her silken hands on Marydyth's face.

"I hope so, sugar."

The church women had made a pallet in the back of one of the wagons and had given their tight-lipped consent when Flynn insisted on tending Marydyth.

He wasn't about to let her out of his sight—not now.

Something had happened to him while he was in the mine, facing the possibility of losing her. He had realized that life without Rachel and Marydyth wouldn't be worth living. It wouldn't be worth getting out of bed in the morning or drawing another breath if these two precious souls were not in his life.

"Flynn?" Marydyth reached up and rubbed her fingers across his cheekbones. "Are you—are you crying?"

"Me?" His husky voice caught and broke. "Now, do I look like the kind of man who would cry?" Flynn said gruffly. "I just got some sand in my eyes." He coughed and rubbed roughly at his eyes.

"Oh." Marydyth smiled weakly, content to let him tell

the lie in order to save his pride in front of Rachel. In that moment she knew she would love him all of her life.

Flynn gently picked up Marydyth's hand. He kissed the back of her knuckles, ignoring the taste of dirt and grit upon her skin.

"It's a pretty sorry way to end up—Ted Kelts, I mean."

"I don't know," Flynn said. "I think it may be more than the dirty bastard deserved."

"I was so scared."

He laid his hand over hers. "It's over now. And I want you to know I'm going to get Moses and Victoria to change some things."

"What kind of things?" she asked.

"I am going to demand that the terms of Rachel's guardianship be changed. Victoria shouldn't have any objection once everyone understands the circumstances and truth about J.C.'s death."

"No. I don't want you to change a thing," Marydyth said.

"But, Marydyth, it isn't fair to you. The way things are I would always be around, and you would always feel *beholden*. That is not how I want it—not how I want you."

She touched the side of his lean jaw. "I was sort of hoping that you liked being around."

"I do," he said softly.

"I was kind of hoping that you had…some feeling for me." She drew her hand back and waited, holding her breath, hoping against hope.

"I have strong feelings for you, Marydyth. I have the very strongest kind of feelings for you—but I am going to get those papers changed."

"Oh," Marydyth said as disappointment rolled over her.

"I'm going to get them changed because when I ask you to marry me I want to know you are doing it because you love me and not because you feel you have to in order to be around Rachel."

"Marry?" she repeated dumbly. "Marry you?"

"Are we going to marry you, Unca Flynn?" Rachel climbed over Marydyth's legs and clung to Flynn's neck while she peered into his face.

"If you two angels will have me. But Lord knows I am a rough old cob. It won't be easy living with me."

"We both know exactly what it is like to live with you," Marydyth whispered.

Flynn swallowed, and a little color rose to his face. "Yep, I guess you do."

"There have been times..." Marydyth stuck her knuckles in her mouth.

Flynn drew himself up and nodded. "I understand. It was just my heart talking—I should've known better."

"Oh, Flynn, of course we will marry you," Marydyth said.

"Honest? No reservations?"

"I might have just one," she said with a shy smile.

"You tell me what it is and I promise I'll take care of it."

"Could—could you say that you love me? Just once I'd like to hear it."

He grinned and shoved his battered, dusty hat back on his head with his thumb. "Honey, if it will make you happy I'll stand in the middle of Hollenbeck Corners and shout it for all the world to hear, 'cause I love you, Marydyth Hollenbeck, I surely do love you."

"I love you too."

"Me too, Unca Flynn, me too." Rachel chimed in.

Then Flynn wrapped his arms around the two females who were more precious to him than life.

＊ ＊ ＊ ＊ ＊

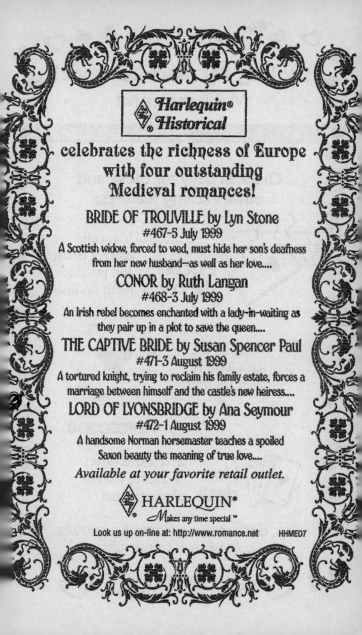

◈ Harlequin® ® Historical

celebrates the richness of Europe with four outstanding Medieval romances!

BRIDE OF TROUVILLE by Lyn Stone
#467-5 July 1999
A Scottish widow, forced to wed, must hide her son's deafness from her new husband—as well as her love....

CONOR by Ruth Langan
#468-3 July 1999
An Irish rebel becomes enchanted with a lady-in-waiting as they pair up in a plot to save the queen....

THE CAPTIVE BRIDE by Susan Spencer Paul
#471-3 August 1999
A tortured knight, trying to reclaim his family estate, forces a marriage between himself and the castle's new heiress....

LORD OF LYONSBRIDGE by Ana Seymour
#472-1 August 1999
A handsome Norman horsemaster teaches a spoiled Saxon beauty the meaning of true love....

Available at your favorite retail outlet.

◈ HARLEQUIN®
Makes any time special ™

Look us up on-line at: http://www.romance.net

HHMED7

Looking For More Romance?

Visit Romance.net

Look us up on-line at: http://www.romance.net

Check in daily for these and other exciting features:

Hot off the press — View all current titles, and purchase them on-line.

What do the stars have in store for you?

Horoscope

Hot deals — Exclusive offers available only at Romance.net

Plus, don't miss our interactive quizzes, contests and bonus gifts.

PWEB

 **HARLEQUIN®**
Makes any time special ™

 WIN A DREAM

In celebration of Harlequin®'s golden anniversary

Enter to win a *dream!* You could win:

- A luxurious trip for two to *The Renaissance Cottonwoods Resort* in Scottsdale, Arizona, or
- A bouquet of flowers once a week for a year from FTD, or
- A $500 shopping spree, or
- A fabulous bath & body gift basket, including K-tel's *Candlelight and Romance* 5-CD set.

Look for **WIN A DREAM** flash on specially marked Harlequin® titles by Penny Jordan, Dallas Schulze, Anne Stuart and Kristine Rolofson in October 1999*.

FTD

RENAISSANCE.
COTTONWOODS RESORT
SCOTTSDALE, ARIZONA

K·TEL

*No purchase necessary—for contest details send a self-addressed envelope to Harlequin Makes Any Time Special Contest, P.O. Box 9069, Buffalo, NY, 14269-9069 (include contest name on self-addressed envelope). Contest ends December 31, 1999. Open to U.S. and Canadian residents who are 18 or over. Void where prohibited.

PHMATS-GR

From bestselling author

Ruth Langan

comes a new Medieval miniseries

The O'Neil Saga

RORY
March 1999

CONOR
June 1999

BRIANA
October 1999

Siblings and warriors all, who must
defend the family legacy—even if it
means loving the enemy....

**Harlequin®
Historical**

Available at your favorite retail outlet.

HARLEQUIN®
Makes any time special ™

Look us up on-line at: http://www.romance.net   HHRL

COMING NEXT MONTH FROM

HARLEQUIN HISTORICALS

DON'T MISS THESE FOUR GREAT TITLES AVAILABLE NOW!

HARLEQUIN · FIVE DECADES OF ROMANCE · CELEBRATES

Starting in September 1999,
Harlequin Temptation®
will also be celebrating
an anniversary—15 years
of bringing you the
best in passion.

Look for these
Harlequin Temptation® titles
at your favorite retail stores
in September:

CLASS ACT
by Pamela Burford

BABY.COM
by Molly Liholm

NIGHT WHISPERS
by Leslie Kelly

THE SEDUCTION OF SYDNEY
by Jamie Denton

Look us up on-line at: http://www.romance.net   H50HT/L